THE HOUSE BY THE FJORD

A touching and atmospheric love story

When Anna Harvik travels to Norway in 1946 in order to visit the family of her late husband, the country is only just recovering from five cruel years of Nazi occupation. So it is with surprise that she finds in this cold and bitter country the capacity for new love and perhaps even a new home...

Recent Titles by Rosalind Laker from
Severn House Large Print

TO DREAM OF SNOW
BRILLIANCE
GARLANDS OF GOLD

THE HOUSE
BY THE FJORD

Rosalind Laker

Severn House Large Print
London & New York

This first large print edition published 2011
in Great Britain and the USA by
SEVERN HOUSE PUBLISHERS LTD of
9-15 High Street, Sutton, Surrey, SM1 1DF.
First world regular print edition published 2011 by
Severn House Publishers Ltd., London and New York.

British Library Cataloguing in Publication Data

Laker, Rosalind.
  The house by the fjord.
  1. War widows--Fiction. 2. Parents-in-law--Norway--
  Fiction. 3. World War, 1939-1945--Social aspects--
  Norway--Fiction. 4. Dwellings--Norway--Fiction.
  5. Norway--History--1945- --Fiction. 6. Love stories.
  7. Large type books.
  I. Title
  823.9'14-dc22

  ISBN-13: 978-0-7278-7993-6

Severn House Publishers support The Forest Stewardship Council
[FSC], the leading international forest certification organisation. All
our titles that are printed on Greenpeace-approved FSC-certified paper
carry the FSC logo.

Printed and bound in Great Britain by the
MPG Books Group, Bodmin, Cornwall.

To Elin Mai with love

One

It was Midsummer Eve when she first saw the annual celebratory bonfires flickering in the curious brightness of the everlasting northern daylight. Landfall had come while she had been in the dining saloon and, when dinner was at an end, she had come up on deck to gaze at the rocky landscape gliding past. The ship had entered the Oslo fjord.

Somebody came to lean on the rails beside her and she saw it was the well-dressed businessman from the same table on the voyage from Newcastle across the North Sea. They had chatted together and his slight accent was not one that she recognized. Yet during World War Two many foreign accents had become familiar, for so many thousands of men and women had escaped Nazi occupation in their own countries to come to the United Kingdom and fight on for freedom.

He nodded towards the shore. 'This is not my homeland,' he said, confirming her supposition, 'but before the war I came here often on business just as I am now. In my opinion – and

7

I have travelled a great deal in my time –
Norway is the most beautiful country in the
world.'

'So I have been told by others.' Anna's heart
contracted at the memory of the beloved man
who had promised to show her all the places in
this country that had meant most to him. But the
Norwegian squadrons had been highly active
with the rest of the Allies throughout World War
Two and he had been shot down only weeks
before hostilities had come to an end.

As a war widow, she had had no difficulty in
getting a passage across the North Sea, the
Norwegian government paying her fare. Yet
ordinary travel was generally restricted, for
Norway was still recovering from five years of
brutal Nazi occupation and was only in need of
those able to help recovery. The businessman
beside her was dealing in tractors and he expected to find a ready market in a land that had
been robbed of almost everything. Although
other war brides had come to their new land
quite soon after Norway's liberation in May
1945, she had needed time to come to terms
with her bereavement. It was why she had
waited for this summer of 1946 to visit her late
husband's country. In the interim she had
finished her teachers' training course, which the
war had interrupted.

'Is anyone meeting you when we dock in
Oslo tomorrow morning?' the tractor dealer
asked. He thought her a striking-looking young
woman with her soft brown hair full of amber

lights, her long-lashed eyes a greenish grey, and her fine complexion tinted by the summer sun.

Anna nodded as she replied. 'Yes, I have an English friend, Molly Svensen, who is married to a Norwegian. She will be on the quay, I know. I'm to stay with them for a while.'

'That will help you get accustomed to your new country,' he said approvingly. 'I wish you good luck.'

'Thank you,' she said. Then he bade her good-night and went to stroll round the deck.

Although he had assumed she had come to settle in Norway, that was not the case. How could she earn a living in a country where she had no knowledge of the language? What was more, her most recent work experience was limited to four years in an armament factory as her part in the war effort, mostly on twelve-hour shifts either from eight o'clock at night or eight in the morning.

Her friendship with Molly had sprung up when they were recruited at the same time into their war work, Molly from a hairdresser's and Anna herself from a teachers' training college. Later, Molly had married Olav Svensen, one of Johan's fellow pilots and his friend since their schooldays. During the Nazi occupation, and in spite of German posters warning that anyone attempting to leave Norway would be shot, the two young men had escaped together in a small fishing boat across the North Sea to the Shetlands. This had become such a popular route to freedom – despite the constant danger of Nazi attack from the air as well as by sea – that it had become known as the Shetland Bus. Many lost their lives on the way over, but the flow of escapees never stopped, and in England the numbers in the Free Royal Norwegian Forces swelled daily. Molly's marriage to Olav had taken place just two months before Anna's own to Johan. Her intention now was to stay a while with Molly and then try to see as much as possible of Johan's homeland before she returned to England.

A smile touched the corners of her lips. On their first date after meeting, Johan had brought her a book entitled *How to speak Norwegian in three months*. He had told her later that he had known from the first moment they had met on the dancefloor that he had found the girl with whom he wanted to spend the rest of his life. She did study the book now and again. But she had had very little time for study and he spoke English so fluently that learning Norwegian was something easily put aside for the future. Sadly, there was to be no future for them.

The day before leaving home near Portsmouth, where she lived with her aunt, she had gone back to the dancehall where she and Johan had met. In those days, with the invasion of the continent drawing near, there was a tremendous gathering of Allied forces in the south of England. As a result there were always long lines of service men and women, American GIs and other nationalities among them, filing in to dance under a rotating sequin ball that had flashed multicoloured lights over the dancers. On the evening of her meeting with Johan she had arrived at the dancehall with Molly, who had immediately been swept into jitterbugging with an American soldier, the two of them soon gaining applause.

The band was playing Glen Miller's *Moonlight Serenade* when a tall Norseman loomed up in front of Anna, blue-eyed, handsome and fair-haired, a pilot's wings on his uniform and, like all overseas troops, his nationality proclaimed on his shoulder flashes: *Norway*.

'Would you like to dance?' he asked with a bow. Later she was to discover that Norwegian men took bowing as a matter of common politeness, but that evening she was further enchanted by his courtesy and seemed to melt into his arms as he swept her into the dancing.

Standing nostalgically outside the closed and deserted dancehall, already in the clothes in which she would be travelling, these were poignant moments of intense memory. Then, full of heartache, she had gone home to label her suitcases and make ready to leave.

Her Aunt Evelyn was waiting for her in the hall when she came downstairs. She was an embittered woman, having lost her husband in the first World War, but she had taken care of Anna after her mother had died soon after she was born and later when her father had been killed in an accident at work. Never demonstrative, Aunt Evelyn submitted to a farewell kiss on the cheek, but pushed away an embrace.

'Well, off you go, Anna. Why you couldn't have married an Englishman I do not know.' She shook her head disapprovingly. 'Then there would have been no gadding off to a foreign country, which you will either like or hate on sight – most probably the latter. Then you'll be glad to come home. At least,' she added acidly, 'those foreigners will be able to see you coming in *that* coat!'

It was scarlet in colour. Anna had bought it from a war bride going to the United States, who was confident that she would get lots of new clothes there. In spite of her aunt's dislike of anything that was not sombre in hue, Anna knew the colour suited her. She patiently ignored the barbed remark as she had learned to do with many other such taunts over the years.

Now here she was on-board ship, seeing Johan's country for the first time. It would not be a case of liking or hating it, because already she loved it for being Johan's land and for which he had given his life.

How warm the evening was and how soft the air! Everybody she knew at home had the idea that Norway was dark and frozen for half the year, but, as Johan had told her, it was only in the very far north, beyond the Arctic Circle, that the sun slipped away in wintertime, creating a short dark period, only to shine again for twenty-four hours a day in summer, which was making this arrival so pleasant for her.

The Oslo fjord was opening up and a few small isolated houses were to be seen now, but she guessed that they were holiday cabins, for she knew from all Johan had told her that his fellow countrymen and women liked nothing better than to get out into the peace and beauty of nature in the mountains or by the sea. All the cabins were built of wood and from a distance they looked like pastel-coloured matchboxes perched here and there.

It was in this sixty-mile long fjord on a dark April night in 1940 that the German invasion had begun without any declaration of war. A skipper on a small fishing vessel had seen the great warship looming out of the darkness and in horror had realized what was happening. He managed to make contact with those manning an ancient fortress farther up the fjord before he and his vessel were blown to pieces by an enemy showing no mercy. At the fortress an ancient cannon was swiftly loaded and when the warship came level it was fired, scoring a direct hit that sent many hundreds of armed soldiers on-board to a watery grave. Most importantly, this delay to the invasion gave King Haakon and Crown Prince Olav and the government time to flee from Oslo with the country's gold and make a stand against the invaders. At the same time, the Crown Princess and the three royal children were able to slip away to safety into neutral Sweden and later to the United States on an American warship.

For three months, Norway, a lengthy country over a thousand miles long with a population of just four million people, who had known only peace for two hundred years, held out against the German invaders. Yet, eventually, the King and his son and the government were forced to flee into exile in England. It was the moment when a resistance movement was born and became so strong that the Germans could be said never to have conquered Norway. As for the country's gold, it was smuggled out to safety in fishing boats to be housed in Fort Knox, while every ship in Norway's large mercantile fleet made its way to an Allied port and served in convoys and performed other wartime activities throughout the hostilities.

With a last lingering look shoreward, Anna turned away from the rails and went down to her cabin.

She was up early in the morning and now there was plenty of activity on shore amid clusters of houses. Almost without exception, every one of them had the red, white and blue flag of Norway or an equally patriotic pennant flying from a flagpole or staff. On the water there were a number of sailing boats and those aboard exchanged waves with those cruising past.

The ship still had not docked at its destination. Anna was full of wonder at the length of this great fjord and gazed ahead as the city of Oslo began to reach out around her, giving her a splendid view of the great red-brown block that she knew to be the city hall lying directly ahead. Soon the ancient Akerhus Castle was sliding along to starboard. The city, bathed in

14

sunshine, its windows sparkling, was truly a fine sight against its background of rising hills. And there on the quayside was her friend, Molly Svensen, waving frantically to get her attention.

Anna responded eagerly, guessing that Molly must have been early to the quayside, because the bunch of flowers she was holding had drooped in her hand. The immigration officers were already coming aboard. With a final wave, Anna went to follow other passengers to the first-class saloon where the officials had seated themselves at tables to check everyone through. Then, ten minutes later, she was descending the gangway to be met by Molly's exuberant hug of welcome, the bouquet of flowers crushed between them.

'You're here at last!' Molly exclaimed with delight, thrusting the bouquet into Anna's hand. 'I'm so glad! I can't wait to hear the news of everyone we know. Olav would have come with me to meet you, but he's instructing pilot recruits today.' Then, with a complete switch of topic and looking Anna up and down admiringly, she declared. 'I love your coat! What a glorious colour! Every woman that sees you will want to snatch it off your back! There is almost nothing to buy in the shops here yet.'

'You said in your last letter that things are getting better.'

'So they are, but not that you will notice. We have ration cards for goods as well as food, but mostly shelves are empty.' Then she turned her attention to the nets of luggage being unloaded from the hold of the ship. 'Now let's hope your luggage doesn't take too long to arrive.'

Fortunately, Anna's two suitcases soon appeared and the custom officer did not ask her to open them, but simply made chalk marks to pass them through. Molly's fluent Norwegian soon gained them a porter quite swiftly and he carried the luggage to the taxi rank. On the way Molly took the crushed flowers back from Anna and dumped them in a rubbish bin.

'They are finished now, but I had to bring them. In this country all arrivals are usually met with flowers and Olav's aunt – with whom I stayed last night – insisted that I bring you a bunch from her garden. Now – as I told you in my letter – we're going to have lunch with her. She is a darling and looking forward so much to meeting you. I have wondered since passing on her invitation whether Johan's father had made some arrangements for you.'

'No,' Anna answered. 'His correspondence has been very brief and crisp. My impression is that he is not overjoyed at having an English daughter-in-law and he has shown no eagerness to meet me. He just suggested that I should visit him at some time in the future and that perhaps Christmas would suit me.'

Molly's eyebrows shot up. 'Christmas! That's months away! I can't believe that if you turned up on his doorstep that he would not welcome you. All the war brides that I know personally have been received most warmly. After all, there are strong ties between our two countries. Not only were we allies during the war, but King Haakon was married to Maud, sister of our George V, until she died some time ago.'

Anna shrugged, but a catch in her voice gave away her disappointment in the coolness of her father-in-law's correspondence, even though she felt immense compassion for him in the loss of his only child. After all, he knew nothing of his son's fate until the war's end and then it was the worst possible news.

'He may feel that the special family atmosphere of the Christmas season would help him to accept me,' Anna said. 'I truly believe that he is so deeply grieved that he still needs more time to adjust to his loss and to having a daughter-in-law who is a stranger, instead of the son he had loved.'

'It is odd that he should have arranged for a lawyer to come after lunch to see you today.'

'Yes, he wanted to know where I would be immediately after my arrival. The tone of his letter suggested an urgent matter, which was why I gave Christina's address after you had given it to me. I have no idea what it can all be about.'

'Perhaps he wants to give you some money. Maybe an allowance? Olav says the Vartdal family has always been wealthy.'

'I have no need of anything,' Anna answered firmly, hoping that money would not be the reason for the lawyer's visit. 'I have my Norwegian widow's pension and that covers all my needs.' She had turned her attention to the passing city, eager to see everything and to change the subject. 'Where are we now?'

'We're on Karl Johan gate,' Molly answered, indicating the wide street along which they were travelling, and then she pointed through the window. 'That's the parliament building we are passing now. But look ahead. There is the royal palace.'

It was located in a fine position on a rise at the head of the wide street, similar in appearance to Buckingham Palace and virtually crowning the city. Although at the entrance there were two guards on duty in their dark uniforms and plumed hats, the vast forecourt lay without walls or railings to keep the public at bay.

'It's all open!' Anna exclaimed.

Molly laughed. 'Yes! Once I looked through a basement window at the side of the palace and saw a royal shirt being ironed! I should not have done it, not because I was committing any crime by walking past there, but because people respect the royal family's privacy.' She settled back in her seat. 'But now I'll finish telling you the rest of the arrangements for today. After we have had lunch and your lawyer's visit is over, we'll catch the train to Jessheim where Olav will meet us with transport. We have one of the little houses – more like cabins really – near the gates of Gardermoen airfield that officers of the German Luftwaffe used when they were there. Their loss is our gain,' she concluded on a triumphant little laugh.

18

'You sound very happy there,' Anna commented with pleasure.

Molly answered thoughtfully, 'Yes, I am, but I have to admit to being a bit homesick at times. The other war brides – or should we call ourselves war wives now? – feel the same way, although only one of us suffered badly from it for a while. After all, although we have parties and dances and meet for drinks or for coffee, bridge or just a chat, it is – by comparison with the hectic wartime years that we all knew – very quiet here. The local people at Gardermoen all worked for the Germans – many had no choice and were secretly loyal to the King, but they had to obey their Nazi masters or get sent to a concentration camp. It is the quislings – those who were Nazi-minded – that show their hostility towards us and towards our men that escaped from the German occupation and went to join the free Norwegian forces in England.'

Anna knew all about quislings. The name had become synonymous with traitors in every Nazi-occupied land, for it had been Vidkun Quisling, a minor member of the Norwegian government, who had welcomed the Germans and grovelled to them. His reward was to be made Prime Minister and they let him take up residence in the royal palace, where King Haakon was now back in his rightful place. Quisling had been the only traitor to be shot after the liberation and, in spite of his crimes and all the terrible suffering he had caused, it

19

had upset many people in a country that had no death sentence in its own laws.

The taxi had arrived at Aunt Christina's house. It was a charming, sun-faded peach-coloured house, built of wood, as were almost all houses in Norway, and it was enhanced by a porch and a flowering garden from which Anna's discarded bouquet had come. The door opened wide and Aunt Christina appeared. She was round-faced and smiling, a buxom lady with curly white hair, her arms thrown open in welcome to the newcomer.

'Welcome, Anna!' she exclaimed excitedly in English. 'I was sure that Johan would have chosen a lovely girl and you have proved me right!'

'You knew him?' Anna asked eagerly as she was warmly embraced. After she had lost Johan, so many people had avoided mentioning his name or anything about him, thinking to spare her more grief and not realizing that talk of him was a comfort to her and kept him in her life.

'Yes, I knew him well. A fine young man! Before the war he and my nephew – Molly's Olav – used to race the Vartdal yacht on the Oslo fjord and they were frequent visitors here.'

Christina swept the two girls into the house, which was full of sunshine through the many windows. There were several interesting wall-tapestries in traditional patterns and every window-ledge held colourful potted plants. Prettiest of them all in Anna's opinion was one with an abundance of small white blossoms cascading from a holder on the wall.

'What is the name of that lovely plant?' Anna asked when she and Molly had freshened themselves up before luncheon.

'It is called the Bethlehem Star,' Molly replied, giving a final touch to her hair before a mirror. 'I have a mauve one. You'll see them in houses everywhere. I'll give you a cutting when you have a place of your own.'

'You are forgetting,' Anna replied with a smile. 'I'm only here on a visit.'

Molly looked unconvinced. 'Wait until you have been here for a little while. These are exceptionally hard times in Norway as they are everywhere else that has suffered in varying degrees from the war, but there is something about the beauty of this country that gets into your blood and you never want to leave it for any length of time.'

At that moment their hostess returned to guide them into the dining room where a round table, covered by a white lace cloth, held an unusual centrepiece of a silver Viking ship filled with flowers, and the napkins were folded like fans. In a silver candlestick a lighted candle, symbol of Norwegian hospitality, flickered in the sunshine. Two large dishes of *smorrebrod* had been placed in readiness.

'What a beautiful table!' Anna exclaimed spontaneously. Until she had met Johan she had only known British sandwiches, which always had a lid of bread, but then he took her to the Shaftesbury Hotel in London, which had been given over to the Norwegian forces for the duration of the war, and where *smorrebrod* had always been available. Yet those had been prepared with whatever meagre food was available, whereas these were piled with pink prawns, smoked salmon and some with lobster, all pleasingly garnished with parsley.

Aunt Christina was beaming at Anna's compliment. 'Please sit down or – as we say in Norwegian – *Vaer so god.*'

It was a phrase Anna knew well. *'Mange takk,'* she replied as she seated herself. During the conversation that followed, Christina was extremely interested to hear that Anna was a trained teacher, for during the occupation the Germans had forbidden the teaching of English in schools.

'The lapse is being made up now, but our children's education suffered, because so many schoolteachers were sent to concentration camps in the far north for refusing to teach the Nazi doctrine.' Christine heaved a sigh. 'Those were terrible times. Even our judges and clergy had their authority taken away from them for refusing to be influenced by Nazism.' She shook her head as if shaking away the past and smiled brightly. 'But we look to the future now. In my eyes, you, Anna, symbolize our new beginning, because you have endured sorrow and have now come to make a new life in this land for the sake of the loved one whom you lost.'

Anna was aware of Molly shooting her a warning glance, daring her to say that she intended to be only on holiday, but deceit was not in her nature and she felt compelled to answer honestly.

'I'm not convinced that my future lies here...' she began.

'Of course you are not.' Christina conceded at once, interrupting her. 'You need to look around and get to know this country before you make firm decisions about anything. Keep an open mind.'

Having been widowed young herself, her kind eyes showed a deep understanding of Anna's dilemma. During the meal she spoke of Johan several times, recalling amusing incidents and how he and Olav had sometimes taken her on sailing trips.

'It was my father who taught me how to sail when I was very young and I had my own little boat and loved it,' she said. 'I used to enjoy watching Johan and Olav racing the Vartdal yacht when they were competing in races on the Oslo fjord.'

Anna recalled how often Johan had spoken of his love of sailing and how he felt that flying was akin to it in some ways. There was the same vastness in ocean and sky, the same power in one's hands, the same intoxicating sense of freedom.

After lunch they moved outside to sit on the veranda, which faced a lawn at the back of the house and was surrounded by trees. When coffee was served, there were crisp little home-made biscuits, known as *sand-kaker*, served in a silver bowl. Anna thought them well named, for they reminded her of the fluted moulds in which she had made sand cakes on the beach during the annual childhood holidays at Margate with her aunt, who never chose to stay anywhere else.

'I had a wonderful visit to London with Nils, my late husband, before the war,' Christina said reminiscently. 'Tell me, Anna, how much of it survived the terrible Blitz. Molly is not familiar with the city, but I believe you are.'

'Yes, Johan and I were often in London whenever he had leave. There were still plenty of places of entertainment and theatres to go to and we had many happy times there.'

'Is the Café de Paris still standing?' Christina enquired eagerly. 'Nils and I had several wonderful evenings dancing under those grand chandeliers to the music of "Snakehips" Johnson and his band.'

'Sadly, no,' Anna replied. 'It was full of people enjoying themselves and defying the Blitz when it received a direct hit from a bomb with the most tragic consequences.' She saw a look of sadness pass across the woman's face. Then, in an encouraging tone, she added, 'But all of London will be rebuilt eventually and then people will dance there again. Where else did you go?'

'Oh, we did a lot of sightseeing. I have kept all the guidebooks. I think I liked visiting West-

24

minster Abbey most of all. There was so much of interest.' At that moment they heard a car draw up and its door slammed. 'That must be your visitor, Anna! Bring him indoors to the other room where you can talk privately.'

Anna went round the side of the house to reach the path and waited to greet him. He was not middle-aged or even older, which somehow she had expected, but was tall, lean and broad-shouldered, a physically attractive man with an athletic look about him, and she judged his age to be about thirty. He had classic and rather fierce Nordic good looks in a straight nose, strong cheekbones and a determined jaw. She was acutely aware of his very blue eyes seeming to pierce into her as he advanced towards her along the path. He had thick and well-groomed, wheat-coloured hair with a healthy sheen to it in the brightness of the sun. As for his mouth, it was wide and well shaped and presently set in a very firm and serious line. With a private smile, she thought it would be easy to picture him in a Viking helmet, with weapons and a round shield, instead of the light-grey suit he was wearing and the briefcase he had in his hand. When he reached her, he took her hand and bowed over it as he introduced himself, his English clear with a strong Norse accent.

'I'm Alexander Ringstad,' he said, his attitude very formal. 'It is a pleasure to meet you, Mrs Vartdal. Welcome to Norway. Please accept my sincere condolences on your bereavement. I know that your late husband was a very courageous man.'

'Did you know him?' she asked eagerly, hoping to gather yet more snippets of Johan's early life to add to Christina's reminiscences.

'Unfortunately not, but I know he was decorated for his bravery by our King.' He seemed to realize that he had disappointed her by not being acquainted with her late husband and promptly explained the reason why. 'Although your father-in-law has had a long association with the firm of lawyers that I represent, it is only recently that I obtained a partnership with them and so I'm relatively new to that part of Norway. Previously I was in Bergen, my home town.'

'I cannot imagine why my father-in-law wanted you to come and see me.' She was still inwardly agitated by Molly's mention of money, for her independence was all-important to her. 'My affairs are wholly in order.'

'I'm sure they are and there is nothing to be worried about,' he replied reassuringly. 'In fact, I have something to tell you that will be to your advantage in a very unusual way.'

She led the way indoors and they sat down on comfortable chairs opposite each other, a coffee table between them. He promptly opened his briefcase to draw out a sheaf of documents, which he placed towards her on the coffee table.

'Do you read Norwegian?' he asked.

'Not very well. I know that a legal document,

such as this sheaf of papers seems to be, would be past my understanding.'

'I thought that might be the case,' he said, 'which is why I had the same document drawn up in English for you. However, I'll explain everything to you. There is an old house on a lower slope of the Romsdal mountains that lies on the opposite side of the fjord from the Vartdal family home in the town of Molde. It has not been lived in for many years. Neither had it been visited recently until at my client's request I went there last week to inspect the property and check that it was still intact. Not that there would have been any local vandalism, because that simply never happens.'

'That's very commendable,' she said with a note of surprise.

'Country people respect one another's property, especially when the same families have lived on their farms for many generations and they all know one another so well, which is the case in all the agricultural valleys. They bring their children up in the same way. The house had been broken into by the Germans during the Nazi occupation when they were searching for a resistance fighter who was on the run from them. They failed to find him there, although later they boasted that he been shot and killed somewhere in the area. The soldiers did some damage to the house, leaving broken windows and a few smashed doors, but Harry Jensen – your father-in-law's nephew – managed to get permission from the local German commandant to personally carry out the repairs. These days he specializes in restoring buildings of historic interest. I found the old house still boarded up and partly hidden by bushes that should be cleared away and a couple of young trees that need to be felled. When that work is done, the house will once again have a wonderful view of the fjord and the valley from almost every window.'

'Why are you telling me all this?' she queried. 'Does my father-in-law want me to see this house?'

'More than that! He wants ownership of it to be yours! It has been handed down to the youngest daughter in the family since 1840 and your marriage to his son makes you the next in line. There has never been a will entailing the property as there should have been and the family has just kept to the old tradition. The last owner, who was childless and lived away, has died without settling who the next owner should be. It has fallen to your father-in-law to settle the matter, and unless you are willing to accept the house, it will go to a distant relative in the United States. That is not what Steffan Vartdal wants to happen to the house for reasons that have not been disclosed to me. All I do know is that it has some special family significance. Did your husband ever mention it to you?'

She thought carefully. 'Not specifically. He talked a lot about the weekend exodus before the Nazi occupation from towns and villages to cabins in the mountains or for sailing in the fjords and, of course, in winter for the skiing. He did once say there was a family property that he wanted to restore, but never said anything more about it.' She let her hands rise and fall expressively. 'Perhaps he would have done one day if time had not run out for us.'

He was still watching her very closely, his blue gaze unwavering. 'Now that you know it was your late husband's wish to restore this property, would you be willing to consider the project? There's a fund available that has not been touched for many years.' He tapped the papers lying on the table. 'This is the document you would be required to sign. It would be your agreement to accept the property and to ensure that it would pass to the next female in line. Hopefully – without any wish to distress you in speaking of a possible event in the future – it could be your own daughter.'

She caught her breath sharply; another dimension of her grief was that she would never have Johan's children, and the pain caused by his words cut through her. 'I can't consider that possibility.' She straightened in her chair. 'If it lay in my power and if circumstances were different, I would gladly fulfil my husband's wish to restore the property, but at the present time I can't make any commitments.'

'You would have professional help and advice.'

She paused before answering him in a firm tone. 'I have come here on holiday with no

29

plans to stay permanently. This is my first day on Norwegian soil. How can I begin to consider such a proposition?'

He nodded immediately in understanding. He had advised his client that it would most surely be far too soon for any decision to be made by the new arrival, but the old man had been anxious to have the matter settled. He slid the papers back into his briefcase, except for one lot clipped together, which he pushed across the table towards her.

'Here's the copy of the agreement in English, which I will leave for you to read through at your leisure. When shall you be meeting your father-in-law?'

'I have been invited for Christmas,' she replied.

He frowned thoughtfully. 'Perhaps after I make my report to him he will wish to see you sooner. If you should decide to view the house, I would willingly take you there.'

'Thank you for your offer,' she said.

They both rose to their feet and he shook her hand again in farewell. 'It has been a pleasure meeting you, Mrs Vartdal. I hope you will decide to stay in Norway.' Then his serious expression changed as he gave a sudden wide grin that unexpectedly made his eyes dance. 'I can recommend it.'

'Time will tell,' she replied, smiling herself as she responded to his sudden, more informal attitude.

She went with him to the door and stood there

as he went away down the path. At his car he gave her a wave before he slid in behind the wheel. As he drove away, she turned back into the house to find that Christina and Molly had come in from the garden and were clearly bursting with curiosity to hear what had been discussed.

'Do tell us!' Christina exclaimed, clasping her hands together in excitement. 'Have you been left a fortune?'

Anna laughed and shook her head. 'It's quite a mystery.'

When she had told them what had been discussed, they were both all for her claiming the property, but she merely inclined her head without replying. It would be pointless to take on the responsibility for the house if she should be far away in England and unable to keep a personal eye on it. Yet, if it should be the house in the mountains that Johan had wanted to restore – and there seemed little doubt about it – then it would be something she could do for him, but not if it proved to be just a casual thought on his part. She would know more when she eventually met her father-in-law, although Christmas, as Molly had said, was still a long time ahead.

Two

The train journey to Jessheim took just under an hour, following what was mostly a gently undulating landscape with farms on both sides and areas of thick forest here and there. Once, to Anna's excitement, she spotted an elk trotting along not far from the track.

'There's plenty of them around,' Molly said, being well used to sightings. 'But, as you will know, there are no reindeer this far south.' Her eyes twinkled. 'Do you remember how during the war some of the Norwegians used to tell tall tales about polar bears roaming the streets of Oslo and gullible people believed them?'

'I'm afraid they did,' Anna said in amusement.

'But it's not surprising that people swallowed their tales,' Molly continued, 'because it was only rich people that came to Norway before the war or went anywhere else abroad on holiday. I remember at school how envious I was of girls whose parents could afford for them to go on trips to France. The rich visitors here came for the salmon fishing in summer and deer hunting in the autumn. Olav says he can remember them arriving in their tweeds with their loud posh voices, and pony-carts or open cars were always lined up to take them to their destinations or on sightseeing trips.'

'So much has happened since then. Perhaps when more affluent times return again, those rich sportsmen will come back.'

'I expect they will,' Molly agreed. With amusement in her voice, she continued to speculate. 'Then there'll be all those relatives coming to see how the war brides are faring and view their new grandchildren. It could mean a whole flood of different tourists!'

'Maybe I'll be one of them, coming to see your children.'

Molly frowned with a change of mood at Anna's light-hearted remark. 'I would want you on the spot whenever I should give birth, because there will be nobody from my family to be with me. Olav would go to pieces if he saw me in labour. He gets frantic if he thinks there is anything wrong with me. It was bad enough last winter when I fell badly on skis.'

'How have you progressed with skiing?'

'Quite well until I had that fall, but I love it. If you stay for the winter, you can have all the skiing you could possibly want – and have a whole mountain slope to yourself for it.'

'I must admit that I would like to learn.'

Molly nodded with satisfaction. She usually managed to get her own way in most things, and keeping Anna in Norway was her new resolve.

At Jessheim station, Olav Svensen, tall,

copper-haired and good-looking in his uniform with two ribbon decorations under his pilot wings, greeted Anna exuberantly. 'Welcome, Anna! It's great to see you again! For weeks Molly has talked of nothing else but your coming to stay.' He picked up her two suitcases. 'I parked over there.' He nodded in the direction of a jeep with the white star of the Allied forces still on its sides. 'I couldn't bring my sports car, because there would not have been room for the three of us and your luggage.'

Anna smiled to herself. The pilots always seemed to get hold of open-topped sports cars in the war. Johan's had been ancient, but he had been vastly proud of it.

It was not long before they reached the outskirts of the airfield, which was flanked on one side by a thick forest. They drove past a little shop, which Molly said was the only local store. Logs for sale were piled along the wall at the side of the shop and some were in sacks, which, with a sense of shock, Anna saw were stamped with large swastikas. Immediately, Molly noticed her reaction.

'I know the sight of those swastikas makes your blood run cold,' she said, 'but the sacks are being used simply because there are no new ones available yet. So many things left by the Nazis are filling gaps in the meantime.' Then she nodded in the direction of a parked truckload of soldiers in greyish uniforms that they were passing. 'You'll have to get used to seeing them too.'

Anna gasped, twisting around in her seat to look at them again through the rear window. 'They're German soldiers!'

'Yes, they and others of them are awaiting repatriation. In the meantime they work on the airfield.'

'But surely they should have been sent back to their homeland by now!' she queried.

Molly spoke patiently. 'Don't forget that Hitler had fifty-seven thousand men under arms in Norway when the war in Europe ended, all because he thought the Allies would invade here. Once, he had five hundred thousand men here until so many more troops were needed on the Russian front. It is taking time to get those here home again.'

Anna thought how gloomy the prisoners look-ed, packed together in the back of the truck, but it was natural that they should be yearning for their homeland and to see their loved ones. She despaired again at the futility of war, although this time there had been no choice but to take up the fight for freedom against a horrific regime.

Olav drew up outside one of the cabins locat-ed near the gates of the airfield. Molly jumped out and led the way indoors.

'It's small and the furniture is what the Germans left behind, but it is home for the time being.' She was standing in the middle of the little sitting room with her arms outflung. 'Do you like my décor? I queued for over three hours to buy this cretonne in an Oslo shop. It was the first stock that had arrived in months.'

'Yes, I like it,' Anna answered honestly. The material was bright and cheerful with a design of multicoloured flowers that showed up well against the white-painted panelled walls. There was just rather a lot of it, for Molly had covered cushions, chair seats and a sofa, as well making it into curtains.

Viewing the cabin took only a matter of minutes. There was a tiny kitchen, and the two bedrooms were narrow and cramped. Anna's room had a single bed and a wall cupboard where once a German uniform would have been housed. There were two single beds pushed together in Molly and Olav's room with the same standard wall cupboard and a stack of boxes that were obviously crammed with their possessions. Anna realized immediately that Molly and Olav would have used her room for storage and that, however welcome she was as their guest, she was causing them great inconvenience. At the first chance she would suggest to Molly that it would be best if she could rent accommodation nearby. She knew her friend well enough to know that common sense would prevail and Molly would not take offence at her suggestion.

By sheer chance, the opportunity to raise the subject came that evening when Molly spoke apologetically again of their quarters being so cramped.

'What was space aplenty for two German officers mostly on duty is not enough for us!' she declared. 'We would apply for an apartment in one of the old houses along the lane, where the rooms are large and there's plenty of space, but that's all very old property. There's no indoor plumbing, except a cold-water tap in some of them, and the loo is always in an outhouse.'

'But would it be possible for me to rent somewhere if I should decide to stay on for a few months?' Anna asked casually. She knew that only the possibility of her extending her visit would sway her friend into allowing her to move elsewhere.

Molly frowned at her. 'I would agree to that only if I knew you were serious about staying on.'

'I'll take Christina's words to heart,' Anna answered, 'which means allowing plenty of time to make up my mind.'

'That calls for a drink of celebration!' Molly declared happily and prodded Olav, who was reading a newspaper and had not been listening. 'Get out that bottle of champagne that we've been saving for a special occasion! Anna is going to give Norway a good try!'

The evening ended merrily. Olav and Molly knew there would be difficulty in getting a place for Anna, for there was a waiting list for all the accommodation. Yet, as a war widow whose husband had flown with all the surviving pilots in the squadron, more than one owing his life to Johan Vartdal's leadership, there was every chance that somewhere would be found for her.

The next day Molly took Anna to meet the

other British war brides. She explained that there were a number of Norwegian wives living on the far side of the airfield, and although they were friendly and sociable, they had formed their own friendship circles just as Molly's own group had done, and to whom Anna would soon be introduced. She would be meeting them in an apartment in one of the old houses that had the large, well-proportioned rooms, but almost no indoor plumbing. These properties all faced the forest on the opposite side of the long lane. As Anna walked along with Molly on their way there, she thought the houses charming, with their filigreed porches and ornamented windows, even though most were in need of paint. All were well spaced and Molly paused once to point out through a gap between them a nearby airfield building beyond the bordering hedge.

'There's the shower unit for the wives and children of the air force. It is a wonderful facility for the war brides living in old properties without civilized plumbing. There's another unit on the far side of the airfield kept for wives and families there. Sally and two or three others with apartments along here go through the dividing hedge to get to this one. It saves going all the way to the main gate to reach it.'

They walked on and soon saw ahead the house they were to visit, for a Union Jack was draped over the balcony's balustrade.

They had been sighted. A young woman, sleek and beautiful with a swirl of shoulder-length fair hair, suddenly appeared on the balcony and called down to them.

'Hi, Molly! Welcome, Anna! Just walk in and come up.'

'Thanks, Sally!' Molly paused in the porch and spoke quietly to Anna, although there was no one to overhear. 'They all know you're a widow and so there will be no thoughtless remarks.'

Then Molly opened the front door and Anna followed her in. There was a buzz of voices upstairs where the wives had gathered. It was easy to see that the house must have known grander days, for there was a wide staircase in the large hall, which was presently cluttered with stacks of packing cases and three prams with a sleeping baby in one of them.

'This is Terry,' Molly whispered as they both peeped in at the pink-cheeked baby. 'His mother is a fellow English war bride, Vanessa Holmsen. She nearly died of homesickness before he was born.'

'Whatever do you mean?'

Molly put her hand on the baluster rail as they began to mount the stairs and again she lowered her voice. 'She literally began to pine away. In fact, she took to her bed and turned her face to the wall, wanting to die. All of us British wives did our best to coax her back to some interest in life, but she would not speak or look at us. Gunnar, her husband, was at loss to know what to do. He was afraid to let her take a trip back to England in case she never returned.'

'Did a doctor see her?'

39

'She refused to see the first one who came, but then in desperation Gunnar called in the medical officer, whom Vanessa knew well. He told her brusquely that she was pregnant, but even that might not have jolted her out of her lethargy if a few days later she hadn't felt the baby give a flutter of movement or imagined that she did.' Molly gave a laugh. 'That did the trick. She left her bed and ate three scrambled eggs with four pieces of toast!'

'How is she now?'

'Still thin as a rake and not really settled, but she is not likely to leave Gunnar or die, as he had begun to fear. They have the ground floor of this house as their apartment.' She paused on the stairs again to impart some more information. 'Sally Brand, whom you've just seen, is Canadian and financially the most well-off of all of us, because her father is a very successful businessman and sends her a generous allowance every three months. She can afford to have almost anything she wants and is the only one of us with a part-time nursemaid. Sometimes she even takes a shopping trip over the border into Sweden where – not having been occupied by the Nazis – the shops do have more goods to sell. She is generous and usually buys us all a gift – sometimes a lipstick or chocolates, and once we all had a bracelet, each one different. You should see her wardrobe! She has some lovely clothes that she brought with her from Canada.'

Molly had spoken without envy, simply setting the scene for Anna. They had reached the open door on the landing and a hush fell as they entered to face a circle of eight smiling young women, all of them curious to meet the newcomer arriving in their midst. One of the two toddlers playing on the floor turned quickly to his mother in shyness.

'This is Anna Vartdal!' Molly announced. 'My friend through thick and thin and more air raids than I care to remember!'

They laughed and greeted Anna while Sally poured coffee into a fresh cup. 'Do you like milk or cream in your coffee, Anna?' she asked. 'We buy our dairy products from local farmers. They are not supposed to sell off ration cards, but they do and charge us a little extra for it.'

'Cream will be a great treat,' Anna replied. 'I cannot remember the last time I had it.'

'Have one of Jane's sugared cookies with your coffee. She is the best cook among us.'

Jane, dark-haired and tall, gave Anna a welcoming grin and offered the plate of cookies. 'It's good to have you aboard.'

'You sound as if you were in the Navy,' Anna replied.

'Yes, I was a Wren, stationed at Portsmouth for most of my time.'

Anna had found the cookie to be crisp and delicious. 'Did you bake these for the sailors, Jane?' she said jokingly.

'I did once for a sailor who was special to me,' Jane answered on a quiet note, 'but he was lost on convoy duty when his ship was tor-

41

pedoed.'

'Oh, I'm so sorry,' Anna said, distressed that she herself should have been the one to make a thoughtless remark.

Jane waved a forgiving hand. 'That was about two years before I met Per on a train. We started talking and that was it. I thought I could never love a second time, but he showed me that it was possible and I'm grateful to him for it.'

Anna thought to herself that Jane was unaware of being a little tactless herself in advocating second love to a widow, but she put it from her mind as she was introduced to Vanessa, who was still pale and very slim from the time homesickness had made her ill. Her appearance was not helped by her thin pointed features and her pale golden hair, which gave her an ethereal look. Anna hoped that she was eating more now than scrambled eggs and toast.

'We'll do our best to make you happy here,' Vanessa said quite shyly. 'I've found everyone in our group to be very supportive.'

'That's very kind,' Anna answered sincerely. 'Thank you.'

She had been waved to a chair and sat down while the next introduction was to Helen Jensen, who had curly brown hair, bright hazel eyes and a very practical look about her.

'We all want to know how you and your husband met. That's why we are telling you how we all matched up. I'm a Scottish lass and married to Kristian. We met in an Aberdeen pub. It was a case of one glance across a crowded room, because as soon as I walked in he said to Wendy's husband, who was with him, that he had seen the girl he was going to marry.'

'That was very romantic,' Pat said approvingly. 'But what a pity it was in a pub! You should have been on an exotic beach somewhere with Bing Crosby singing about love and moonlight in the background.'

Helen laughed. 'Better in a pub than not all!' Then she turned to Anna. 'You are very welcome, Anna. As Vanessa has just told you, we do our best for one another. I've been teaching Highland dancing to our friends here. It's excellent exercise and they are all getting quite good at it.'

'Could I learn?' Anna asked. 'I've always thought the reels look such fun to dance.'

'Yes, they are.' Then Helen addressed the rest of the company. 'Did you hear that? I have a new pupil!' There was applause and some vocal encouragement for Anna.

The war bride sitting near Anna leaned forward, having been waiting for a chance to speak to her. She had abundantly beautiful hair, a rich red-brown, which Anna thought was just like film star Rita Hayworth's shoulder-length hair, a style that so many had copied in the war years as being the epitome of glamour.

'Welcome to Norway, Anna,' she said. 'I'm Rosemary Strom, married to Henrik. I was in the WAF and we were stationed on the same airfield. That's how we met.'

Again Sally offered some information, 'Rosemary is a marvellous needlewoman. She made that gorgeous blouse she is wearing.'

The next introduction was to Pat Andersen, an Irish girl with a naturally happy face, her figure plump and round-hipped and her eyes full of fun.

'I met my husband in hospital where I was a nurse. Where did you meet yours, Anna?'

'At a dance,' Anna replied. 'I had not wanted to go that evening, having danced almost every night the previous week, but Molly begged me, because neither of us ever went on our own. So to please her I went and that's where I met Johan.'

'What a good thing you did go,' Pat said in a matter-of-fact tone.

Anna was thankful that there had been no expression of sympathy and yet she sensed that all felt compassion for her. At times grief would drag at her heart so painfully that tears would come without warning. 'Yes,' she said quickly, 'I'm so thankful that I did.'

'Why was your Rolf in hospital, Pat?' someone asked. 'You've never told us. Was he wounded?'

Pat threw back her head in amusement. 'Not that time! Later he was sent to a military hospital after he was shot down near the end of the war. He had come into my ward that first time to have his tonsils out! When I went to take his temperature, the cheeky devil put his hand up my skirt and snapped my stocking suspender belt! Even though he was my patient, I slapped him hard!' She joined in everybody's burst of laughter as she reached down to pick up one of the toddlers, a pretty little girl, who had made herself sticky with a candy. 'Just look at you, Mandy! It's all round your mouth.'

Matters were put right with a rough wipe by a damp cloth on face and fingers before the child was set back on the floor to continue playing with some cotton reels and a few coloured wooden bricks.

Sally, having refilled everybody's cup, sat down next to Anna. 'I'm from Toronto,' she said. 'Arvid and I met when he was training with other pilots at "Little Norway" in Canada.' She lifted away the toddler that had burrowed into her and held him up in her arms. 'This is Tom, our son and heir. According to Arvid, this little fellow will one day be the world's champion skier with at least a dozen Olympic gold medals.'

The toddler regarded Anna seriously. When she smiled and spoke to him, he just stared as if making up his mind about her. He was a handsome child, blue-eyed and fair-haired. She could guess how his father would dote on him.

Next to be introduced was Wendy Misund, who was quaintly old-fashioned in that she had her straight hair parted on the side and caught back with a tortoiseshell slide such as a young schoolgirl might wear, her only make-up a touch of lipstick. Her whole manner was quiet and retiring, and yet her welcome was warmer than might have been expected.

'I hope you will be very happy here, Anna,' she said quietly. 'We shall all do what we can to make that happen. As for how I met Edvard, it was at a dance, just like you. It was during a ladies' *Excuse Me* waltz. I know the girl he was dancing with was furious when I tapped his shoulder for him to relinquish her for me. She looked as if she would have liked to claw my eyes out.'

Pat was regarding her approvingly. 'It was probably the bravest thing you ever did, because you are the shyest person I have ever known.'

Wendy blushed. 'Yes, I don't know where I found the courage. But Edvard had such a gentle look that I felt magnetized towards him.'

'The enemy didn't find him very gentle,' Pat joked.

'Yes, but he's different on solid ground. We married just before the Allied invasion. I had no clothing coupons left, but I borrowed a white satin evening gown from my aunt, which had been designed for her by Schiaparelli in Paris before the war. It was so elegant. Somebody loaned me a veil and a coronet of pearls.'

Sally gave a nod of approval. 'That's how a bride should look. I had no such luck. Arvid and I had arranged everything to marry on a certain date, but then only a day after he had finished his training and gained his wings he was suddenly told in the morning that he would be shipped back to England that same evening. So we married in a rush that afternoon with no time to wait for any of the finery still being made for me. I wore a blue suit and a wide-brimmed hat of the same colour. Not at all what I always thought I should wear as a bride.'

'I'm sure you looked beautiful,' Anna said sincerely, thinking that Sally would have looked elegant even if clothed in the proverbial sack.

Then Wendy spoke up. 'I met Edvard at an Anglo-Norse wedding when I was one of the bridesmaids and he was the best man. I had to wear a pre-war white evening dress at my own marriage too,' she said, 'but I covered it from the waist with some white net that an aunt gave me to give it a bouffant skirt.'

'That would have looked pretty,' Anna said. 'What flowers did you have?'

'A Victorian posy. It was made for me by a cousin, who had been a florist before she went into an ammunition factory for her war work.'

'I carried pink roses,' Jane said, putting down her emptied coffee cup. 'I had wanted white ones, but in those days one had to take whatever was available. In any case, I married in uniform.'

'So did I,' Helen said. 'I was a sergeant in the ATS. Sverre and I met in an air-raid shelter during a night of bombing when we were both on leave in London. Needless to say, we spent the rest of that leave together and were married three months later.'

Rosemary spoke up. 'I met Henrik when I was collecting for a Wings for Victory appeal. I

47

was working in an aircraft factory then, although I never knew which part I was making! When I spotted Henrik, I shook my collecting tin at him and not long afterwards I was wearing my grandmother's chiffon wedding dress from the 1920s. It had a low waistline and was covered with pearls. I loved it.'

Anna thought to herself how wartime had been a time of quick decisions, for nobody in the services or in civilian life knew what might lie ahead and happiness was never taken for granted. During the talk of weddings she had noticed that all the women wore their wedding rings on the third finger of their right hands as Norwegians did, but there was no need for her to change hers from her left hand, for here in Norway it showed – being the same for both for men and women – that the wearer was widowed.

'How is your Norwegian, Anna?' Pat was asking her. *'Snakker deg Norsk?'*

'No, I'm sorry to say that my knowledge of the language is almost negligible, but I'm sure each one of you is fluent,' she answered, making a sweeping gesture to include them all.

'Some of us are better than others,' Sally replied, 'but we all make mistakes.'

'Funny ones sometimes,' Pat said. 'At my father-in-law's farm I went for a walk and came to a field where a truly gigantic ox was tethered in a field. I was so impressed that when I returned to the farmhouse I wanted to tell my mother-in-law and sister-in-law what I had seen, but I

48

couldn't think of the word for "bull" or "ox". So I translated it literally into Norwegian by saying that I had just seen what must surely be the largest ever man-cow in the world.' She chuckled. 'They had been so very polite and restrained about previous mistakes I had made, but this time they fell about laughing, unable to help themselves.'

The others laughed and Anna spoke up with interest. 'So what was the right word?'

'Ox! Oxen! Just the same as in English!'

'At least you made yourself understood,' Anna said, amused as all the others had been by the error. 'That would have been beyond my ability.'

'Then you should have some lessons in Norwegian from Fru Eriksen,' Sally suggested. 'She is a teacher by profession, but because she was a quisling and taught the Nazi doctrine during the occupation no school wants her now. She served a prison sentence as did other traitors. Her home is just near the shop. I went to her for a little while to improve my Norwegian and so did Vanessa and Wendy.'

'I did too,' Helen said. 'She was very helpful.'

'I should like to do that,' Anna said, thinking that even if she were only in Norway for a short time, it would be useful to build on the smattering of the language that she had already learned. What was more, if she should meet her father-in-law before leaving, it might help to build a better relationship between them if she could speak a little to him in his own language.

49

'Then we'll go to see her when we leave here,' Molly said quickly, not wanting Anna to have the chance to change her mind.

The morning ended pleasantly with various social events discussed and arranged. Anna was included in everything. She and Molly walked back along the lane with Pat and Vanessa, who were pushing their young ones in their prams. Both of them lived in the German cabins, all of which were exactly the same as Molly's, and they were neighbours. It was there that the four of them parted company, Molly and Anna going off to see the retired teacher.

Fru Eriksen was a trim, slender woman in her fifties, but with a fine bone structure that would carry her good looks into old age. She spoke excellent English in educated tones that were almost free of a Norsk accent. Her home was as neat and spotless as she was herself.

'So you wish to have lessons?' she said to Anna when the three of them were seated. 'How advanced are you?'

'I'm a beginner,' Anna answered, 'but I'm very keen to learn while I'm here.'

'Then we can start tomorrow morning if my terms are agreeable to you.'

Anna thought them reasonable, especially as she was to be taught individually and not in a class. Just before she and Molly left the house, Anna asked Fru Eriksen how she had learned to speak English so perfectly.

'When my father was working abroad for a German company, he sent me to an exclusive

50

school for young ladies in England,' she replied. 'Good speech and good manners counted for more there than education. A ridiculous situation, but I endured it and spent school holidays with him in Germany. Nevertheless, one particular teacher in England inspired me with an interest in languages, which I have studied ever since.'

When they had left the house, Anna asked Molly about Fru Eriksen's husband.

'He was a patriot and she was too fond of the Nazi doctrine. He went to sea just before the German invasion and never came back. On the day of the liberation, Fru Eriksen was one of the women seized for collaborating with the enemy. That's when her head was shaved to mark her out as a traitor.'

'It was a tough punishment,' Anna observed.

'Fru Eriksen went to prison for six months with other traitors,' Molly said. 'It would have been for much longer, except that on one occasion when she was entertaining some Nazi officers she had her cousin, a resistance fighter, hidden in her attic. He spoke up for her at the trial. Fru Eriksen has a large strawberry field and sells her fruit, but she must be aware that when people buy them, they always call them Nazi strawberries. Those berries in my kitchen are some of hers. We are having them for *middag* later today.'

'They looked delicious.'

'Her Nazi raspberries are big and juicy and equally good.'

Anna's first lesson went well. She had brought an English–Norwegian dictionary from home, one that Johan had given her, and she took it with her. Fru Eriksen must have known that Molly would have filled in her Nazi background, but made no reference to it in any way. The woman began by explaining the basic rules of the language, the grammar, the pronunciation and why there was such an abundance of dialects in which people took a great pride.

'It is like the national costumes in that a dialect can vary from valley to valley,' she said. 'It makes it easy for fellow Norwegians to spot exactly where a person comes from in this country. You may find it hard to believe now, but there will come a day when you will be able to do the same.'

The lesson ended with some basic social conversation, for Fru Eriksen believed in helping a pupil feel at ease early on when in company.

When Anna left at the end of her lesson, she paused to look in the window of the little local shop. There was a display of tins and cardboard trade signs, but no food on view. She had a newly acquired food ration card, which had been organized for her, but she had given it to Molly, who needed it for an extra person to feed. Yet perhaps there could be something in the shop that she could buy without a ration card for her friend. Maybe the shop sold bunches of flowers or had a choice of blossoming plants.

A little bell tinkled over the shop door as she

entered. As the airfield was in the midst of farmland, she was not surprised to see there were swastika-stamped sacks of seeds propped along one wall and a stack of wooden hay-rakes. There was a box of potatoes and another of cabbages, but that was all. As for the shelves behind the counter, they were only displaying packets of dried vegetable soup and a number of wooden items such as spoons, mugs and plates, which Anna guessed were locally produced by a carpenter as they were very basic. There were a few sepia postcards of local views and a comical one of a girl sitting astride a pig, all of them slightly curled by age and the sun. None was suitable to send her aunt, who would judge Norway anew by the dreary views, and so she decided to keep to writing dutiful letters.

A woman in a spotless white apron had come to stand behind the counter and was eyeing Anna with curiosity, knowing her to be a new arrival.

'Vaer so god?' the woman said enquiringly.

Anna tried to think what she could say from her lesson that morning, but only one suitable phrase came to mind

'It is a beautiful day,' she said in Norwegian.

'Ja,' the woman replied, still with an expectant look on her face. She was surprised when the young woman bade her good day and left again.

Anna told Molly about it afterwards. 'There was nothing to buy.'

'No, there wouldn't be anything today, but

when there's a delivery of food products, a long line of people wait to get whatever is available. Just like it was at home during the war. It's the same in Oslo when goods come in. Would you like a day's sightseeing there next week?'

'I'd love it!'

'We won't be able to have any military transport, but fortunately there's a local milk delivery truck that leaves for Oslo at seven o'clock in the morning with four seats behind the driver and we can book two of them for us. Now tell me about your first lesson with Fru Eriksen and try out what you have learnt already on me.'

Anna did her best and Molly applauded her.

'Well done,' she said encouragingly. 'You should do well.'

The next day was Sunday when the wives and children of the officers were invited every week to lunch in the officers' mess. Molly and Anna set off together through the airfield's gates to pass by innumerable huts and offices. Anna was busy talking to Molly and did not notice the two cages at her right hand until suddenly there was a great snarling and barking as two large Alsatian dogs threw themselves against the wiring, wanting to get at these intruders. Anna gave an involuntary cry of fright, seeing their fangs in a shower of saliva only a foot away, and Molly pulled her on quickly.

'I should have warned you about those monsters, even though they can't get at you. The Germans left them behind. They were used to hunt down resistance fighters after cases of

54

sabotage and other acts of defiance. Now at night they are put into the hangers to prevent thieving, because there are always outsiders that will still help themselves to anything that is not nailed down if they get the chance.'

Anna gave the dogs a wary backward glance over her shoulder. They were still snarling and barking and leaping up as if they wished to tear her limb from limb. She shuddered at the thought of what must have happened to those brave people who were caught by them.

There was a family atmosphere in the officers' mess, which Anna thought must most surely contrast with the rest of the week when it was a male domain. There were children and toys everywhere and she enjoyed it. She was introduced by Molly to several of the Norwegian wives, all of whom bade her welcome to Norway and told Molly to bring her to have coffee with them.

To Anna's surprise, one of the chefs, a dark-haired, good-looking Frenchman named Jacques, came from the kitchen to welcome her by kissing her hand before a curt nod from an officer sent him back where he belonged. She learned that during the occupation he had been brought to Norway against his will by a high-ranking German officer, who had enjoyed his cooking in Paris and wanted that enjoyment to continue. It was said that Jacques had raged and stormed at his compulsory exile, but was too much of an artist to spoil with extra salt or anything else the food he presented. Yet since the *Boche* – as he called the Germans – had been defeated, he had settled down and showed no wish to return to France for the time being. As a civilian, he did not sleep in air force quarters, but had comfortable lodgings with a family in the village.

'Sally hates him,' Molly said to Anna as they walked home, 'and makes no secret of it. He tries to flirt with her at every opportunity and will serve her personally whenever he gets the chance. He seems to find her irresistible and that's not surprising, because she is beautiful, but – knowing how Sally likes to be admired – I'm not entirely sure that she is as averse to his compliments as she makes out.'

Next morning, Anna did not find it difficult to get up early, for the weather was still glorious and the sunshine streamed into her room. After breakfast she and Molly went to the roadside where the milk truck would pick them up. It was on time and they clambered up into it. There were gaudy cushions on the seats, which had long since ceased to be comfortable, and the other two passengers were local farmers, who talked between themselves, once sharing a mild joke with the driver.

The dropping-off place in Oslo was near the town hall, which was convenient for catching a bus as Molly wanted Anna to visit the Viking Ship Museum before they did anything else.

'You might as well start with the beginnings of Norway's history,' she said. 'Then we'll search the shops and find out if anything new has come in.'

In the museum, it was as Molly had anticipated. Anna stood gazing almost in awe at the
long dark sweep of the dramatic-headed, bow-
keeled Viking ship in the pale, cavernous
arched hall that housed it.

'It's such a beautiful shape,' Anna said softly,
'and such a great length! Like a vast work of
art.'

Unbidden, Alexander Ringstad had come into
her mind. She had thought to herself at the time
of their meeting that he had the looks of a
Viking and now, staring up the proud prow of
the ship, she thought that it was easy to imagine
him standing there with his dangerous gaze
fixed ahead on a distant horizon.

Molly broke into her thoughts. 'That's how
the Vikings went to rape and pillage in other
lands a thousand years ago! Come along now.
There's another ship and much more to see,
because it was a burial ship and when it was
dug up it was found to be full of artefacts.'

After half an hour they caught a ferry back to
the city. On the quayside Molly bought a bag of
freshly cooked prawns from one of the fishing-
boats tied up there. As breakfast was already a
distant memory, they sat on the steps of the
town hall and ate them with relish, other people
doing the same.

'Those were the best prawns I've ever eaten,'
Anna declared happily when they had disposed
of the rubbish in a bin. 'Now for the shops.'

They went first to Stein og Strom, Oslo's

biggest department store, but the shelves were empty except for some grey embroidery silks on one and on another some small oval wooden plaques, each of which had been decorated with a painting of a girl in national costume, all different from one another according to the district where they were worn.

'Which one would be the costume of Johan's county of Romsdal?' she wondered aloud. Molly inquired for her and the assistant picked out one where the figure was wearing a deep-blue costume encrusted with embroidery on the skirt hem and the bodice, and also on the little cap worn on the back of the head. Even as Anna opened her purse to pay for it, the assistant took another plaque from the shelf behind her and placed it on the counter for her to see. It was a male figure in the scarlet jacket, dark knee-breeches and knee-high white woollen socks that was the Romsdal costume for men.

'Now you can have the pair,' Molly said.

With a pang, Anna thought how fine Johan would have looked in such attire. Maybe they would both have had these costumes to wear on special festive occasions. She paid for the plaques and held them to her as they explored the rest of the shop. There was a long queue at one counter for some imported crockery that was patterned with a flowery design. Neither of them wished to purchase, but they looked at it with interest, for it was a change from plain white crockery, which was all that had been produced throughout the war.

They did go to other shops afterwards, and one shop selling glass had some stock to offer. Molly bought a jug and some wine glasses, which made a bulky parcel to carry. As they came out into the street again, Molly pointed to a neighbouring shop.

'Aunt Christina told me that on the day of liberation, when the Nazis were finally defeated, the whole country went wild with happiness and there was a notice in that window that said "Closed because of Joy".'

'What a wonderful reason to shut shop,' Anna said, smiling. 'I can't think of a better one.' They had come to one of the open street cafes where they sat down to eat a couple of *smorrebrod* and have a coffee each before they rounded off the day's outing by going to the cinema. The movie was *Caesar and Cleopatra*, starring Vivian Leigh, which they both enjoyed.

'We get films once a week in the officers' mess on the airfield,' Molly said as they made their way to the railway station, the milk lorry having departed the city long since. 'Occasionally we get a fairly new film, but mostly they are old. That doesn't really matter as it makes an evening out.'

When they arrived back at Gardermoen, there was a letter waiting for Anna from Johan's father. It was as brief and cool as his first letter. He wrote that he fully understood that she wanted time to consider taking on the ownership of the old house, but he was sure that by Christmas she would agree to it. As before, the whole tone of the letter was that of someone well used to getting his own way.

Molly seized the chance to use her powers of persuasion again when Anna had read the letter to her. 'You'll just have to spend Christmas with your husband's family now. You can't possibly not go, whether you accept the responsibility of the old house or not.'

Anna nodded. 'Yes, you're right. My original intention was to stay a couple of months this time and visit again next year. It was something of a shock to have Christmas defined as the earliest I could meet my autocratic father-in-law. Naturally, I want so much to see Johan's home in Molde where he grew up and the mountains that meant so much to him.'

'The west coast in itself is something that should never be missed. It's unbelievably beautiful with its peaks and its fjords. I landed in Bergen when I arrived in Norway, and as Olav had two weeks' leave, we had a wonderful time touring in his old car before we came south to get to Gardermoen. At that time hotels were still having to use paper sheets and pillowcases, because early on in the occupation the Germans had commandeered all their linen.' She laughed. 'In the morning it was like waking up in a waste paper basket!'

The days began to slip by. Then there came the news that Vanessa's husband was leaving the air force to return to civilian life. It meant that their apartment in one of the old houses along the lane would become vacant. It was allotted to Anna with the agreement of the elderly couple that owned the house and lived downstairs. She already knew the layout of the apartment with its tiny kitchenette and a single cold tap from visiting at coffee gatherings and card parties. Before moving in, Anna met Vanessa there to have the eccentricities of the pre-war electric cooker explained to her, and from the window she was shown the best place to get through the hedge to the shower unit.

Finally, blushing scarlet, Vanessa gave Anna some personal advice.

'I know this probably will not apply to you in any way,' she said with embarrassment, 'but these old wooden houses creak like mad and the bed most of all, which means any activity in it can be heard downstairs, even though the old couple are a bit deaf.'

Anna was amused. 'Thanks for the warning. I'll wear slippers by day and I can assure you that I will not be disturbing anyone at night.'

Vanessa gave a nod. Yet she wondered if a beautiful girl like Anna could remain immune to the attractiveness of some of the determined young officers at the airfield.

Three

There was the crispness of autumn in the air when Anna settled in her new quarters. Her landlady, Fru Dahl, was a picture-postcard old lady, with white hair and a round apple-cheeked face, and always wore black with a little crocheted lace at the neck. She was delighted to find that Anna, who had been studying hard in her lessons to master Norsk with Fru Eriksen, was able to converse with her, albeit hesitantly at times and not without mistakes that made it difficult to hide a smile. Her husband was an ugly old man with a grey moustache, who was known to regret the end of the Nazi regime in Norway since he had done well working as a tailor for the Germans, but had been obliged to retire, the Royal Norwegian Air Force having its own tailors in the ranks to care for the uniforms.

The old couple had a dog, named Odin, a beautiful, fierce-looking elkhound that was as mild and kindly in his nature as the old lady, and Anna made friends with him on the first day. He was kept tethered on a long chain, but she was allowed to release him to accompany her on walks and she was glad of his company.

The first thing that Anna did in her new home, after the furniture had been arranged to her liking, was to hang the national costume plaques side by side on the white wooden wall, where they made a bright highlight of colour. Molly had given her a potted white Bethlehem Star in a container that was also hung on the wall to display its cascade of flowers. A second house-warming gift had come jointly from the other wives and was a flowered chamber pot. Everybody laughed and applauded as it was presented to Anna.

'It's for those winter nights,' Sally said, 'when otherwise you would have to dig your way through the snow to the outhouse!'

The apartment was heated by a black floor-to-ceiling stove that gave out a wonderful heat and presently had a small stack of logs for refuelling beside it. The windows were double-glazed as was customary, and the ancient furniture included high-backed, leather-upholstered chairs and bench seat. There was also a coffee table, which Vanessa's husband had made and which they had left behind for her. It was stained with rings from beer mugs, but Anna soon washed it clean and gave it a much-needed polish afterwards. The wall-bed was in an alcove, which could be closed off by two ancient doors. Fru Dahl supplied the snow-white bed linen and her daughter dealt with the laundry.

Best of all, in the apartment was a beautiful old cupboard that was decoratively painted in soft, aged colours. Anna knew what this particular form of painting was called, because she had seen similar decoration several times during a visit that she and Molly had made one day to the large open-air museum in Oslo. The design was very Nordic, with links to the country's Viking past in its interpretation of roses and symbols in what was known as rosemaling, a skill that dated far back in the country's history, and this cupboard, standing in a rented room, was an antique treasure in itself.

She remarked on it to Fru Dahl. 'It is so beautiful!'

The old woman nodded agreement. 'That was my grandmother's cupboard and her mother's before her, but I have no idea how many more women in the past owned it. I expect it was made as a gift for a bride. That used to happen.'

Anna thought what a wonderful gift it would be for any bride of today, too, and made sure that it had pride of place in her living room, where its beauty could be fully appreciated.

On the first day of moving in, she had gone to inspect the loo in the outhouse. There were two steps up to a wooden, boxed-in bench with lids covering three apertures, the third being the right size for a child. The walls were decorated with picture pages from magazines that had not been renewed for a long time, judging by the yellowing of the paper and the fashions in some of them. Suitably sized pieces of newspaper had been patiently strung on a piece of string and suspended from a nail. It was a strange economy when the right paper was available for almost everything, even for what Molly called monthly 'essentials' and which were among the very few items amply stocked by the local shop. Anna shut the door behind her as she left. It had a heart painted on it, a guidance symbol that she was soon to see in barns and houses elsewhere.

The front windows of Anna's apartment gave her a view of the thick forest bordering the opposite side of the lane, while the rear window's view was of the airfield, and she could see miles across it to the distant hangars and the coming and going of the planes. One day, she saw the first brand-new fighter jet plane land there, which all the pilots had been eagerly awaiting. The propellers of the past war years were to be no more in a fighter squadron. She felt a pang for the Spitfire that had won the Battle of Britain and would now be confined to museum status.

She was watching from the front window when she saw the first of her guests arriving for her house-warming party. At last she was getting the chance to return some of the warm hospitality she had enjoyed since her arrival. All the men were in uniform as usual, for a civilian suit or even a jacket was still virtually unobtainable. A bachelor officer named Karl Haug had come along too. He was tall like most of his fellow countrymen, with healthy good looks, smiling eyes and fair hair, a strand of which flicked across his forehead.

'Hope it's OK with you that I've invited

myself this evening, Anna,' he said with a grin, his eyes twinkling as he handed her a bottle of wine, 'but Molly was sure you wouldn't turn me away.'

'No, of course not,' she replied, liking his open, friendly attitude. 'You're very welcome.'

All the men had brought bottles that had been purchased in the officers' mess, and Pat's husband, Rolf, had brought a gramophone with records of Crosby and Sinatra and various dance bands. Anna had met him several times before this evening and he was as likeable as his wife, having a round boyish face with an impish grin, and she could quite believe Pat's account of the suspender snapping.

Fru Dahl had asked that the party should not continue beyond midnight, and Anna had fully intended to respect that request, but time slipped by unnoticed with talk, laughter and dancing. Karl flirted with Anna, making her laugh, and he kept her dancing or chatting with him until two minutes past midnight when there came a thunderous knock on the door of her apartment.

Anna opened it to find Herr Dahl nearly as red-faced as his scarlet flannel nightshirt. He spoke so quickly in the local dialect that she could only guess at what he was saying, but his meaning was very clear. He ignored her sincere apology as he stumped away downstairs, his slippers flapping. She turned back into the room.

'Sorry, everyone!' she said, 'but we've run

over time.'

She waved from the window as the last of her guests made their way merrily homewards. She did not envy the war brides still having husbands that had survived the war, for she was deeply thankful that these courageous men had been able to return to their homeland. Yet her yearning for the man she had loved never eased. It was as if her heart had been permanently damaged.

Karl called on her the next day. His sports car was parked outside. 'Come for a drive,' he invited, leaning his shoulder against the door jamb. 'I'll take you into Oslo. I know a place where it is possible to get some really good food and we can do a show afterwards. The new American musical *Oklahoma!* has opened at the theatre and has had some great reviews.'

It proved to be one of the best days she had had for a long time and the show was all it had promised to be. When he saw her to her door, he kissed her lightly on the cheek and then his gaze lingered on her.

'I'm on flying duties tomorrow,' he said, 'but I could see you in the evening.'

'I'll make supper,' she said.

After that they saw each other often. He never made any demands on her, but would turn up unannounced to lounge on the hard leather-backed bench with his long legs crossed at the ankles, relaxed and content, while they enjoyed a glass of wine or two from the bottles he brought her. They enjoyed each other's company. He had known Johan as his squadron leader and Anna could tell that, through being aware of her late husband's qualities, he was not attempting to rush into a close relationship with her, and neither would she have wanted it. They sometimes lunched with Molly and Olav on family Sundays in the officers' mess and were now always invited to parties together. Anna was well aware that the other war brides were watching with speculation this growing closeness between her and Karl, but she only thought of him as a good friend, favouring him in her mind because he had flown with Johan.

Then there came the evening when he could no longer hold back his desire for her. It was the first extremely cold night of autumn and he had his arm around her to huddle her up to him and keep her warm in the short distance between the car and the house. When they reached the porch, he did not release her, but bent his head and kissed her fiercely and passionately. Inevitably he reignited a long forgotten fire in her and she seemed to come alive in his arms, responding in a way that was as much a surprise to her as it was a pleasure for him.

He whispered to her, his breath warm on her lips. 'Don't send me away tonight, Anna. Let me stay.'

Her hand shook as she inserted the key in the front door and she left him to close it after them as she led the way upstairs. The tall black stove gave warmth from its embers as they undressed in silence, she keeping her back to him. She

68

was remembering painfully that only Johan had ever seen her naked and it was only with him that she had ever made love, but loneliness had taken hold of her in an icy grip and for the moment she did not know how to withstand it.

Karl came up behind her and ran caressing hands over her shoulders and down her arms. Then he cupped her breasts and fondled her nipples as he held her back against his chest, his body strong and warm and eager for her. He kissed the nape of her neck.

'You're beautiful, Anna,' he murmured.

She shivered. 'The bed creaks,' she said despairingly, almost as a last pathetic effort to halt the inevitable from happening.

'That's no problem.' He turned, whipped the duvet off the bed and spread it on the floor, adding a pillow for her head. Then he drew her down on to it and her rebel body responded to his kisses and caresses as he awoke long suppressed passion in her. He gave a low groan of triumph as he brought her to fulfilment.

He slept almost at once, but she lay awake, thinking how mechanical the encounter had been, with none of the truly loving tenderness, the fiery, heartfelt passion and the soft, adoring words that had filled her nights with the man she knew she would love for the rest of her days.

After a while she sat up and carefully lifted aside Karl's arm that was encompassing her. Then she reached for her dressing robe. Slipping it on, she went to put two logs into the stove, feeling the warmth of the red-gold embers that glowed through the grating. Then she padded into the kitchenette where she switched on the light and made herself a cup of tea.

Sipping it, as she perched on a wooden stool, she thought how very English it was of her to turn to tea to help soothe her tangled thoughts. In air-raids, or in any other crisis, it had always been a cup of tea offered to survivors or those otherwise in some kind of crisis.

What had happened tonight had not been a crisis, but emotionally it had shown her that fondness for someone like Karl, no matter how deep, was not enough and never would be.

She finished her tea and put the cup aside, but she sat on, gazing through the window at the coloured lights of the airfield blinking under a canopy of stars. Now that autumn was here, the skies were dark and the days were getting shorter; the temperature had already fallen sharply and the lovely brightness of the summer nights had faded away until next year.

With a little sigh she returned to look down at Karl where he slept. Then, still in her robe, she lay down on the bed and after a while sleep did come to her.

She cooked scrambled eggs for his breakfast and he was buoyant and happy. He did not become aware of her sober mood until he was about to leave and spoke of picking her up that evening for a party in the officers' mess.

'Not this time,' she said quietly, 'and not

70

again. I realize that I'm not ready for any new relationship and truly I don't think I ever will be.'

He was distressed and full of questions, but in the end he accepted her decision. As he left, she thought it would not be long before he found someone else to take her place. To her embarrassment, she saw from her window old Herr Dahl come bursting out of the house to shout at him and shake a furious fist after him as he drove away.

Having offended the old man's moral code, she fully expected to be given notice to leave, but nothing happened. There was no clump of his boots on the stairs. She supposed that as he had demanded a higher rent from her than he had charged the Misunds, he had no wish to lose her as a tenant.

She was restless that morning, feeling confined by the walls that surrounded her and wanting to get out into the open air. She decided to go and pick some wild cranberries that were showing like bright jewels amid their foliage in the forest. Previously she had had some good pickings of wild blueberries, enough to share with Fru Dahl and Molly. She took up a basket and went downstairs

Outside, Odin came trotting up to accompany her and she talked to him as she unfastened his leash. Then they crossed the lane and entered the clean ferny atmosphere of the forest, the tall fir trees seeming to touch the sky as she looked up at them. She found picking the cranberries therapeutic. All the tenseness in her soothed away in the total peace of her surroundings and she failed to realize that she was going deeper into the forest than ever before.

It was as she paused to stand up and rest her back that she realized that Odin was no longer with her. He had drawn back earlier on, and even when she had spoken to him encouragingly, he had not followed her willingly. She had thought it strange. Now he was nowhere to be seen. It was as she looked about for him she saw something glinting through the distant trees.

Full of curiosity as to what it could be, she moved forward and became aware at the same time of a new kind of silence, as if the forest were holding its breath. There was not the faintest rustle to be heard. Then she saw that it was a high wire fence looming up amid the trees that had caught the light, and even then she did not guess what it might be, only wondering who would keep farm animals enclosed this far into the forest, for she could not think of any other explanation.

It was as she held aside a branch to go forward that the full horror of what was exposed made her cry out in distress. It was a long-deserted concentration camp with the grey huts, the guards' high lookout posts and the gates still standing wide where they had been flung open to freedom on the day of liberation. All the terrible images she had seen in newsreels and in newspaper photos of the tragic inmates of

Auschwitz and Belsen and other such concentration camps flashed through her mind, causing such a cramping hold of pity on her that for a few moments she could not move. Then abruptly she swung about, the basket of cranberries flying from her hand, and broke into a run, heedless of the direction she was taking. Yet somehow she emerged on to the lane to find she was only a short distance from the Dahls' house.

She could see Fru Dahl on the porch, talking to a tall civilian, who was informally dressed, his traditionally patterned ski cardigan in black and white. A car was parked by the gate. As she approached the house, the old lady sighted her and would have smiled, but Anna's tortured expression and total lack of colour made her throw up her hands in alarm.

The man turned immediately to follow Fru Dahl's gaze and Anna saw it was Alexander Ringstad. He came towards her at once, his strong gaze full of concern.

'What's happened?' he demanded. 'Are you ill?'

She shook her head. 'In the forest,' she said, horror straining in her voice. 'A concentration camp!'

'Ah, yes,' he said quietly in understanding, putting his hand lightly on her back to guide her into the house. Fru Dahl went swiftly ahead to open the door to her own parlour where she promptly poured some brandy into a wine glass.

73

Anna sat down and took it with a trembling hand. 'I knew about the notorious Grini concentration camp near Oslo and the dreadful one in the far north, where the schoolteachers and others died of cold and ill treatment, but I never expected to see one here almost on this doorstep.'

She had spoken in English, but Fru Dahl exchanged a word with Alexander and gained the gist of what had been said.

'A terrible place!' the old woman continued in her own tongue to Alexander, not realizing quite how much Anna would understand. 'We used to hear the firing squad at four o'clock in the mornings. The bodies were buried in a clearing in the forest.' She let her hands rise and fall expressively. 'Such terrible years! Then, on liberation day, the quislings were made to dig up the bodies for identification, which were then given a proper Christian burial. All our Jewish people – about five or six hundred of them in all – were taken off to Germany by the Nazis as soon as our country was occupied.'

Alexander noticed that Anna sat as though frozen with her head bowed. He rested a hand on her shoulder in a protective gesture as he tried to stem the old lady's flow of tragic reminiscences.

'Yes, Fru Dahl,' he said, not sure how much Anna would gather from the woman's rapid Norwegian dialect. 'I'm well aware of what happened in those camps and can guess what happened here.'

74

Yet the woman proved unstoppable. 'There's a small hut in there where they kept the condemned the night before their execution. The walls are covered with last messages to people named, such as "Give my love to my parents" – "Tell my beloved wife and children that my last thoughts will be of them"—'

The stem of the wine glass snapped in Anna's hand and she looked up tragically as the brandy spread out on the wooden floor. 'I'm so sorry, Fru Dahl. I've broken your lovely wine glass.'

The woman declared it was of no importance and would have poured her a measure in another glass, but Anna shook her head, wiping her eyes, and Alexander intervened.

'I'll take Anna for drive. I don't want her to think of the forest as being wholly ruined by what she saw.' Then he added to her, 'It will heal itself with new trees and bushes, ferns and flowers, but there will be a memorial to those that lost their lives there. They will never be forgotten.'

They drove quite a long way and she saw aspects of the forest that she had never seen before. There were the bare slopes where local people would ski in winter, and nearby there was a ski-jump, and farther on a lake that would become a skating rink for children when temperatures dropped. They saw several elk, which regarded them from a distance with long mournful faces, their antlers widely magnificent.

'It is beautiful around here, Alex,' she said,

for they were now on first name terms.

He had stopped the car and they had got out to sit on a fallen tree trunk, drinking coffee in mugs from a vacuum flask that he had produced.

'Wait till you see where your father-in-law lives in the town of Molde,' he said, 'because there it is possible to look out across the fjord and see eighty-seven mountain peaks. You'll never want to leave.'

'Johan told me about them. He was skiing up in those mountains when he saw Molde being bombed.'

'The Nazis knew that the King and the Crown Prince and the government would have reached there on their flight from Oslo. It's why German bombers tried to destroy every defenceless little town along the route. Wooden houses soon blaze like torches.'

She shook her head at the tragedy of it, wondering if Alex would now tell her why he was in England during the war and which service he was in, but it did not happen and she was reluctant to question him. Then they returned to the car.

She had recovered from her initial shock and was glad that the beautiful forest had not been lost to her through the horrific deeds that had been carried out in one heart-torn part of it. With time, when all sign of the camp had been removed, the forest would heal again, as Alex had said, and it would be as if nothing had ever violated its quiet peace and beauty, but the men

76

that had died there would always be remembered by those who had loved them, as well as
those who had respected them.

'Are you still coming to Molde at Christmas?'
Alex asked her before they parted outside the
Dahls' house.

'Yes,' she answered without hesitation.

'Then I'll look forward to seeing you.' He
gave her a wave as he drove off, and she felt
extremely grateful for the help he had given her
as she went into the house. Although he had
said that business had brought him to Oslo
again, she thought it significant that he had
gone out of his way to visit her. It seemed as if
her father-in-law was keeping a close check on
her, and yet on reflection she realized that Alex
had mentioned Steffan Vartdal only in a passing
reference and neither had he asked her if she
had read the document that he had left for her to
study. Perhaps he had come of his own free will
just to see her. It was an interesting thought.

Four

Before winter set in, workmen and trucks
appeared further up the lane from where Anna
was living and she realized that the concentration camp was being dismantled. Bonfires
flickered through the trees and the trucks
carried away loads to be destroyed elsewhere. It
had been announced that a memorial was to be
erected there and she thought that very soon the
beautiful forest would heal its terrible scars.

Every day the weather was getting colder.
One morning the forest was covered in hoar
frost and sparkled as if every tree had been
decked dazzlingly for Christmas. Soon afterwards the snow came and Anna awoke that day
to a new vista and the sound of her elderly land-
lord clearing the steps of snow. She ran to the
window and there she stood gazing across at the
gigantic cones of snow that now covered every
tree in sight. Then she heard sleigh bells and
watched in delight as one of the local farmers
drove past on his sleigh, the first of many that
she was to see in the days and weeks ahead.

As soon as Anna had had her breakfast, she
wrapped up warmly in a thick jacket that her
aunt had sent at her request, with some other

items of winter clothing for her extended visit. Then, pulling her woollen cap well down over her ears, she went outside. The cold air stung her nostrils and nipped her cheeks, but she was so delighted with the glorious scene all around her that she scarcely noticed. Odin, seeing her, began jumping at his leash, eager for a walk, and she released him to let him go bounding along beside her.

She made two discoveries as they walked the lane, which had already been cleared by a snowplough. Firstly, the dry cold did not penetrate her warm clothing and, secondly, the snow did not have the wet texture of the snow she was used to in England, but due to the low temperature it flew up like grains of rice when she kicked it.

She walked as far as Molly's cabin where she was welcomed in for a steaming cup of coffee while Odin settled down on the porch outside. Later they would go off to learn a Scottish dance new to them under Helen's supervision. Anna was enjoying the lessons. The war brides had been given permission to hold their lessons in an old shed on the airfield, which was not used by the air force. The Highland music was supplied by a gramophone, Helen having brought the records with her from Scotland.

All the war brides agreed that their first winter in Norway had not been as cold as this one was proving to be. For some time now officers and ranks alike were wearing well-fitting greatcoats and handsome round fur hats with the insignia of the Royal Norwegian Air Force. Pat and Sally took their toddlers, well wrapped up, out on little sleds just as the local people did. Anna decided that one of these sleds, which were sold in the local shop, was just what she needed. She could pull along her purchases whenever foodstuffs were on sale there or elsewhere on the farms, for she had discovered that even a well-gloved hand soon became stiff and chilled to the bone when carrying anything and was agony to thaw in lukewarm water. It would be easier to pull a sledge by straps over her shoulders, even though it would make her feel as if she were ready to accompany Amundsen to the South Pole.

When Fru Dahl, whose daughter did her shopping for her, saw Anna about to set out with the sled, she beckoned to her to wait. A few minutes later, the old lady reappeared with a dog's sled harness for Odin. Afterwards, to Anna's delight, he pulled the shopping effortlessly for her.

The daily temperature at Gardermoen began to average well below zero. Soon it was said generally to be the coldest winter in living memory and even Oslo fjord had begun to freeze. Anna's aunt wrote from England that it was the coldest season that she or anyone else could remember and the whole of Europe seemed similarly afflicted by the merciless weather.

Everything carried on as usual in Norway. Trains kept running and snow ploughs kept the roads clear, although the former were not always on time due to unusual avalanches of snow blocking the lines and having to be cleared. Military flying was often curtailed, for heavy falls of snow were frequent, obliterating everything, but the social life of the airfield continued unhampered and many people went around on skis. Olav and Molly taught Anna to ski and she was quick to learn, in spite of many falls in the process.

It was because she was unused to such cold weather that it played tricks on her. She had been warned never to touch metal outside with her bare hand or else she would stick to it, which she was careful to remember, but she had given up hanging out her washing because it became as stiff as boards in a matter of seconds. One day the local shop had had some jellies for sale and she had made a raspberry-flavoured one, which she put outside her apartment on top of a cupboard on the landing to cool, knowing that it would set quicker there in the unheated area than in her warm apartment. A little later when she was on her way out to visit Molly, she found it had frozen to solid ice, giving her an indication just how cold it could be indoors as well as out when there was no stove to keep everything warm.

Karl Haug had been posted elsewhere and so Anna did not see him more than a couple of times after the night she wished to forget. His gaze had lingered on her and they had spoken, but he had made no attempt to restart what had happened between them.

81

Another purchase Anna made was a *spark*. This was a simple form of transport that every-one seemed to possess, for these were every-where. It consisted of a simple wooden chair fastened on to two metal runners, which ex-tended behind it, and it was on these that one scooted along the icy roads while holding on to the top of the chair, with sometimes either a passenger or purchases on the seat. Anna had come on her *spark* on the evening she and Molly had decided to go to the airfield cinema to see the Marx Brothers in *A Night at the Opera*.

'You sit and I'll scoot,' Anna said as they were about to set off. Molly was wearing an ancient fur coat that her mother had sent her. She would not wear it in daylight, having once caught a glimpse of a customer in an Oslo shop mirror and thought what a terrible sight the woman presented in a ginger fur coat and a woolly hat, until she had realized with dismay that it was a reflection of herself.

The runways, illumined by the airfields lights, gave a wonderful surface for a good pace as they swept along between the high banks of cleared snow on either side. They had covered quite a distance when an unexpected happening took place. Two young airmen, bundled up like polar bears in their thick jackets and fur hats, who had spotted them from a distance, came darting forward with a whoop of triumph.

'Want some help?' one joked as he and his companion leapt one behind the other on to the runners with Anna, and promptly increased the pace of the *spark* to a tremendous speed. Molly uttered a piercing shriek, which was drowned by the airmen's noisy cheering, and Anna clung desperately to the back of the passenger-chair, her cries to slow down unheeded. The runway was skimming away under them until suddenly there was a deafening crack as one of the metal runners snapped. The next moment all four of them were sent flying on to the runway.

Anna felt like a spinning top as she slid across the icy surface. As she sat up, she was relieved to see that nobody was injured. Molly, who was sitting with her legs stuck out in front of her, her fur coat split from shoulder to hem, was laughing helplessly at the stark expressions of the two airmen as they recognized her as the wife of one of their senior officers. It was obvious they had mistaken her and Anna for two civilian girls from the kitchens, homeward bound on the *spark*.

Molly cut short their apologies as they helped her up, Anna already on her feet. 'Just find us another *spark*,' Molly said in Norwegian, wiping tears of mirth from her eyes, 'and then I'll forget I ever saw you.'

They bolted off to do her bidding and returned very soon afterwards on another *spark* at almost the same speed. They saluted smartly as Anna and Molly set off again, both of the young men still awed by what they had done. Afterwards, on a leisurely homeward run, Molly declared she had laughed far more at them than at the

Marx brothers.

It was at this time of freezing temperatures that Anna saw the Northern Lights for the first time. They were pale and wispy, but they were there, brushing long fingers of feathery light over the whole night sky in a way that was both beautiful and strange. She gazed at them in wonder. Then, when it became still colder, and on the nights when the sky was clear of clouds, there were waves of beautiful colours sweeping majestically across the skies.

For some time now the war brides, cooperating with the Norwegian wives, had been planning a big party all together early in the New Year when they had returned from their various Christmas destinations. The husbands would be their guests and any other of the single officers wishing to come with girlfriends would add to the enjoyment of the party. To this aim, the British and the Norwegian wives met once a week to drink coffee and give a regular donation to the funds, which were in the care of Sally as treasurer. Soon a good sum began to accumulate that was well on the way to covering all the food and drink for the evening. The commanding officer had given his permission for the party to be held in the mess hall where once German air crews had been briefed for bombing sorties.

In Oslo the shops had made their premises and windows as festive as possible, and the department store of Stein og Strom had a beautifully decorated Christmas tree that reached through an upper floor almost to the ceiling.

On a shopping trip Anna and Molly found that a great deal of Christmas stock had come in or had been saved for the festive season. There were plenty of pretty tree ornaments to buy, most of them artistically fashioned in paper. At one counter, silk ties were being sold, and after waiting in line for half an hour Anna was able to purchase one for her father-in-law, and Molly bought the same for hers too. There was another long wait to buy some very good costume jewellery, and Anna managed to get a pretty green enamelled necklace for Steffan Vartdal's housekeeper.

There was one small shop that they always visited ever since Sally had made a very special purchase there for herself. The shop owner had had a sudden delivery of some stock that had been brought personally into the country by a friend from the States. By chance, Sally had travelled into Oslo that same morning and was passing the shop just as the blinds went up to reveal, in a kind of unveiling, a lovely pale-grey coat with a sumptuous fur collar. She had gone into the shop instantly and her purchase of the coat had been a source of wonder for many of the war brides. They could only guess at the price and would not have been able to afford it in any case. Yet, ever since that day of Sally's good fortune, every war bride going into Oslo would always make a point of looking in that particular window, if only to gaze at the un-attainable, but so far there had not been a repeat of that wonderful delivery.

Anna and Molly, having made their usual pilgrimage to look in the window, finished their Christmas shopping by each buying a flowering plant for Aunt Christina, for they knew there was nothing she would like better. They went straight to deliver their gifts to her, always calling on her whenever possible, and as usual she welcomed them warmly and plied them with refreshment.

Anna had been given several good recipes for bread by Aunt Christina, for like most of the war brides she had begun making her own loaves and rolls. There was a bread van that delivered, but often it had run out of supplies before it reached Gardermoen. Anna had had an amusing experience the first time she wanted to buy yeast from the local shop, for she had forgotten her dictionary. So she mimed kneading dough and puffing out her cheeks until understanding dawned on the shop-woman, who was promptly convulsed by giggles that she could not overcome. She was still giggling when she handed over the yeast to Anna, who was equally amused.

Although bread deliveries were erratic, it was never difficult to buy fresh fish. The fish van came every Thursday, the fishmonger hooting his horn at every halt to let housewives know he had arrived. Fru Dahl and Anna were regular customers, for meat was still in short supply and the fish was always the day's catch and the choice excellent. There were times when Anna

86

thought to herself that she had never eaten so much fish in her life before, even though she had grown up in a seaside town. Once she had remarked to the fishmonger that it must have been a great help for people to have fish off ration during the Nazi occupation, but he immediately corrected her.

'No, that was not the case. We had to supply daily quotas of our catch to the German troops and there was very little left – and sometimes nothing – for our own people.' Anna thanked him for enlightening her. There seemed to be no end to the privation that the Norwegian people had suffered during the occupation. Yet nothing had shaken their united defiance.

Five

It had been arranged that Anna should travel by train with Pat and Rolf and little Mandy to the west coast at Christmas. Rolf's parents lived in the family farmhouse on the outskirts of Andalsnes, the town that lay at the head of the Romsdal fjord, and from there it was either a ferry ride or a drive to the town of Molde, which was Anna's destination. Correspondence with Johan's father had resulted in an arrangement that she would be met by car at the railway station upon her arrival. Whether he would be driving or somebody else at the wheel he had not stated.

'Train tickets are going to be hard to get,' Pat told Anna, 'because there are still only comparatively few trains due to sabotage during the occupation and general neglect during those years. As long as German troops could be moved about, the travelling public had to take whatever was available. What's more, the Norwegians are all like homing pigeons when it comes to Christmas! As for the traditional Christmas tree, I don't know what any one of them would do if they didn't have one! I remember so well from last year – my first

Christmas in Norway.'

'Johan and I only had two Christmases together in our lives. I remember how jubilant he was when the news came to the squadron that King Haakon had received his annual Christmas tree, brought back by Norwegians returning from secret sorties there.'

'Yes, he had one every year throughout his exile. I read in the paper it's why Norway is sending a tree to London this year, and intends to do it in perpetuity in appreciation of all the UK did for the King and Norway during the war.'

'I'm glad of that. Did you enjoy Christmas here as much as at home?'

Pat answered thoughtfully. 'I missed my parents and my brother, but otherwise I thought Christmas a lovely time to be here. Rolf is going to line up early for our train tickets, because it will be a case of first come first served. He intends to take up a place at four o'clock this afternoon at Oslo's railway station before the sale of tickets starts tomorrow morning at eight o'clock. He wants to be sure of getting a sleeping compartment for you with me and Mandy, because it is a long overnight journey.'

'Do we have to go into Oslo to catch the train?'

'No, we'll get on it at ten o'clock when it stops at Eidsvold, which is the nearest railway station for us.'

'Is that what you did last year?'

'No, we were too late to get train tickets and travelled by bus, which took forever. I couldn't face that again.'

Anna was not present when Rolf returned home with the sleeping-compartment tickets, waving them triumphantly, and he had also managed to book a seat for himself. She heard later what an ordeal the long wait had been; there had been a fiercely bitter wind constantly gusting snow from across Oslo fjord in a night temperature that was far below freezing, making the long row of those patiently waiting look like an endless row of snowmen. Pat was concerned that Rolf would suffer after-effects, but a hot shower and a substantial breakfast soon put him right again. All that remained was to book a taxi to take them to Eidsvold for their departure.

This proved to be difficult too, for there were not many taxis in the area and all had been booked long before. Eventually one taxi driver, wanting to be helpful, called in a friend, who agreed to take Rolf and his family with Anna to Eidvold railway station on the night required.

The temperature continued to drop steadily in the final weeks before Christmas. It was thirty degrees below zero when the substitute driver and his car arrived half an hour later than the time that had been arranged for him to come. Pat had begun to panic, thinking he was not going to turn up, and was so relieved when he did arrive, tooting his horn to announce his arrival, that she declared herself ready to kiss him. Rolf, in his haste to get the girls and his child out of the cold night into the vehicle failed to notice that there were no chains on the car wheels to prevent skidding. Neither did he realize that the driver, silently and solidly wrapped up, who had not moved from his seat to help with the luggage, was drunk. That became all too obvious to Rolf when he took the seat in the front beside him and was assailed by the man's alcohol-imbued breath. But it was too late to do anything about it now, and Rolf had grave fears as they set off into the blackness of the night amid the swirling snow.

It was a dangerous drive in every way, the wheels constantly sliding from one side of the road to the other on the icy surface, and there were no lights along these country roads to aid the journey. Rolf wanted to change places and drive the taxi himself, but the drunken driver stubbornly refused, gripping the wheel with a relentless strength. He was a large man, greatly overweight, and there was no way he could be budged single-handed out of the driving seat. He refused utterly to give up the wheel.

'No,' he declared stubbornly, his speech slurred. 'You've no licence to take passengers.'

'Neither have you in your alcoholic state!' Rolf retorted. 'If the police stop us, you'll lose the one you have!'

But persuasion and threats proved useless and the nightmare journey continued. Fortunately there was very little traffic, but they were still a distance from Eidsvold railway station when the taxi finally skidded off the road into a bank of snow. The girls screamed and Mandy, warmly wrapped in a plaid shawl, woke with a start and began to cry. Rolf leapt out to view the damage with the light of a torch he had previously used in loading the luggage. The snow had softened the impact and he could see no real damage apart from a buckled fender, but there was no way the taxi could be brought back on to the road without a tow rope.

There followed a seemingly endless wait for a vehicle to come along that could be of help, and all the while the time ticked away to the arrival of the train at Eidsvold. If they missed it, it would be end of their getting to their destinations for Christmas. Rolf paced up and down, watching for headlights to appear. Normally of a jovial nature, he could be angrier than most at incompetence and carelessness. He did his best to soothe the girls' anxieties.

'Don't worry. Someone will come along soon. Then we'll be on our way again.'

Yet he looked surreptitiously at his watch whenever he was out of their view.

Suddenly the glow of headlights appeared, and to his relief he saw it was a van. He waved it down and the driver was quick to jump out and help a fellow motorist. It was not an uncommon accident.

He produced his own tow rope, which most drivers kept in their vehicles for emergencies, although Rolf had failed to find one in the taxi.

The car was soon back on the road and by

now the driver had sunk into a drunken stupor. With further help from the van driver, Rolf managed to heave him out from behind the wheel and into the neighbouring seat. He would have liked to dump the fellow at the side of the road, but he could not let him freeze to death. Then, after thanks and an exchange of Christmas greetings with the van driver, Rolf drove off on the last lap of the journey. It was already past ten o'clock and he hoped desperately that the train would be a little late and give them some leeway to get there. On the back seat the girls were silent, as if holding their breath in suspense.

At last they arrived at Eidsvold railway station. Rolf darted ahead, prepared to halt the train if it should still be there. Within minutes he was back again and opened the car door for the girls.

'No need to hurry,' he said wryly. 'There's been an avalanche on the line, which has delayed the train for clearance, and there'll be a wait of at least four hours.'

Relief that they were still able to get the train made the long wait ahead seem negligible to the girls, but even though they waited in a warm waiting room with a big black stove kept refuelled by a porter, they soon found that time dragged by. The wooden wall-seats were uncomfortable and not an inducement to sleep. Like the other passengers waiting with them, they dozed, ate sandwiches they had brought with them and drank hot coffee from a vacuum flask. All the time Mandy slept as snugly as if in her own cot at Gardermoen.

It was more than four hours later when the train eventually came thunderously into the station, hissing steam. Everybody grabbed luggage and rushed out on to the platform. It was snowing heavily and the sleeping cars were at the far end of the train. Rolf hurried the girls forward and helped them aboard into the entrance compartment, but Anna found that the connecting door into the sleepers was locked. Although she and Pat hammered on the door and Rolf shook it, there was no response.

'The attendant must be at the other end of the car,' he exclaimed in exasperation. 'I'll find him!'

He leapt out on to the platform again, but as he slammed the door after him the train began to move. Pat gave a shriek.

'He'll be left behind!'

Anna cupped her hands against the glass and peered out, but it was impossible to see anything in the thickly swirling snow. She turned back to Pat, both having the same anxious expression at the seriousness of the situation, for the temperature in this narrow space was the same as outside.

'How long before we get to the next halt?' Anna asked.

'It could be two hours,' Pat answered tremulously.

'We must keep Mandy warm at all costs.'

Although the child was still wrapped in the

plaid shawl over her winter coat, Anna knelt to open her suitcase and take out a thick cardigan, which they added to the wrappings around the child as well as a spare scarf. Then they both sat down on their upright suitcases and tried not to think how long they might have to wait before they gained the chance to change to another part of the train. Now and again Anna banged on the connecting door, but there was no response.

They had fully resigned themselves to Rolf having failed to reboard when half an hour later there came the sound of a key being turned in the connecting door. As they sprang to their feet, the door opened with a gush of warmth and the sleeper-attendant stepped aside to let Rolf come rushing in to gather them up.

'It's taken me all this time to search the train for this lazy devil right here behind me!' he declared angrily. 'He was sleeping out of sight in the luggage car! He's lucky I didn't murder him! Now,' he added as he shepherded them into the corridor of the sleeping compartments, 'I'll get you settled into number thirty-two.'

But the uniformed attendant, an officious-looking little man, was holding up his hand and blocking the way. 'There are no sleeping compartments or seats left, but you ladies can sit on the floor with other people without seats further up the train.'

Rolf looked as if he might explode with rage and held up the tickets. 'I waited sixteen hours in the worst of Oslo weather to get these sleepers and I mean to have them!'

The attendant answered with smug satisfaction. 'You were not here to claim them by the booked time of ten o'clock and therefore you have forfeited your right to them. Two other passengers are occupying them now.'

'Your damn train wasn't here at ten o'clock!' Rolf roared. 'It was still halfway up the line from Oslo! I'm having those sleepers no matter how much the occupants tipped you to let them in there!'

He charged off along the row of doors until he came to number thirty-two, where he banged a furious fist on the door. The attendant had come rushing after him, shouting at him to stop, but as Rolf hammered on the door again, it slid open from inside and a sleepy young man on the lower bunk raised himself on an elbow.

'Yes?' he mumbled. 'What is it?' Then before Rolf could answer the young man's eyes opened wide as he recognized the intruder. 'Rolf Hansen! I thought you were dead! Shot down over Germany!'

Rolf laughed, equally astonished by this unexpected meeting with a former comrade-in-arms. 'So I was, Nils, but although they shipped me back to England and patched me up, I wasn't able to return to 332 Squadon before the liberation came.'

By now the other young man on the top bunk had stirred to see what was happening and was introduced as Nils's brother, Kurt.

'Great to meet you, Rolf,' he said sleepily, extending a handshake, 'but did it have to be in the middle of the night?'

'Yes, it did,' Rolf replied, 'because I want your bunks for my wife and her friend and my little daughter.' Briefly he explained the situation and before he had finished both brothers slid from their bunks in their pants and vests and began to dress. They were soon ready, their ties loose around their necks to be adjusted later. Both of them attempted to straighten the bedclothes, but Pat stopped them.

'Don't bother to do that! Anna and I will do it. If I stand here another minute after all I've been through tonight, I'll collapse on the floor.'

They emerged hastily with rucksacks. The attendant had disappeared, not wanting to return the generous tip he had received from them earlier. Brief introductions took place and then Pat, Anna and Mandy were finally able to get to bed.

Six

When Anna awoke, the small compartment was filled with a greyish light filtering through the window blind. Pat and Mandy were still asleep on the bunk below. Propping herself up on her elbow, she reached out and held back the edge of the blind to look out. There they were! The great mountains of the west coast soaring up in all their splendour, fierce and beautiful and snow-clad, all a-glitter with frozen waterfalls, and on a level with the train was a wide, wildly rushing river adding its own beauty to the scene.

Now Molly and Mandy were awake. The three of them took turns with the facilities and were ready when Rolf arrived to take them along to the restaurant car for breakfast.

By chance, their table was on the opposite side of the aisle to where Kurt and Nils were seated, and at first the conversation between the men continued across the aisle as if had not been interrupted the previous night. They exchanged news of comrades and also discussed events that had taken place in the post-occupation period.

Anna had not taken any part in the general

conversation, just listening with interest, but suddenly Nils turned his gaze on her, his eyes merry in his cheerful face. 'I heard Pat say earlier that you'll be spending Christmas in Molde. That's not far from our family farm where Kurt and I will be. Let's all meet up some time in the festive season.'

'That's a great idea,' Pat endorsed. Then to Anna she added, 'We can always pick you up in Rolf's ancient Ford.'

'Ancient?' Rolf echoed. 'It's only about ten years since I bought it.'

'Yet the Germans never took it,' Pat teased, her eyes dancing at him over the rim of her coffee cup. 'They commandeered all the best cars.'

'They also took all the best horses from the farms to pull their gun-carriages and wagons,' Nils intervened soberly. 'That was hardest of all for my father. It was a family joke that he cared more for them than for the rest of us.'

'Did he ever get them back?' Anna asked with concern. So far she had only seen a few of the *fjordings*, the unique Westland ponies that were the sturdiest of workers, patient and intelligent, all of them a distinctive cream colour with a black streak through the mane and down the tail. They were also the breed that the Vikings had ridden, and that fact appealed to her sense of history.

Nils was shaking his head. 'He is still looking. The Nazis just abandoned them at the docks when being shipped home. Some farmers

99

did find their own.'

The conversation then turned back to arranging a get-together, but Anna had to refuse, explaining that she no idea yet what her father-in-law would have planned for her. Uppermost in her mind was the house in the mountains that awaited her inspection. She pictured it dark and gloomy, smelling of damp and cobwebs, perhaps overrun by mice after being neglected for so many years. In a way, she was dreading that viewing, especially since she knew what a disappointment it would be to her father-in-law when she almost certainly would refuse to accept it. As she reminded herself yet again, he had lost enough in losing Johan. She had no wish to add to his sorrow, but she could not commit herself to an impossible obligation.

When the train pulled into Andalsnes station, the steam billowed over the platform, making ghostlike all who were milling about there. Rolf's brother had come to meet him and his family, and Anna looked around to see who was meeting her. Suddenly a tall figure appeared before her. It was Alex Ringstad and he grinned at her surprise. She warmed to the friendliness in his eyes again.

'Welcome, Anna,' he said, picking up her suitcase. 'I volunteered to meet you.'

'That was good of you, but have you been waiting here long?' she asked with concern. 'This train is hours late.'

'I telephoned a couple of times before I set out, because I had not expected it to be exactly on time, and so I was prepared to wait a while.'

She guessed that, in spite of what he had said, the waiting had been long, but she was making swift introductions to Pat and Rolf and, as always in Norwegian company, there was a great deal of handshaking. Christmas greetings were exchanged as they went their separate ways.

'*God Jul!*'

'Happy Christmas!'

When Anna was in Alex's car, she asked after her father-in-law. 'How is he?'

'I suppose he is as well as can be expected,' Alex replied as he drove out of the station yard. 'Winter is never a good time of the year for him when the roads and pavements are icy. He has to be careful not to fall. He has never fully recovered from the ordeal he suffered at the hands of the Nazis.'

'Why? What happened?' Immediately she was concerned.

'Has Gudrun, his housekeeper, never written about it to you?'

'No. Should she have done?'

He inclined his head, his gaze on the snow-bordered road gleaming in the headlights. 'I just thought she might have prepared you for his frailty. An incident took place in 1943 on June 7th, King Haakon's birthday. Steffan was forty-six then and in his garden he picked a carnation – the national flower of Norway – and put it in his buttonhole before going into town. Other Norwegians would have recognized the flower's significance as a symbol of unity against the invader, but unfortunately a Nazi officer did too and snatched the flower away before striking him to the ground. Then he was hauled to his feet and made to run round and round the market square until he collapsed from exhaustion. He would have been left there if local people had not lifted him up and taken him home. It was then that he suffered a stroke, which affected his walking.'

'Why didn't you tell me this when you came to Gardermoen, on the day you showed me different parts of the forest?'

'Steffan Vartdal is a very fierce, proud man, who likes to ignore his disability, even though now he always has to support himself with a cane. I had to be sure that he wanted me to prepare you in advance and it was only recently he let me know that he did.'

'It sounds to me as if he trusts you implicitly.'

'I believe he does, but he has a nephew, Harry Holmsen, who is his late sister's son. Since Johan's death, Harry has done his best to fill the great gap in Steffan's life, but now you, his daughter-in-law, have the chance to take the place of his nephew and – more importantly – his much loved son.'

She shivered. 'That is an impossible task and too much to ask of me. I'm not here to stay.'

'You may have no choice.'

She did not reply, unable to foresee any circumstances that could persuade her against her will to make her residence permanent. 'I always have a choice,' she replied firmly.' Nobody can take that away from me.'

As they drove along, she was surprised how little snow there was on the lower slopes in comparison to all the heavy falls and freezing temperatures she had left behind in eastern Norway. She questioned Alex about it.

'That is because we have the Gulf Stream all the way up the west coast,' he replied. 'It helps keep our climate mild here in comparison with the eastern part of the country, and it ensures our harbours are ice-free. That's one of the reasons the Germans invaded – they could keep their U-boats in these waters ready to attack Allied ships in the Atlantic.'

'Another was that they wanted the heavy water for their atom bomb,' she replied. 'I read all about that small band of the Norwegian resistance destroying the German chances of getting the atom bomb before the Americans, which they would have done otherwise.'

'Yes, it was a wonderful achievement that will go down in history.'

She thought to herself that in time Hollywood would probably make a movie about those courageous young Telemark heroes, but it was too frivolous a comment to make when remembering the extraordinary bravery that had literally saved the free world.

'Is the district of Telemark far from here?' she asked with interest.

Alex glanced at her. 'It's not too far if you would like to see where it all happened. I'd take you there.'

She thought how quick he was in his offers of assistance and she made her usual excuse. 'I can't make any plans yet.'

The drive took them out of town and then the road followed the still, grey waters of the fjord westwards all the way, the mountains soaring high on either side of it. She had no wish to talk, fascinated by all she was seeing, and he respected her silence.

Then, at last, they drove into the little town of Molde, which was clustered on the lower slopes overlooking the fjord. She could see that some of the houses on the outskirts had escaped the bombing, but the heart of the town still had the simple wooden buildings that Alex explained had been erected in the aftermath of the air raid to keep trade and businesses going in place of the shops and offices that had been burnt to the ground.

'The church here was lost too,' Alex said, 'and so throughout the occupation people used the mediaeval one in the local open-air museum. On the day of liberation, its bell was rung so hard in jubilation that it cracked!'

She smiled. 'It was a great day to celebrate.'

'Molde used to be known as the Town of Roses,' Alex continued as they drove along the main street. 'It had a red rose that was unique to this town and had such a delicate and yet so powerful a scent that it could be inhaled by those on-board ships coming up the fjord. The bombing and the resulting fire destroyed every rose bush in the streets and private gardens. I'm sorry to say that the Molde rose has been lost forever.'

Anna was silent for a few moments. 'That is very sad,' she said quietly. 'To lose such a rose. I would have loved to see it in bloom.'

'They were a fine sight. I only saw them once. That was when I was on a cycling trip during my university days.'

By now they had reached the far side of the town, and Alex turned the car through a pair of open gates and up a drive to come to a halt outside a large and very fine white house with an elegant porch and windows on three floors. It was just far enough out of the town to have escaped the fire, although Alex told her that it had almost reached the Vartdal house.

'So here we are,' he said, switching off the ignition and turning in his seat to look at her with an encouraging grin. 'Don't worry. You will be welcome in spite of your fears.'

'Oh, do I look nervous?' she asked anxiously.

'No, but I'm getting to know you well enough to guess your feelings at this moment. Incidentally, I'm giving a party on New Year's Eve and I'd be very glad if you would come. Your father-in-law already knows and approves that I'm inviting you. I believe I was just in time as I was told that quite a few invitations are awaiting your arrival.'

She smiled. 'In that case, I accept your invitation. It will be wonderful to celebrate New Year's Eve here in Norway.' Then she drew in a deep breath and nodded towards the house. 'Now the time has come.'

He took her suitcases out of the car as she went up the steps of the porch. She reached out and pressed the bell firmly.

Seven

They must have been sighted from a window, for the front door opened immediately, golden light flowing out to them. In the entrance stood a slim, grey-haired woman in her sixties, neatly attired in a green woollen dress, and she greeted Anna with a delighted smile.

'Welcome, Anna,' she said in English. 'I'm Gudrun Eriksen, your father-in-law's housekeeper over many years. Please come in. We have been looking forward so much to your arrival. Alex telephoned us to say you had been delayed.'

'For a while it seemed as if we would never get here,' Anna replied, appreciating the housekeeper's welcome as she and Alex entered the warmth of the wide hallway, where a number of modern paintings adorned the walls and there was the sweep of a grand staircase. She saw Steffan Vartdal immediately. He was silhouetted against a glass door at the end of the hall, a tall figure with his right hand resting on a cane. Gudrun stepped aside for her as she went forward to where he stood, since he made no move to come towards her. Although he was approaching fifty, he was still a handsome man with hawklike features, his hair thick and white, and his eyes were the same deep blue as his son had possessed.

'*Velkommen*, Anna,' he said, formally shaking her hand. Although the words were welcoming, his gaze was cold. It was also as if he had set a clamp on her, and momentarily she was unnerved.

'I'm very glad to be in Johan's childhood home,' she managed to say in Norwegian.

He gave an impatient nod and answered her unhesitatingly in English. 'I judge from what I know of you already from Alex that you are an independent young woman with a mind of your own. You will meet your match in me, for which I'm sure you are prepared.' Then as if bestowing a great favour he added, 'You may call me *Svigerfar*.'

It was Norwegian for father-in-law, and Anna was thankful that he had made it clear from the start how he wished to be addressed by her. 'Thank you, *Svigerfar*.'

Gudrun had come forward to help Anna off with her coat and gathered together her woolly hat, gloves and scarf. 'I'm sure you would like some refreshment now after your long journey.' She glanced up at the staircase where Alex was descending after taking Anna's suitcase upstairs. 'Shall you stay for coffee, Alex?'

'Not this time, Froken Eriksen, but I'll call in tomorrow to see how Anna is settling in.'

Anna wished he was staying, but he was already at the door. Steffan raised a hand to him

108

in farewell. 'I thank you for meeting my daughter-in-law.'

'It was a pleasure.'

Anna did not think it could have been much of a pleasure wasting time in a waiting room that would have been as crowded as the one in which she and her friends had been confined at Eidsvold, but it was kind of Alex not to have minded about the lengthy wait.

Steffan had turned to lead the way into a large and pleasant room where the coffee table had been spread with a lace cloth, and there was a large plate of waffles and a variety of cakes. In a corner fireplace, logs were burning brightly, the flames dancing. On the table there was also a silver candlestick with the customary lighted candle that symbolized welcome whatever the hour of the day.

Anna had learned long since that to be offered a cup of coffee in Norway always entailed food as well, frequently waffles and often *lefser*, which was a kind of pancake, buttered and sprinkled with sugar, that she liked immensely. The coffee and cakes were being served with the finest china in accordance with an old tradition that guests must always receive the best of everything. The war brides had all taken up the Norwegian custom, so everything was familiar to Anna as she sat down while Gudrun poured coffee into the delicate cups.

Anna's glance was caught by the portrait on the wall of a lovely woman that was clearly painted by a very accomplished artist. She guessed the sitter's identity even before Steffan followed her gaze and told her.

'That is my late wife, Rosa – Johan's mother. She was younger than me and yet she was the one to leave this world first when it should have been me. Now my son has gone before me too.'

Anna was aware of the underlying depth of sadness in his calmly delivered words. She recalled Johan saying that his parents' marriage had been a love match in spite of the difference in their ages.

'Your wife was a very beautiful woman,' Anna said.

'Indeed she was. We have an accomplished artist among our forebears, but he was gone long before this portrait of her was commissioned. There is some of his work in the hall and another in the room you are to occupy.'

'I'll look forward to studying each one in turn. I caught sight of them out of the corner of my eye as I arrived.'

'They are not easily overlooked,' he remarked drily. 'Magnus Harvik had a style that was uniquely his own.' Then, changing the subject, he looked at her under his white brows with some concern. 'You must have had a very difficult journey to arrive so late.'

She explained the circumstances of the trip as Gudrun offered her a glass bowl of home-made cloudberry preserve from which she took a spoonful for the waffle she had chosen.

'How delicious!' she said, handing back the bowl. 'I have only tasted this preserve once

110

before when an English friend's Norwegian mother-in-law gave her a pot to share with the rest of us.'

She knew it was a great delicacy for its rarity, the reason being that these golden berries, much like a raspberry in shape and appearance, although not in colour or taste, grew high in the mountains, sometimes almost inaccessibly.

Although Steffan listened keenly to all Anna told him about the journey, it was not with any lessening of the coldness in his eyes. Gudrun exclaimed over all the setbacks that Anna and her friends had endured before asking what life was like for British women at Gardermoen. It gave Anna the chance to say how she enjoyed the company of the friends she had made and how interesting it would be to hear how they had all spent Christmas when she returned. She thought it fortunate that she had been given the opportunity to make her position clear from the start, and Steffan would now know that her stay was only temporary.

Although earlier she had wished that Alex would be staying with her for the first hour or two, everything seemed to be going along very well, which was quite contrary to her expectations. Yet, apart from her initial mention of being in Johan's home, his name had not come into the conversation again. She longed for Steffan to talk about the man she had loved and still loved, for there was so much more she wanted to know about Johan's childhood, as well as his schooldays and his time at univer-

111

sity, before he escaped to England in spite of all the posters warning that anyone attempting to leave Norway would be shot.

She thought there must be photographs of Johan somewhere in the house and she had glanced in vain around the room in the hope of seeing one. She had a framed photograph of him in her suitcase and some snapshots in her purse, but she sensed that the time must be exactly right for when there could be talk of him between the two people who had loved him most.

When the coffee session came to an end, Gudrun suggested that she show Anna to her room. 'I've prepared Johan's room for you, Anna,' she said as she began to lead the way up the curving staircase. 'I was sure you would like to sleep there.'

'Oh, yes! How thoughtful of you!'

'It was recently redecorated with some other rooms in the house, but it is the same as it was in Johan's time.'

'Was there some smoke damage from the fire?' Anna asked. 'Alex told me that the flames almost reached this house.'

'No, the redecoration was not for that reason,' Gudrun paused with her hand resting on the banister rail to look back over her shoulder at Anna following behind, 'although Steffan and I did make a dash for safety up the nearby slopes. I grabbed something blindly as we fled, instinctively wanting to save something from what I thought was our doomed home, and it was not until we stopped to draw breath that I saw what I had snatched up. It was an empty birdcage!' She laughed and her amusement made Anna smile too.

'Do you still have it?'

'Yes. We had just lost a little canary. Although we never replaced it, I have a flowering plant in the cage now and it hangs outside the kitchen window. It is also a reminder of when we saw the King and Crown Prince Olav that day. It was when they were being pursued up the coast by the German Luftwaffe. They watched the bombing and burning of Molde from where they stood by an old birch tree. They were not far from where we were sitting on the grass and catching our breath. Steffan did not think it was right for us to sit in the royal presence, but we were both so exhausted from running that we couldn't do otherwise.'

'Were there other people taking refuge there too?'

'Yes, people were sprawled everywhere. Nearly everyone had grabbed something as they rushed from home. There were dolls and umbrellas and a vase or two – one man had snatched up a wedding top hat. When the fires were under control and it was safe for many of us to return to what was left of Molde, he wore it as he went down the slope. We all saw that as an act of defiance.'

'Yes, I can see that it was.'

Gudrun continued her way up the stairs. 'It was the first show of defiance that I witnessed, but during the Nazi occupation there were all sorts of ways in which we showed our unity against the enemy.' She paused to talk again. 'The paper clip was popular as it was a Norwegian invention, and we wore it on our lapels as a symbolic sign of togetherness. When the Germans realized what it meant, they would snatch them away until some men started putting a razor blade underneath their lapels! That soon deterred the overzealous Nazis!'

Anna made a little grimace. 'I'm sure that it did! Alex told me about Steffan and the carnation.'

'Ah, yes. It was a very worrying time afterwards, because it seemed for a while that he would never recover, but thankfully his strong will pulled him through. We were able to get the paint for redecorating the whole house because of the way it had been used during the occupation. The Germans always commandeered the best houses for officers' quarters and this house suffered an even worse fate. They blocked off the small wing for Steffan and me, which included Johan's room, only allowing us to stay here for me to be their house-cleaner. Then they turned the rest of the place into an officers' brothel. There was noise both night and day.'

Anna raised her eyebrows in dismay. 'That must have been dreadful for you both.'

Gudrun nodded wearily. 'They had brothel ships too, coming up and down the coast.' Then she smiled. 'The only amusement we had during that time was when a load of French

114

prostitutes was brought here. They had been gathered up in Paris against their will and put on one of the brothel ships where they were so seasick and so rebellious that eventually they were taken ashore and brought here instead. That did not last long as they were a constant trouble to the Nazis, always singing the Marseillaise and making French flags to wave in their captors' faces. Finally the commanding officer had them sent to the women's section of the concentration camp at Grini.' Gudrun continued leading the way upstairs. 'I hope no harm came to them, because they had so much spirit and refused to be dominated.'

'Who came after them?'

'Some poor Russian women, most of them young and pretty. They were so sad and homesick, not knowing what had happened to their men or their families or their invaded country. Although it was forbidden to have a radio, Steffan and I used to listen secretly to one that we kept hidden in the cellar and we heard the BBC broadcasting the news from London. Yet, for everybody's safety, we could not pass any information on to them, not even when things were going badly for the German invasion force in Russia.' They had reached the landing and she went ahead to open one of the doors. 'This is Johan's room, Anna. Just as he left it.'

Picking up her suitcase that Alex had left on the landing, Anna entered a simply furnished room with colourful rugs on the pine floor and a view of the garden, with the wide fjord stretching beyond to meet the mountain range filling the horizon. Johan had once described this scene to her, saying that it was possible from Molde to see eighty-seven mountain peaks. She was not at the right viewpoint to see them all now, but it was still a magnificent skyline of which she could never tire.

'When Johan was growing up,' Gudrun was saying, 'Steffan and his late wife had a summer home on the island of Ona, which lies off the coast not far from here. Johan loved it there for the fishing and sailing and swimming, often having a pack of school friends there too. So as soon as it was possible after the liberation Steffan rid this house of anything that he felt the Nazis had contaminated by their presence. People who had lost everything in the bombing were thankful to have all that he gave away. At the same time he replaced what was missing with furniture brought from the Ona summer house.'

'He and his wife must have lived very grandly there,' Anna commented, having thought downstairs what fine furniture there was everywhere.

'Steffan comes from a well-established family that made its money in shipping and he still has business interests in that line.'

Anna had been drawn to the framed oil painting on the wall. The strong colours and something of the artist's style reminded her a little of Van Gogh. She peered at the signature. 'Magnus Harvik,' she said aloud. It was a dramatic view in sweeping brush strokes of a wide fjord

116

hemmed in by great mountains, which seared across the canvas. 'This looks like Geiranger fjord. Am I right?'

'Yes, you are. Have you been there?'

'No, but I have seen pictures of it.' Anna drew back a few paces to gaze anew at the painting. There was a blob of orange paint high up on a wandering path that looked as if it might be representing a woman, which seemed to emphasize the drama of this work of art. 'I think this painting is extraordinarily beautiful. So those paintings in the hall are by the same family artist?'

'Yes. Steffan gave Johan this particular painting during his last Christmas before he escaped to England. It was one that he had long wanted to own.'

'I'm glad to know he had pleasure from it all the time that he could,' Anna said quietly.

Gudrun, although moved to sadness by Anna's tone, managed a smile. 'Naturally the painting belongs to you now.'

Anna caught her breath on a piercing heartache. It was like receiving a gift from Johan himself, one to treasure, although it should have been shared with him. If Gudrun had noticed the anguish in Anna's face, she made no sign.

'Steffan will tell you all about Magnus Harvik soon, but let him choose his own time. Now I'll leave you to unpack. Come downstairs when you are ready.'

Gundrun closed the door behind her and Anna gazed again at the painting, marvelling once more at the skilful use of colour. Then she turned to her unpacking and took out the framed photo of Johan in his uniform, which she held against her as she looked slowly around the room. Here was a set of shelves crammed with his books. There was a mirror that would have reflected his handsome face, and by the bed a lamp by which he would have read at night. She pondered as to where she should place his photograph. Finally she decided on the top of a chest of drawers, turning the photograph slightly so that she would see it from the bed before she slept and again as soon as she opened her eyes in the morning. It also faced Johan's beloved mountains.

She finished her unpacking, placing the contents of her suitcase into drawers where Johan's clothes had once been folded away. Before leaving the room, she went to the window again and studied the view. As she stood there, she did not know how to bear the anguish of being in Johan's home without him. He had had such plans as to where he would take her and what she should see in all the places that had meant so much to him. Then she left the room and went downstairs.

In the hall Anna looked carefully at the Magnus Harvik paintings in turn. The use of colour was also intensely dramatic in each one of them and she was full of admiration for the work. One of them showed a young woman laughing as she turned her head sharply towards the artist, mischief in her eyes, and her rich golden hair was a swirling swathe in the air. She was not beautiful in a conventional sense, but she had a hauntingly sensual presence. This was not a woman who would be easily forgotten by anyone; even her likeness in a painting seemed destined to linger in the mind.

Turning away from the paintings, Anna went into a room that was not the one in which she had had coffee, but she could see Steffan waiting for her in what was probably his favourite chair. It was more library than living room, comfortably furnished and with two walls filled with books from floor to ceiling.

'Come and sit down, Anna,' he said, indicating a chair by the fire of crackling birch logs that gave a cosy atmosphere. She had noticed immediately that there were two more paintings here, not by Magnus Harvik, but by another accomplished artist. Both were portraits and dominated the room. One was another of Steffan's wife when she was older, the other of Johan painted when he was about sixteen years old, with all the signs of the good-looking man he was to become. Steffan followed her gaze and then turned to her again as she sat down, still unable to take her eyes from Johan's portrait and cherishing this glimpse of his earlier years.

'It was difficult to get Johan to give up his leisure time to sit for the artist,' Steffan said. 'He would have preferred every time to be on skis or climbing a mountain somewhere, but his mother wanted a portrait of him and for her sake he suffered the boredom of sitting.' He shifted slightly in his chair as he settled himself to discuss other matters with her. 'Now, there is so much that I want to ask you.'

She expected to be questioned about Johan's time in England and how they had met and so forth, but he avoided all mention of his son whenever possible. Anna deduced that it tore at him to consider his loss at any time, an attitude of mind that she fully understood.

It was the first of several conversations that she was to have with Steffan during the days left before Christmas. His stern expression, which was normal to him, did not encourage light chatter, but he was keenly interested in hearing how the United Kingdom was struggling back to normality after the terrible war years and how she herself had survived the bombing raids. British politics also had his interest and he was full of praise for Winston Churchill. He had strong opinions about his own country's parliament, which he aired forcefully and with displeasure. Once, she asked him about the portrait in the hall of the woman with the golden hair.

'That was Ingrid Harvik, the artist's wife. You shall know more about her another day. Now there are other topics I wish to discuss with you.'

Although he seemed to like talking to her, his frosty attitude did not ease. It was almost as if a veil of hostility hung between them, and Anna was puzzled and chilled by it. Was she such a disappointment in being an English daughter-in-law instead of a Norwegian one?

Alex called to see Anna several times during this time. At the weekend he introduced her to his friends and generally made her feel welcome, in contrast to her father-in-law's chilly attitude. The local cinema had yet to be rebuilt, but a hall that had escaped the fire offered seating on hard chairs, where one night she and Alex viewed a very funny pre-war Norsk comedy, which was worth the discomfort. Anna enjoyed Alex's company, which enabled her to relax whenever she was with him.

Eight

The next few days passed quickly. Anna spoke on the telephone to Molly a couple of times and said that, contrary to her fears, she had been welcomed by her father-in-law, albeit not all that warmly. People came to the house to meet Johan's widow and to invite Anna to coffee or some social event they were holding during the festive season, and she had the chance to go to two different New Year's Eve parties other than Alex's; however, she had accepted his invitation after mentioning it to Steffan. He had encouraged her to go since he never stayed up for New Year's Eve and neither did Gudrun, who preferred to go to bed and listen to the festivities broadcast on the radio.

Anna received another invitation that took her by surprise. The doorbell had rung and, being nearby, she opened it. A tall, thin man, well-dressed in a thick winter coat with a fur collar and hat, his eyes very alert behind horn-rimmed spectacles, greeted her immediately.

'Mrs Vartdal, I believe,' he said in English. 'My name is Daniel Andersen. I am the headmaster of a school situated a little way out from Molde. I wonder if you could spare me a few

122

minutes of your time? I expect you can guess the reason for my visit.'

'Perhaps I can,' she said, his mention of his school having alerted her. 'Please come in.'

He thanked her and entered, removing his fur hat. She took him into the library where they sat down.

'I have heard that you are a qualified teacher,' he said, coming straight to the point of his visit, 'and I have come to offer you a teaching post in my school. English is already spoken all over the world and I believe the time is coming when not to speak such a universal language will be a great disadvantage. That is why I want my pupils to have the very best tuition and to have full command of it. So what could be better for them than an English teacher qualified to teach it well? During the five years of the occupation we were only permitted to teach German and many of the older children fell far behind in their English studies.' He paused, regarding her hopefully. 'Have I said enough to convince you how gladly we would welcome you into our school?'

Anna inclined her head. 'Indeed you have,' she said at once, 'but I have no plans to live in Norway. I am here visiting my father-in-law and hope to make such visits in the future, but those will be from England.'

His disappointment was obvious. 'I know these are hard times in Norway, but we shall recover.'

'I'm certain of that too, but at the moment I

cannot foresee a future here for myself.'

He saw that her mind was made up and he shook his head regretfully. 'If ever you should reconsider, I would always be glad to discuss this matter with you again.'

He departed soon afterwards. She did not tell either Steffan or Gudrun about his visit, not wanting it used as further persuasion towards making her consider staying permanently in Norway.

Anna had soon realized that Gudrun was making sure she was not overwhelmed by local invitations. At the same time she guessed that Steffan was pleased that she was being absorbed into the community.

On the morning of Christmas Eve, Steffan's nephew, Harry Holmsen, called in, having returned from a business trip into Sweden. Anna had been told about him in preparation for his frequent visits to the house. He was the only son of Steffan's late sister, of whom he had been very fond. Harry had trained as an architect, but had become interested in the restoration of old buildings, particularly those of historic interest. Presently he had a project in Sweden, which was taking him there from time to time.

Anna had looked forward to meeting him, being sure that he would be an interesting man, but now that he was here she felt an instinctive dislike of him. He bade her welcome to Norway as everybody did, but she did not feel that he was sincere in his greeting.

'Now,' he continued in his rather lordly manner, 'how are you settling down here, Anna? Everything must be very different for you.' He was in his late twenties, broad-framed and straight-backed, with a chiselled face and sleekly controlled brown hair. 'I had begun to think you would be going home to England without ever coming to see us.'

'It would have been foolish never to have seen this lovely part of Norway,' she replied, not liking his patronizing air, 'quite apart from not meeting Johan's father.'

'How are you getting on with the old devil?' he asked bluntly.

She resented his attitude. 'He has been very kind and hospitable towards me,' she said truthfully. She did not intend to mention the coolness that still lingered in Steffan's attitude towards her.

'Wait until you cross him and then you'll see a different side to his character. I know from my own experience.' He turned towards Gudrun as she returned from placing the gifts that Harry had brought under the tree.

'I see you have included a box of Swedish chocolates for us too, Harry. That's very kind. Have you time to stay for a little while?'

He shook his head. 'I've a lot to do. I only arrived home yesterday afternoon.'

'But you have time to put the sheaf of corn up for us?' she persisted.

He frowned, glancing at his watch. 'I'd forgotten about that. Yes, I'll do it.'

Anna followed them outside, where Harry set up a stepladder by the corner of the house. As he mounted the first steps, Gudrun held up what she had told Anna was a traditional sheaf of corn purchased at the end of a local harvest. Harry took it from her and fastened it on a hook that had probably been there for years and was specifically used for this custom of feeding the wild birds in winter. Some of the neighbouring houses already had their sheaves in place and little birds were fluttering around them, the tits among them adding their colours of blue and green to the festive sight they presented. This Christmas feast would be there to last them throughout the hardest months of the year.

As soon as his task was done, Harry left again, his Christmas gifts from Steffan and Gudrun tucked under his arm, and leaving the stepladder for Gudrun to remove. Anna helped her carry it back to the old *stabbur*, where it was stored with a lawnmower and various other items. The *stabbur* was like a little house, built of logs with a turf-covered roof and standing on rat-proof stone supports. It was much older than Steffan's residence by two hundred years or more and had a lower and an upper floor. Anna remarked that it looked as if it had come out of a fairy tale. She had seen them on old farms as well as in Oslo's open-air museum, and she thought that every one of them looked as if it had been plucked from a magical time.

'I love these old buildings,' she said appreciatively.

'Steffan saved this one from being destroyed,' Gudrun said. 'Some farmers are careless about casting out or demolishing old things, but he cherishes them. Harry is just like him in that way. In the old days these *stabburs* would have been guests' quarters and all the best tapestries, bed linen and draperies would be on the upper floor for them, and the lower floor would used to store corn and other such crops, hence the rat-proof supports and the gap between the steps and the building.' Gudrun nodded wisely. 'The housewives of the old days weren't silly – they knew how to keep guests from being under their feet all the time.' Then she added hastily, 'Not anyone like you, of course.'

'I'm reassured,' Anna said teasingly in amusement as they turned for the kitchen entrance of the house. Then, before they reached it, Anna felt something soft and cold alight on her cheek and she looked up in delight. Large white flakes were falling without a breath of wind to disturb their descent.

'It's Christmas snow!' she exclaimed joyfully.

Gudrun looked surprised at her delight. 'But you've seen plenty of snow at Gardermoen.'

'Not like this, without the bitter cold. This snow is going to transform Molde into the most beautiful Christmas card ever seen!'

'What a romantic you are!' Gudrun declared kindly with a smiling shake of her head. She thought to herself how much Johan must have loved this girl with her wide-eyed appreciation of all that was beautiful. Again, Gudrun personally mourned him anew for his father's sake and for her own private loss in no longer having his friendship. He must have known that she and his father became lovers after his very sick mother died, but he was never judgemental.

She remembered so well the night he was planning his escape to England. So many young men were going, little groups of them taking fishing boats under the cover of darkness to cross the North Sea to the Shetlands while the boat owners deliberately looked the other way. Quite a number went with the escapees, but others had too many domestic commitments to risk the danger of being shot for trying to escape, or being drowned in the North Sea when their vessels were attacked by patrolling German ships or by the ever watchful Luftwaffe from the air.

It was four o'clock on the dark, snow-clad February morning of Johan's departure in 1941 when she went downstairs in her dressing robe to find him putting the last items that he was taking with him into his rucksack. They exchanged a long look with each other, but she spoke as if nothing was out of the ordinary.

'I'll make you breakfast,' she said, fetching the coffee kettle. She had managed to get three eggs from the grocer the day before and she fried all three for him. Then she wrapped two loaves, which would have been the mainstay of her and Steffan's diet for the week, and added a last hoarded tin of meat-cakes.

'I can't take this food—' he began when he had finished breakfast and saw what she had made ready, but she silenced him with a gesture.

'You may be glad to have it,' she said. 'That's all that matters.'

He thanked her and packed it away. Then he shouldered his rucksack and kissed her on the cheek. Still they had not exchanged a word about his departure, and she understood that it was because the less she knew of his exploit, the safer she and Steffan would be if interrogated. Then, as he went out of the house, she darted after him into the porch to clutch at his sleeve in desperate appeal.

'Don't let the Germans get you!' she implored.

He gave her a reassuring grin. 'Just let them try!'

She had watched him go off down the road with his quick and easy stride, the darkness soon swallowing him up. It was to be five long years until the liberation, when she and Steffan wept together at the news that he was never coming home again. Gudrun's thoughts turned to Anna, for there was mounting up in her a determination to confront this young woman with the future instead of letting everything dwell on the past. The opportunity presented itself when she was busy in the kitchen and Anna came in after taking a brisk walk.

'What are you making now?' Anna asked with interest, pulling off her hat and gloves before dropping her jacket on to the back of the chair. Gudrun, standing by the table, was beating hard the mixture in a bowl that she was balancing on her hip.

'A *blotkaker*,' she replied. 'Want to help?'

'Yes! Those cakes are the most delicious I have ever tasted and I've had a fair share of them since I arrived here in Molde. Tell me what to do.'

'There are five eggs in this bowl and – in your English measurements – five ounces of sugar. Carry on whisking until the mixture trebles in size and becomes thick enough for you to trail a figure eight in it. Then lightly fold in three ounces of plain flour sifted with two ounces of potato flour. I have greased and lined the baking tin already.'

Anna took up the whisking with enthusiasm, thinking how she would make one of these glorious cakes for her next coffee gathering at Gardermoen. It was not long before the mixture was ready to be poured into a tin, which she estimated to be about ten inches in diameter. Then into the oven it went at 150 degrees centigrade for ten minutes and then the heat was lowered to 140 degrees for half an hour.

Gudrun came into the kitchen just as the cake was ready. She took it from the oven and turned the feather-light sponge upside down on to a rack, explaining that it would not sink.

'When it is cold,' she said, 'you turn it out the right way up, slice sideways through it and put whipped cream on the bottom half, sprinkle on some fruit, and then put on the top half and cover it with whipped cream. Make a design on the top with a fork or decorate with more of the fruit. I always think that strawberries or raspberries in season are the best choice.'

'What are you using today?'

'Some very nice canned apricots. Harry brought us a couple of cans from Sweden after one of his trips there.'

'This cake will be food for the gods!' Anna declared happily, proud over the part she had played in the making of it.

Suddenly the words which Gudrun had had uppermost in her mind over several days burst forth as if of their own volition. 'You should be making cakes like these for a husband and family!'

The colour drained from Anna's face. 'How can you say that to me here in Johan's home?'

'Because he would never have wanted to block your happiness for the rest of your life! And that is what your memories are making him do! Love him still! Remember him always! But make way for the future. It's where you belong!'

For a few seconds Anna stared at her. Then she rushed from the kitchen up to her room, slamming the door behind her. She went across to the window and stared out, as if to draw strength from the view. Gudrun's words were to haunt her for the rest of her stay, the truth of them burning into her. Yet how could anyone ever take Johan's place?

131

Nine

It was Christmas Eve and Anna put on a green silk dress that she had kept for the occasion. It was not new, having been bought with clothing coupons saved up towards its purchase during the war. 'It matches your eyes,' Johan had said fondly the first time she had worn it.

They were both so happy that evening. They had come home from a dance to her room in the accommodation provided for workers at the nearby munitions factory. Ahead of them stretched a whole night of love-making, but it was to be the last of their short married life together.

Before leaving the room, Anna picked up the framed photograph of Johan to take downstairs with her. Although Steffan had brushed aside every attempt she had made to speak of Johan, this was a special night of the year, and he should be remembered and spoken of with love in what was a truly a family occasion. Unlike Steffan, Gudrun had been pleased to share her memories of Johan, showing her an old album full of black and white family snapshots of Johan from babyhood to his university days. Some had been taken with friends when sailing or skiing, often with plenty of pretty girls in tow, as well as earlier ones with his parents on childhood family picnics in the mountains and elsewhere. Then, when all the snapshots were viewed, Gudrun closed the album and handed it to Anna.

'I'm sure Johan would have wanted you to have these pictures.'

Beyond words, Anna hugged her in gratitude.

Now, as Anna went down the curved stairway, she was surprised to see that Steffan was waiting for her. He was wearing what she guessed to be his best dark suit with a diamond-headed gold pin in his tie. There was also the sparkle of diamonds in his cufflinks.

'We shall go in together to dine,' he said formally, offering his arm.

She hesitated. 'But first of all, because it is Christmas Eve, there is something I want so much to share with you.'

He raised his thick white brows enquiringly, not having seen that she had been holding the photograph at her side. 'What could that be?'

She raised the photograph with both hands to show it to him. His face revealed no change of expression, although a nerve twitched in his tightened jaw as he studied the likeness of his son. He half lifted a hand as if to take it from her, but changed his mind to let his hand drop back.

'I can see that the war took Johan's boyhood from him,' he said quietly. 'This is the likeness of a man that faced and overcame a terrible

133

enemy. There is a heavy responsibility in his eyes that was never there before. Yet he found love too.' He turned his gaze on Anna. 'I'm thankful that you brought happiness into his life when he needed it most. It is why you should stay in Norway. Without you as a constant reminder of his life, he would be totally lost to me.'

She was dismayed, never suspecting that he would turn the moment to put an obligation on to her shoulders. He had offered his arm again and she took it hesitantly. Together they went towards the open double doors where Gudrun was waiting for them. The whole dining room was shining with candlelight from the silver candelabra on the table, setting the glassware sparkling and giving a rich ruby glow to the crystal decanter of Gudrun's home-made wine. Earlier, Anna had been asked by Gudrun to do a centrepiece, and she had trailed greenery and bright rowan berries along the white cloth that was embroidered around the hem by some long-ago hand with a motif of little Christmas gnomes riding reindeer or driving sleighs or dancing to the music of an Hardanger violin. She had been shown by Gudrun how to fold the napkins into fans and these added to the pleasing scene.

Anna set Johan's photograph on a side table, and out of the corner of her eye she saw Gudrun's flash of surprise, although nothing was said. Then the three of them sat down together and bowed their heads as Steffan said grace. First of all they drank aquavit from tiny glasses, saying *Skal* to one another. The spirit almost took Anna's breath away as it was very strong, although she had experienced it before at Gardermoen parties and knew what to expect.

The first course was smoked salmon and this was followed by *pinnekjott,* a dish customary to this part of the west coast at Christmas, consisting of lamb chops that had been salted and prepared much as had been done in Viking times, accompanied by a selection of vegetables. The meat had a distinct flavour that was uniquely delicious, and Anna was surprised by how much she liked it. She thought how different this dinner was from the turkey and Christmas pudding in England, for there followed the famous *ris krem.* Gudrun explained that it was thick cream whipped to hold its shape and then a little cooked short grain rice was stirred in for texture, and the whole served with a pouring fruit juice, which this evening came from raspberries bottled by Gudrun in the summer. Throughout the dinner the Scandinavian custom had prevailed in which nobody drank alone, but always raised a glass to another, who responded.

'What a perfect Christmas feast, Gudrun,' Anna said appreciatively as the meal ended.

'I'm so glad you enjoyed it,' Gudrun replied, looking pleased.

'We cannot leave the table without a toast,' Steffan said, rising to his feet, and both Anna and Gudrun did the same. He held his glass high and spoke clearly and strongly. 'To the memory of Johan and those of his fellow pilots, who also lost their lives in the cause of freedom!'

They drank the toast. Surprise had kept Anna dry-eyed, but Gudrun turned aside to wipe her eyes surreptitiously. Then, as they drew away from the table, Steffan turned abruptly to Anna in a sudden and tremendous burst of fury, emphasized by his fist crashing down with such force on the table that the candelabras tilted, scattering lighted candles. Gudrun cried out in dismay as the decanter crashed to the floor in a river of wine. Anna stood shocked and motionless.

'Why did you not have a child?' he roared at Anna, his face tormented.

Now she understood the coldness that he had maintained towards her. His resentment had finally built up beyond his control. If he had had a grandchild, it would have been some consolation to him, particularly if the child had been a boy. Instead, he had nothing but a foreign daughter-in-law likely to leave Norway at any time and he had no power to compel her to stay.

Anna remained frozen by shock. 'I wanted a baby,' she said, the words stumbling from her. 'I never knew from day to day if Johan would return safely and I would have loved his child dearly. But it did not happen, and so I was left doubly bereft when I lost him.'

After standing as he was for a minute or two, Steffan covered his eyes with his hand while with the other he clutched the back of a chair for support. Deeply moved, Anna went forward and put an arm about him.

'Don't cry,' she implored desperately. 'I don't know how to suffer more tears and yours are breaking my heart all over again.'

After a few minutes he straightened up and faced her. 'That is something I would never wish to do.' He was seemingly in control of himself again. Gudrun had managed to extinguish the candles before any damage was done and had been quick to get a cloth to mop up the wine. He waved his hand slightly to indicate that she should leave the mess for the time being.

'Let us go to the tree,' he said.

Gudrun glanced uncertainly from him to Anna and rose up off her knees. Then she obeyed him, going ahead to open the double doors into the next room, but closing them again after her. Steffan offered Anna his arm. She was still trembling from the shock she had received and could feel that he was shaking from the exertion of his outburst. Together they went towards the closed double doors, which Gudrun threw wide as they approached, presenting a perfect sight of the beautifully decorated tree. It was aglow with lighted candles fastened to its branches, and many small decorations glittered and shone amid strings of little Norwegian flags. At the top of the tree was a sparkling star of Bethlehem.

'It's perfect,' she said almost in a whisper, knowing that she was seeing this tree exactly as Johan would have seen the trees of his youth, right up until the last Christmas before he left home, never to return.

'Would you like to distribute the gifts from under the tree, Anna?' Gudrun was asking her.

'Yes, I should like that very much,' she replied, her thoughts still full of Johan.

The gifts were opened in turn. Steffan thanked Anna courteously for the tie and for the bottle of aquavit she had purchased in the officers' mess. Gudrun was clearly pleased with her necklace and put it on at once. There was a bottle of whisky for Steffan from Harry, which he would have bought on his trip to Sweden, and also a gift for Gudrun, which turned out to be her first pair of nylon stockings. She was delighted with them. Women everywhere had heard about this new type of stocking, but few had seen them. Anna smiled to remember that the best gift any girl could receive during the war had been a pair of nylons from a GI, for the American troops seemed to get them supplied together with chocolate and chewing gum and other things that were rare treats for everybody else. She had never had a GI boyfriend and was as eager as Gudrun to see these fine stockings, but their excited discussion ended when Steffan tapped his cane to remind them that there were other gifts to open.

Anna was pleased to find that Alex had given

her a book with very fine photographs of Norway. She took a quick glance at some of them before she turned to her other gifts. Gudrun had knitted her a matching set of woolly cap, scarf and gloves. In addition, on Steffan's behalf, Gudrun had knitted her one of the classic Norwegian cardigans of homespun wool, which every Norwegian – man, woman and child – possessed in various colours and design. Anna's was blue and white with a pattern of snowflakes over the shoulders. She was extremely pleased with it, having long wanted one. She tried it on and it fitted her perfectly.

There were two gifts left for her to open. She was surprised to find that one was from Harry and he had given her a pair of nylon stockings too. He would have known that Steffan's daughter-in-law was coming for Christmas and clearly he had not wanted her to feel left out. Perhaps he had even guessed at the cool reception she would have to face.

'How very kind of Harry to include me,' she said, feeling that she must revise her initial opinion of him.

Her final gift was from Steffan. When it was unwrapped, a jewellers' box was revealed. She opened it to find a beautiful gold necklace and matching earrings. It was easy to see it had been a craftsman of exceptional skill that had made this exquisite set.

'How can I begin to thank you, *Svigerfar*!' she exclaimed. 'It's a wonderful gift.'

He watched as she put on the earrings and

Gudrun fastened the clasp of the necklace for her. Then she darted across to a wall mirror and gave a deep sigh of pleasure at her reflection. Then she turned back to Steffan. As it was the custom always to shake the hand of a donor when a gift was received, she took his hand into hers.

'*Tusen takk, Svigerfar*,' she said, almost in a whisper from the depth of her feelings, which somehow created a moment of intimacy between them, even though she sensed that his resentment was still there. It was too deep-rooted even on this Christmas Eve for him to show any compassion for her sorrow that she had never conceived. Apart from the circumstances of the Nazi occupation, she supposed it was the first time he had been denied what he had wanted most in his life.

He went to bed soon afterwards. Gudrun was unable to relax until the untidiness in the dining room had been cleared up. Anna helped her and it was soon done. They also washed the dishes, for although Gudrun had help in the house, she had given the girl time off to spend Christmas with her own family. Anna, remembering Sally's letter that had told how she had a dishwasher in her kitchen, she wondered how long it would take before those machines could be purchased here or anywhere else struggling to recover from the war.

They returned from the kitchen to sit by the corner fireplace, where birch logs crackled cosily and danced with flames. There they enjoyed several chocolates from the box that Harry had included with his gifts. Gudrun talked for a while about him.

'He's the only son of Steffan's late sister, of whom he was very fond. As I have mentioned to you, Harry has always been generous. During the Nazi occupation he often managed to get food for us. I did not let Steffan know, because it was against his principles to have anything denied to others, but I could not refuse when so often the shops had nothing to meet the ration cards and our own cupboards were empty. Only the Germans were well fed, and what they did not eat was shipped back to Germany.'

'At least you can be pleased to know that in caring for Steffan you kept him well after his stroke.'

'But that was his second stroke, which is why I dread him having a third one. He suffered the first one after Johan had escaped to England and we received a false report that he had been captured, which meant the death sentence. It turned out to be another young man named Johan, but the damage had been done. Steffan was in a very poor state and unable to leave his bed, when the Germans began rounding up the fathers of the escapees as hostages and putting them in concentration camps.'

Anna was shocked. 'Was Steffan arrested?'

She shook her head. 'Fortunately the two young soldiers who came to get him were reluctant to drag a sick man from his bed. I could see that they were kind-hearted boys, as I'm sure many of them were, but they had to obey the Nazi orders that turned them into thugs. These two reported back to their medical officer, who came strutting into our small section of the house to inspect the patient. He took one look at Steffan and told the soldiers to leave the old man as he was going to die anyway.'

Anna gasped. 'Did Steffan hear that?'

'Yes, he did, and maybe it was a turning point, because he rallied afterwards, determined to hold on to life until Johan returned. Yet it took him a long time to recover. That was when Harry was particularly helpful, getting eggs and other foodstuffs to help Steffan's recovery.'

'Did Harry ever try to escape to England?'

She shook her head. 'Harry was in the resistance, although that is all I know. Naturally he does not talk about what he did, but I do know that when one of the resistance leaders was being hunted in this area, Harry endured being labelled a quisling when he pretended to fraternize with the Germans in searching for the fugitive. After that – as he explained to us and to a court after the liberation – he had gained the Germans' trust enough for them to put him to work in one of their offices. This enabled him to thwart them in minor ways, such as alerting those about to be arrested and so forth.'

'How did he clear his name after the liberation?'

'It was difficult for him and he only escaped prison by sheer luck when a few people spoke on his behalf, telling how he had warned them when the Germans were making raids on property and so forth.'

Anna was reminded of Fru Eriksen at Gardermoen, who had also been spoken for by someone she had helped. Now she tried to revise her opinion of Harry. That instinctive dislike of him had not been entirely erased in spite of his generosity, which she had genuinely appreciated.

'What of Alex?' she asked. 'What did he do here in Norway? He has never mentioned being in England.'

'He was there!' Gudrun exclaimed with emphasis. 'And he was in and out of Norway too! Not that we would have known, except that he had a special award from the King and another from Winston Churchill when that great man visited Oslo not long after the end of the war. Alex was in the SOE.'

Anna caught her breath. Those in the Special Operations Expedition – men and women specially trained in the UK who returned to their own Nazi-occupied countries and organized branches of resistance to carry out vital sabotage and take great risks themselves in various operations. Such men and women had done as much to win the war in their own courageous way as the armed forces.

'I asked Alex once about what he had done,' Gudrun continued. 'He simply said that his worst moment had been when he was in Oslo on a secret mission and saw his own parents coming along Karl Johan gate. He had to turn away and look in a shop window, because on no account could he let them see him. Too many lives depended on his remaining totally inconspicuous. He watched their reflections pass by. Sadly for him, he never saw either of them again as both died before the occupation ended.'

Anna felt a deep pang of pity for him. He lingered in her thoughts when at last she and Gudrun went upstairs to bed. They said goodnight in whispers on the landing, not wanting to disturb Steffan. Then Anna closed her door silently and stood in thought for a few moments. She had had an insight into the lives of three very different men that evening. She now understood and sympathized with Steffan's frozen attitude towards her, which she doubted would ever really thaw. As for Harry, he had much to commend him which she had not suspected before, and she hoped her initial uncertainty about him would fade as she came to know him better. Yet it was Alex who had done most for his country. Now that everything had been made clear to her, she felt more in control of her own life. She found this a comforting thought as she made ready for bed. Yet before getting under the duvet, she went to the window and parted the curtains to look out at the snowy scene. It was a clear night and the fjord looked almost luminous under a sky of stars.

On the far side of the fjord were the twinkling

lights in the villages of Vestnes and Vikebukt. Again, the feeling swept over her that all was more familiar to her than she would previously have believed possible. She could only conclude that Johan had described everything to her so vividly that he had given her this extraordinary awareness of the beauty and history of his homeland.

Christmas Day dawned bright and clear, the sky a cloudless blue. Anna smiled to think how her aunt had thought this land was dark by night and day. When she went downstairs, she saw immediately that several framed photographs of Johan had been placed here and there by Gudrun. Most importantly of all, the portrait of Johan had been moved to the drawing room wall near another portrait of his mother. Gudrun found Anna studying it.

'Steffan told me to put it back in its original place,' she said. 'I have missed it there so much. He had everything shut away when we received the terrible news about Johan. He just could not endure reminders of what he had lost. It was the same when he lost his wife. I believe his grief will begin to heal now.'

'I hope so much that you are right,' Anna replied thankfully.

Then it was time to get ready for church. Anna had expected it to be a service at the museum church, but that was not to be. Instead, Harry was coming in his car to take them across the fjord to Vestnes, and from there they would attend the service in Tresfjord church. Gudrun

145

explained that Steffan's wife, Rosa, had grown up on a farm in Tresfjord, and she and Steffan had been married in the church there. Her last resting place was in the churchyard.

'It is Steffan's annual pilgrimage,' Gudrun explained. 'It is a physical strain on him to make any journey these days.'

Harry arrived promptly. He jumped out of the car to help Gudrun settle Steffan into the front passenger seat. They all exchanged the season's greetings.

'*Gud Jul!* Happy Christmas!'

Then, as Harry held the rear door for Gudrun and Anna, they both thanked him for the stockings.

'Are you wearing them?' he asked.

'I am!' Anna extended her foot for display. He grinned approval. 'You've the right ankles for them!' Then he bent his head to look in the car, where Gudrun had taken her place on the back seat. 'What about you, Gudrun?'

'I'm saving them for a special occasion. Perhaps for Anna's wedding, if she should ever find someone to match the best young man that any of us ever knew.'

'That's impossible!' Anna answered firmly, taking her place beside Gudrun in the car. She was surprised at such tactlessness. Then she caught a glance that Harry threw at Gudrun. Did either of them suppose that he had a chance with her?

It was not far to the quay. After Harry had driven on-board the waiting ferry, Gudrun took

146

Steffan into the warmth of the saloon, but as the ferry began to move, Anna went to an upper deck and stood at the rails to gaze at the panoramic view unfolding before her. The great mountains ahead seemed to glide towards her, bringing their own reflections with them. Although the air was sharp and icy cold, there was not a breath of wind to ripple the surface. Harry came to lean on the rails beside her.

'How does this view match that of your home vista?' he asked.

'My personal vista where I grew up was of a seaside promenade and the English Channel, which can capture all the colours of the fjords at various times.' She glanced at him. 'If you are expecting me to praise one country before another, I would never do it, even though Norway is special to me as it is Johan's land.'

He was silent for a minute or two. 'Are you still leaving here after New Year's Eve?'

'Yes, my train ticket is for travelling by day this time, and I will probably return to England soon afterwards. Steffan and Gudrun are aware of my plans and that I intend to return to Norway to visit them from time to time.' Then she seized the chance to change the subject. 'Tell me the names of these wonderful peaks.'

Once on land again, it was only a short drive to the church. It was a white octagonal building with an air of tranquillity about it in its setting of mountain and fjord. Its flagpole held the Norwegian flag high in honour of Christmas Day, and although it hung limply in the still, cold air, it made a brilliant splash of colour against the snow-white scene.

They went first into the churchyard where Steffan took the sheaf of flowers that Gudrun had bought for him the previous day and went alone to stand by his wife's grave. Neither Gudrun nor Harry made any move to follow him, and Anna realized that this was a time when he needed to be on his own. She saw how tenderly he brushed away the snow on the gravestone and then how carefully he laid the flowers in place. Then, unexpectedly, he looked across and beckoned to her.

She went to stand by his side and she read the inscription on the gravestone as they stood in silent respect. Then he spoke quietly.

'Johan would have been standing where you are now.'

After a few more moments he turned to retrace his steps and she followed him to the church door where Gudrun and Harry were now waiting. There Steffan was greeted by people he knew and others used to seeing him once a year. Anna sat next to him in the third row of the pews, with Gudrun and Harry seated on his other side. She was fluent enough in Norwegian to follow the service easily, but she was unfamiliar with the hymns and during the singing she studied the simple but very colourful decoration of the church, wondering what long-ago hand had first painted stars on the vaulted ceiling and decorated the four pillars that supported it. The carved altar piece, which she

148

had been told dated back to the seventeenth century, as did the very handsome pulpit, was of the Last Supper and was clearly the work of a country craftsman more devout than skilled, the figures of Christ and the disciples standing proud at their table. On the wall nearest her was an equally antique angel with outstretched arms, the left one charmingly longer the right one, and Anna appreciated seeing these unusual works of country art.

Harry stayed to dine when they returned home to Molde. He was a good talker and – as Anna had noticed before – Steffan clearly enjoyed his company. She wondered again what it was about this good-looking, friendly man, whom she knew to be generous by nature, which made her wary of him. It caused her to remember how Odin had slunk away in the forest, refusing to go near the concentration camp, but that was a foolish comparison when this man had done so much for his country in difficult times.

After he had gone home, Gudrun went to write some letters and Anna was left alone with Steffan. He regarded her with the stern expression normal to him.

'Are you still resolved to return to Gardermoen and afterwards to England?'

'I'm not going forever. You know that I have promised to visit from time to time.'

'You will always be welcome, but I had hoped that by now you would at least have decided to stay until the Spring when Ingrid's house in the mountains will no longer be hidden by snow.'

'Ingrid?' Anna echoed. 'You have never mentioned a name before.'

'She was my grandmother, and I have in my possession a journal that she kept for a number of years. It dates back to the 1870s, and because it was written in the old style *Norsk* and her handwriting was sometimes difficult to read, I transposed it myself into today's Norwegian. Then, when I heard I had an English daughter-in-law, I had it translated professionally into English.' He rose from his chair and took a red leather-bound book that had been lying in readiness on a side table. Holding it in both hands, he presented it to her quite formally. 'This is the English copy for you.'

'Thank you so much!' She saw that the title in gilded letters read *Ingrid Harvik's Journal.* 'I'll take great care of it.'

'I'm sure you will. It is for your eyes only, because Ingrid was a strong and determined young woman, who writes frankly of her desires and emotions. It is as well that none of her descendants ever read it, because I do not doubt they thought of her as an eccentric old lady, never considering that once she was young and passionate. She is the girl with the swathe of yellow hair that you have seen in the painting hanging in the hall.'

'I have looked at her every time I have passed that painting! Now I am to read her journal!' Anna paused. 'How can you be sure that her journal was never read by others?'

'Because when Johan was a boy, he found it accidentally in its original hiding place.'

'How did it happen?'

'Johan was twelve years old at the time and we were at the old house, taking a look around before going on up to the mountains for the day. I used to check occasionally to see if any repairs were needed. Then I heard a crash and Johan, who had been jumping about upstairs, had knocked over a small cupboard, sending a drawer shooting out to smash down on to the floor. Amongst the debris was a package, wrapped in a dusty drawstring bag, which had been fastened to the back of the drawer. I remember that Johan was disappointed that it was not buried treasure, and yet it was to me. The opening page made me realize that it was a very private journal written by Ingrid Harvik, who made a home in the old house after it had stood uninhabited for many years.'

'Does anybody know why she came there?'

'A reason is given in the journal. I have always respected her privacy, which is why Harry had the other copies printed for me when he was living in the north in Trondheim before the occupation, and where her surname and mine would never be connected. It meant she could retain her anonymity.'

'Did Johan ever read it?

'Once, when he was home from university. His outspoken comment to me was that she would have been formidable in war and a delight in bed.'

151

Anna smiled to herself in amusement. Johan had never minced his words.

'My wife was too ill to read it when it was found,' Steffan continued, 'but I read it to her. At the end of it, she said that she felt Ingrid had the power to draw people to her. Perhaps Ingrid will draw you back to Norway so often that in the end you will have to stay.'

She was intrigued, although she guessed that the journal would just be an account of the life of a strong-minded woman that had passed by in childbearing and domestic happenings. She would wait to read it until she was back in Gardermoen when she could sit quietly in her own apartment and, for Steffan's sake, give her full attention to it. She smiled again at Johan's comment. She knew she had been a delight to him at all times, quite apart from the joy they had shared in their bed.

Ten

The rest of Christmas Day was spent quietly, Anna found a children's book on the bookshelves that had belonged to Johan and in which he had written his name. She passed her fingertips gently over the spot. The book was full of tales about trolls, with splendid illustrations showing these long-nosed creatures peeping around mountain crags or rearing up alarmingly out of rivers and waterfalls.

The remaining time she spent chatting with Gudrun and in the evening listening with her and Steffan to a concert on the radio. It was the following day, which the Norwegians called Little Christmas Day, when friends called on one another, and there were coffee parties and even, in one house, a concert performed by family members and, in another, a talented young man played his violin. Anna met Alex twice at different functions during the day. On both occasions he was with a pretty girl whose looks reminded Anna of Sonja Henie, the Norwegian Olympic skater and film star. He introduced them to each other, but Anna had no clue as to whether the girl, whose name was Eva, was a steady girlfriend or, perhaps, something more. Later she asked Gudrun about her.

'They go around together whenever she comes home to Molde. But that is not very often as Eva has a lovely singing voice. She does a lot of broadcasting and concerts.'

Usually Gudrun and Anna went by themselves to these gatherings, for Steffan preferred a quiet time at home. He even declined an invitation from Harry the following evening and Gudrun did the same, thinking she should stay with him. Anna had already accepted and Harry came in his car to collect her.

'Has Steffan spoken any more about the ancient house he wants to load on to you?' he asked as they drove along.

'No,' she said. 'I think he is beginning to understand that I'm not under his thumb and that this may be my only visit to Molde before I return to England.'

'So how much do you know about the property?'

'Alex explained it all to me soon after my arrival in Norway.'

'If my advice is of any value to you, don't get involved with anything to do with it. Nobody has been in that house for years, and although these old log buildings can stand for centuries, it doesn't mean to say they don't deteriorate in one way or another.'

She enjoyed the evening, for the other six guests were lively and interesting. There was a long discussion about the marvel of Scotsman Baird's invention of television. There had been some televising from a building known as the Alexandra Palace in London before the war, but Anna had never seen any of it. It was said that one day there would be a television screen in every household, but that possibility seemed very remote.

Harry drove Anna home after the others had left. She was afraid he might become amorous when they said goodnight, but she kept her distance and he made no attempt to embrace her.

'I'll see you again before you leave,' he said as he stepped away from the porch, 'even though you haven't much time left now.'

As she entered the house, she thought to herself that Harry was the only one who kept referring to her departure. It was almost as if he wanted her gone in spite of his obvious wish that they should be friends.

New Year's Eve was the last highlight of her visit. Alex gave a good party in his apartment on the outskirts of town. There was plenty to drink, lots of talk and laughter, and a *kalt bord* that offered a number of delicacies, including roasted venison, which she suspected might be reindeer, but she did not want to know and did not ask. His pretty girlfriend was not present, and when she made a casual enquiry, she was told that Eva was singing in a New Year's concert in Oslo.

Dancing took place on the polished floor to the music of gramophone records, although one of the guests played the piano for some of the time, and Anna had no shortage of partners. After earlier dances with her, Alex returned to claim her in the waltz that was the last to be danced in the old year.

'This has to be mine,' he said with a smile, 'since you are my guest of honour.' She thought to herself that he had a way of looking into her eyes as if he were trying to see into her very being. She had noticed it at their first meeting in Oslo. She supposed it was because, as a lawyer, he was always trying to root out the truth. Whatever did he suppose she might be hiding from him?

'It's been a great party – one I shall remember,' she said.

Time had been slipping away and glasses were refilled as Alex switched on the radio. Then from Oslo came the striking of midnight and the greeting: *Godt Nytt Ar!* There was cheering and music. The year of 1948 had arrived. Anna missed the old custom from home of singing *Auld Lang Syne*, and there followed in the room more handshaking than she had ever seen in England, but there was kissing too. Alex's lips were firm and warm and altogether enjoyable. As they drew apart, they looked at each other with a kind of understanding of what might have been if they had chosen to look for it and if her heart had not been swept away long since. She was going home to England and that would be like a door closing between them.

One of the young women there came to touch

156

Anna on the arm. 'Are you ready to leave, Anna? Lars and I have to get back to our baby-sitter and we can give you a lift.'

She accepted, thanked Alex, and left him with his other guests. She was privately thankful that he would not be taking her home as he had expected. One kiss was enough, and she was sure another would have been forthcoming when they were alone.

Eleven

Anna packed Ingrid's journal into her hand baggage when she made ready to leave on the final day of her stay in Molde. She would not risk letting it out of her immediate care. Now she would be travelling back by day with Pat and Rolf and little Mandy in the train seats that had been booked at the same time as the sleepers. It was an early morning departure and Alex arrived in good time to drive her to the railway station.

'All ready?' he asked, picking up her suitcase to put in the car.

'Yes,' she answered, not liking this moment of goodbye. She had said her farewell to Steffan the night before, because he did not rise as early as her departure. He would only have shaken her hand, but she had kissed him lightly on the cheek. Now, under the light in the porch, she and Gudrun exchanged a hug. There was an imploring look in the woman's eyes.

'Come back to us soon, Anna,' she whispered. 'Please don't stay away.'

'I'll visit again, but whether it will be after I have been back to England or before I can't say at the present time,' Anna said. She did not feel able, even at this time of an emotional farewell, to promise anything more.

Alex was holding the car door for her and she went quickly down the porch steps to take her seat. As they drove away, she and Gudrun waved to each other. It was still dark, but already the sky was lifting. Fresh snow had fallen in the night, but the snowploughs had cleared the road. Anna looked from side to side as they drove through the town centre where early lights were appearing in the shops.

'What are you thinking about?' Alex asked, noticing how attentive she was to the passing scene,

'I'm wondering how much Molde will have changed when I see it again. I hope it will be the town of roses all over again, even though it has lost its most important treasure.'

They continued talking as they drove along. At first it was mostly about his New Year Eve party, she wanting to know more about the people whom she had met.

'It was a great evening,' she said.

'Let's make it a date for next year,' he said.

She glanced at him. 'If I'm in Norway,' she said.

'You will be,' he replied confidently.

At Andalsnes railway station, Pat and Rolf were waiting for them, Mandy clutching a new rag doll that had been her favourite Christmas gift. The train was on time, already at the platform. Pat looked anxiously at Anna.

'Did all go well?' she asked at once, her tone

full of concern. 'I thought you sounded all right when we talked on the telephone.'

'Yes,' Anna replied reassuringly. 'Speaking figuratively, I have crossed a bridge with my father-in-law. I know I'll always be welcome whenever I return.'

Rolf had exchanged New Year greetings with Alex and was impatient to get his charges on to the train. 'Come along. You girls can talk all you want when we're aboard.'

As Anna turned to have a final word of fare-well with Alex, he took her by the shoulders, drawing her dose to him, and kissed her deeply for a matter of seconds. She felt totally cap-tured, held as much by the pleasure of his mouth as she was by the firmness of his hold on her. Then he released her with a smile that met hers before she entered the train and followed Pat to the booked seats. She sat down by the window and looked out, expecting to see Alex, but he had gone. Yet his kiss lingered with her in a most pleasing sensation well into the jour-ney.

Back in her apartment at Gardermoen, Anna found mail waiting for her. There were some Christmas cards from friends in England that must have arrived after she had left, a letter from her aunt, who had not been well and emphasized how much she had needed Anna's attention, closing as always on the question that came in every letter: when would she be return-ing home? Interestingly, there were two notifi-cations from her training college of interviews for teaching posts, one in Kent and the other in Derbyshire. Either post would have suited her well, but she would have to be on the next ferry back to England if she wished to be in time to attend the interviews and she was not quite ready yet for departure. She thought again about the offer to teach that had been made to her in Molde and how well that appointment would have fitted into her life if she had not been going back to England before long.

After tucking the college letters back in their envelopes, she opened the door of her stove and thrust them into the flames.

From then onwards her social routine began again with pleasant gatherings and – at first – much talk of how they had all spent Christmas and New Year. Then, soon, the favourite topic was the party they were to hold, and there were various discussions about the decorations for the mess and the food to be served; some of the girls planned to make their own special recipes that everybody would like. It would still be an expensive evening, but enough had been collected to cover everything – even a band of air force musicians, who would play during the meal and for the dancing afterwards.

Recently there had been a movie at the airfield cinema starring Betty Grable, which had been set exotically in Havana with plenty of palm trees, music and dancing. All had enjoyed it and at a meeting the next day the suggestion had been put forward by one of the Norwegian wives that there should be a tropical theme to the party. The idea met with everybody's approval, being particularly welcome when outside the snow was halfway up the windows.

From the start it was agreed that everyone at the party should have a garland of flowers to wear as in the movie, although these would be made of paper. Anna and Molly were to make the table decorations, and others were already pondering how they could create a few palm trees and what colours should be chosen for the garlands, lots of yellow and orange being the favourites. The money already collected and held by Sally as treasurer would cover everything, including the band. At first it seemed as if there might be a problem for those wanting babysitters, because normally the mothers took turns with one another. Yet even that was solved eventually by the young local girl, who had been hired some while ago by Sally to be a nursemaid for Tom. She organized her friends into becoming babysitters for the evening. Everything seemed set for a perfect party.

Then the afternoon came when Anna could be sure of nobody calling or any other interruptions. She took up Ingrid's journal and settled back in her chair against the cushion that Molly had given her for Christmas. On the coffee table beside her she had placed a notebook and a fountain pen in case she wanted to make any notes. Yet before she could read a word there came a frantic knocking on her door. In exasperation Anna put the journal in a drawer, not wanting to be questioned about it. Normally, books in English were willingly loaned, but this one was not to be seen by other eyes.

The desperate knocking had increased. Anna reached the door and opened it to find Sally looking distraught and frantic. 'You have to help me, Anna! I'm in terrible trouble!' she cried, thrusting past into the room and throwing off her coat and scarf before dropping down into the nearest chair.

'Whatever is the matter?' Anna was extremely concerned. There was a wild, untidy look about Sally that she had never seen before. Then, even more distressing, Sally began to sob noisily, her words tumbling from her.

'Before Christmas I received a private word from the owner of the little shop in Oslo where I bought that beautiful coat,' she managed to say between sobs. 'She had had some more lovely stock delivered. Naturally, I went into Oslo that same morning and bought well, but not wisely. Oh, what a fool I was!'

Anna stooped down by the chair to be on a level with her, impatiently seizing her wrists and shaking her into attention. 'You're not making sense! Are you owing her money? Is she threatening you with a summons?'

'No, it's worse than that! The only ready money I had that day was what I had been entrusted with as treasurer for the party and I took it with me.' She looked up now, her eyes stark. 'There were two beautiful and terribly expensive designer dresses that I just had to have or else they would have been snapped up by somebody else! I only meant to borrow from that party fund and repay the amount from my allowance, but the Canadian money still hasn't come through this month and at the next meeting I'm due to show my party fund receipts. I've just enough in my purse to reimburse those who have paid out for a few little things, but that is all! It is bad enough that I shall have to confess what I have done to our friends, but whatever will the Norwegian wives think of me! They will condemn all of us as thieves! That must not happen! That is why I've come to you.'

'I can't help you, Sally!' Anna exclaimed in dismay. 'I spent out in the run-up to Christmas.'

'But everybody knows you have a rich father-in-law. One of the Norwegian wives told us that he was once head of a shipping company. You could telephone him and ask him to send you the amount we need. Then I'll repay the loan when my allowance arrives, as it must do soon.'

Anna straightened up and stood back from her. 'You are asking for the impossible. He is the last person I would ask for anything, especially since I cannot agree to his wishes in a family matter. You must return the dresses to the shop and get a refund.'

'I tried, but the woman refused. She said if I had only had them for two or three days, she would have returned my money, but I have had them since before Christmas and I wore them at various parties during the festive season at my in-laws' home.' Her expression became pathetic. 'How could I not when they were so lovely?' Then her tone became wheedling. 'I'm sure your father-in-law would oblige if only you would ask him.'

'No,' Anna stated firmly. 'My relationship with him is still on a tentative footing, and as yet I've no idea what the eventual outcome will be. Surely Arvid would back you financially until your allowance comes through? After all, he is your husband for better or worse.'

Sally groaned aloud, raising her stricken face. 'I would not dare to ask him! We have had so many rows about my so-called extravagance, because my allowance always seems to run though my fingers and then I get into debt with ordinary things.' She threw up her hands. 'I can't help it! I've always had money to spend and I can't manage on a budget. Arvid is always wanting me to save!' She repeated the word scornfully. *'Save!* As if anybody could do that on our income!'

Anna thought to herself that the other wives whose husbands held the same rank seemed to manage very well. Sally's complaining voice followed her as she went into the kitchenette to make a pot of tea. As Sally continued to moan and groan, Anna shook her head despairingly. It was as Sally had said: all the British wives would be tainted by her theft. It was that thought that made her determined to find a way out of this trouble.

She returned with the tea. She poured a cup

for Sally before sitting down with one for herself. 'I don't want your action to spoil things for others, and so I have a suggestion to make.'

'What is it?' Sally demanded sullenly, still furious that Anna had disappointed her.

'The most important expense other than the drinks is the food, and the caterer has stipulated that he wants to be paid on delivery. But I think we could get what we need from another source that would extend the time of payment. You cannot ask any of the Norwegian chefs to collude with you, but there is one who I'm sure would be glad of a chance to win your favour by doing everything in his power to get you out of this trouble.'

Sally paused after sipping her tea and frowned. 'Whom do you mean?' Then understanding dawned and she looked horrified. 'Not that lecherous Frenchman!'

Anna nodded. 'He is your only hope. Go and see him. Tell him what has happened and how your allowance has been temporarily delayed. Ask him to provide the same food as we have on order with the Oslo caterer, which can then be cancelled, and tell him that payment will come to him just as soon as you're in the money again. The barman will keep account of what is drunk at the bar, but I'm sure Jacques could find a way to get settlement for the drinks delayed by a few days. Your allowance will probably have come by then.'

Sally was torn between relief at Anna's solution and abhorrence at having to humble herself to the Frenchman, who undressed her with his eyes whenever he saw her. Yet she realized that Anna had presented the only solution. Most important of all – both for Arvid's sake as much for her own – was the protection of her good name. Otherwise, it could go against his promotion if a whiff of a money scandal hung about them both. Then their income would never improve and that mattered a great deal to her.

'I'll do it,' she said reluctantly.

Anna sighed with relief as Sally departed, but the interview had distressed her and she was in no mood to start reading Ingrid's book.

She thought later that if it had not been for that interruption by Sally, she would have been reading and might never have thought of inviting Alex to the party. Yet the idea came to her as she was picking up the teacups to take them into the kitchenette and her glance fell on the book of Norwegian photographs that he had given her and which she kept displayed on the coffee table. After the upsetting time with Sally, she was reminded of his powerful presence, which seemed to her at this moment to have the calmness of those same mountains in the book. Yet there was most certainly the fierceness of those mountains too. She had found his kiss of farewell at the railway station impossible to put from her mind. Maybe that was what had been intended. She doubted that he would come such a long way for one evening, but she would ask him anyway.

The letter was sent the next day and a reply of

acceptance came back by return of post. Molly offered her small spare bedroom for his accommodation overnight if he would not mind the storage boxes now housed there. Anna accepted on his behalf.

Anna did not see Sally again until the next meeting. She supposed all had gone well as she had heard nothing more from her. This was confirmed by Sally's sharp and serious nod as Anna entered the room and took a chair beside her.

'I've seen Jacques and he is going to deal with everything,' Sally said stiffly and low-voiced in order not to be overheard, although there was such a babble of voices in the room among the other women that even normal conversation was difficult to hear. 'He is even going to settle the drinks bill temporarily until my allowance arrives.'

'He is being more helpful than I ever dared hope he would be,' Anna said with relief. 'Another bonus is that his food will be better than that of the caterer. So it is a case of all's well that ends well.'

'Not for me.' Sally spoke icily to her. 'I had to give him something on account.'

Anna stared at her in growing understanding, meeting the frantically distressed look in Sally's eyes. 'How could he have dared to make such a demand on you!'

Sally's lips twisted wryly. 'Because he saw as soon as I arrived at his lodgings that I was at my wits' end and desperate for his help. When he stated his demand that I go to bed with him, I nearly went mad with rage, but he remained adamant and made a final ultimatum, saying that otherwise he would report my visit to Arvid. I could not risk that happening and I consoled myself with the thought that it would be a matter of a few quick awful minutes.' She took a deep breath as if it were a struggle to go on. 'But I soon discovered that he prides himself on being an artist in other matters beside food. That was the dreadful part of it. I have never had so much sexual pleasure in all my life!'

'Sally!' Anna gasped. Then she was at a loss for words, having caught an undercurrent in her friend's voice that she did not trust. Sally seemed to guess at Anna's thoughts.

'No, I don't intend to go to him again, but if fate ever threw me in his path at some other time, I cannot vouch for what I would do.'

Anna, dismayed by what had happened, reluctantly turned her attention across the room to Molly, who was on her feet ready to open the meeting. After welcoming everybody to what was to be the final gathering before the party, she commenced with a happy announcement.

'Chef Jacques has volunteered to provide the food at cost price, giving his time and his skill free of charge!'

There was enthusiastic applause from all but two in the room.

Twelve

It was late afternoon when Alex arrived in Gardermoen on the day of the party. He had driven all the way from Molde in falling snow and was glad to enter the welcoming warmth of the Anna's apartment, where she had coffee and *smorrebrod* waiting for him. Most of all he was pleased to see her again and it showed in his eyes. He had good news of Steffan and Gudrun in that they were both well.

'They sent greetings to you,' he said, comfortably settled in a chair, his cup of coffee in his hand. 'What have you been doing since I last saw you?'

'Mostly it has been making paper flowers and doing other things for the party. Incidentally, I have been giving thought to when I go back to England and I have come to the conclusion that I should wait for the Spring. It's not just for the purpose of viewing the old house, although I would do that when I'm in Molde, but because everyone tells me that the Spring is so beautiful here.'

'That must mean you'll be taking a trip to Molde to view the Spring and not just to visit your father-in-law.'

170

She smiled. 'Are you saying that the Spring is more spectacular there than anywhere else?'

He looked seriously at her. 'Yes, I am. All over the country wild flowers appear everywhere and there's a small windflower that makes a white carpet on every forest floor, but in addition on the west coast every waterfall bursts through its ice, many creating a fantastic torrent with clouds of spray. There's a spectacular one not far from the old house that you have yet to see.'

She was sharply interested. 'You say the waterfall is not far from that house? Can it be seen from the windows?'

'Yes, of course, and – except when it is frozen – it can also be heard by night and day.'

'I should like that,' she said, nodding approvingly. 'One would never feel lonely at that time of year.'

He thought it an odd remark to make about a waterfall, but he was glad that he had aroused her interest. 'Don't forget that once I offered to take you to see the house. That offer still stands.'

'Thank you, Alex. I have not forgotten. More coffee?'

He refused, glancing at his watch. 'I must find my way to the Svensens' house. It was good of them to offer me accommodation.'

Anna was glad that he had accepted without question that he would not be staying with her. After her experience with Karl, she wanted to keep sex out of her life for the foreseeable

171

future. She gave Alex directions, and his headlights went sweeping away down the lane. Then she went to take out her green silk dress and put it ready.

Alex came on time to collect her. They arrived at the mess hall to find it transformed by sunshine colours in the garlands around the walls, which were echoed in the decorations and lighted candles on the buffet supper table. There was some skilful draping of orange net that one of the Norwegian wives had discovered in her grandmother's attic during the Christmas holiday. Two of the husbands had made palm trees out of plywood with paper leaves, and these, set against the walls, were very effective. Already the band had started to play as people were arriving early, and very soon talk and laughter and South American music filled the air.

Sally wore one of the two dresses that had caused all the trouble. It was black silk and elegantly cut, suiting her slim figure, with narrow pleats swirling out at knee level and the neckline cut low, revealing her beautiful cleavage. She looked sensational. Anna noticed that Jacques, who was presiding over the buffet table, followed Sally with his gaze whenever it was possible.

During the dancing, a couple of British wartime dances were included, everybody lining up merrily for the Palais Glide and the Lambeth Walk, but mostly the band kept to the theme of the evening. Sally, seductively dancing a tango with one of the younger officers, caused other dancers to drift from the floor and stand to watch and applaud. Anna had the impression that Sally's uninhibited display was as much to torment Jacques as it was to please others watching her.

Eventually, it was the last dance of the evening and the band surprised all the British brides by playing 'Goodnight, sweetheart', which had closed countless dances in Britain during the war. As Alex held Anna close to him, he said how well he remembered the song.

'So you had time to go dancing in England,' she said lightly.

He smiled, looking down into her eyes. 'Yes. Sometimes.'

'I wonder if our paths ever crossed without us being aware of it.'

'I doubt it. I would have known.'

She was unsure of the significance of his words, but there was the realization that his presence had been a pleasure to her ever since he had been compassionate in his understanding after the shock she had experienced on seeing the concentration camp. She said no more and gave herself up to the sheer enjoyment of dancing with him to such a nostalgic tune.

Soon afterwards they were parting company in the porch of her present home.

'I'll have to make an early start back to Molde in the morning,' he said, holding her lightly by the arms. 'So I'll not see you again this time, but it's not long until the Spring. I can be patient when I need to be.'

She knew now that he was not just referring to the time until her return to the west coast, but she did not acknowledge it in any way. Yet when he drew her to him, she thought how pleasurable it was to have a man's passionate mouth on hers and, losing all inhibitions, she responded almost with a kind of joy. As they drew apart, they smiled at each other, aware that their relationship had taken a new turn. She waved to him as he left her, but as she entered the house she shook her head regretfully, for the kiss he had given her was one very close to loving. She did not want him to waste his time waiting for her.

At the first coffee gathering of the British brides after the party, the talk was centred almost entirely on its success. Sally was radiant, having whispered to Anna that her delayed allowance had come through together with the one presently due.

'Have you settled what is owed to Jacques?' Anna asked at once.

'Not yet. He knows that I'm getting cash in Oslo tomorrow. I don't want Arvid to see by chance that the money has come from my personal account instead of the one for the party funds.' Sally glanced about to make sure no one was listening. 'I had thought of asking you to hand the money over to Jacques, but I think I have to do it. He does deserve a word of thanks.'

'Let me do it,' Anna said firmly. 'I'll thank

174

him on behalf of all the wives – Norwegian and British.'

Sally shook her head determinedly. 'No, it's only right that I should be the one.'

'Then deliver the money to him next Sunday at the family luncheon in the mess and thank him publicly for giving up his time to prepare that delicious buffet supper. Nobody will know that the money is not from the lost party funds.'

'Yes,' Sally answered vaguely. 'I could do that.'

Anna hoped that Sally would keep her word. Yet when Sunday came, there was no vote of thanks from Sally, but after the luncheon was finished her husband, a tall, straight-backed and serious-looking man, stood up as Jacques was summoned from the kitchen.

'On behalf of all of us who were at the party,' Arvid began, 'I want to thank you, Jacques, for everything you did to help the ladies give us such a memorable evening. I understand that we arc no longer in your debt financially, but we are certainly still indebted to you for being responsible for much of the pleasure of the evening. *Vive la France!*'

Everybody clapped so heartily that one of the babies woke and began to cry. Jacques acknowledged the applause, bowing and spreading his hands as he encompassed everybody in his smile. Anna looked across at Sally, wondering how she could have let her unsuspecting husband make the speech. But Sally deliberately avoided her eyes, which at least suggested she was feeling some shame about it, although that would be an entirely new experience for her. Anna hoped that Sally would never again commit such a folly.

For a while it seemed to Anna that all was well and everything had drifted back to normal. She had not opened Ingrid Harvik's journal since the day that Sally had burst in on her. She knew it was foolish to associate the book with a hysterical woman's intrusion, but in the aftermath the feeling remained and grew steadily stronger until she began to wonder if Ingrid did not want a stranger to read her words.

One afternoon, when Anna was playing a light-hearted game of cards with Molly, Jane and Wendy, the conversation turned during a break for tea to the topic of serious bridge playing, for Jane was known to be an experienced player. Molly looked at her appraisingly.

'I don't know how you can endure playing this silly whist-type game with us. Not when you are such an expert bridge player.'

Jane laughed. 'This is just a fun afternoon and I enjoy it, but I do take playing bridge seriously. That's why I joined the Norwegian wives' bridge club when they invited any of us war brides to become members. They are all excellent players and there's no laughter there until the game is finished.'

'It's quite a distance to come home from there.'

'It doesn't take long if I cut across the airfield on my *spark*, but I've been reprimanded twice for being seen on the runway. Sally was with me the second time and so I expect she got a second ticking off from Arvid if he had heard about it.'

'Has Sally become a member?' Anna asked in surprise.

'No. I overtook her just after I had left my Norwegian bridge friends. She was on her way home too.'

Molly, ever curious, raised her eyebrows. 'Wherever had she been right over there?'

'She said something about calling in on a Norwegian friend.'

Anna was seized by a terrible suspicion. Jacques's lodgings were in that region. Surely Sally had learned her lesson and was not playing with fire again. Then, a few days later and from a far distance, she saw Sally standing in close conversation with Jacques. Neither of them saw her. Afterwards she hoped it had only been a chance encounter, but not long afterwards Rosemary commented on seeing them walking together near the mess.

'She was laughing and seemed in no hurry to walk away,' she said to Helen, Anna and Pat when the four of them were playing cards again, 'and yet I thought she was supposed to dislike him so much.'

'She probably still does,' Helen answered, 'but she can't be rude to him when he did that wonderful buffet at the party.'

'Then that must have changed her attitude towards him.'

Anna made no comment, but she despaired that Sally seemed to have become careless of being seen with the Frenchman. There was no one with whom she could discuss her concern, but she was now having a regular correspondence with Alex and was able to disclose to him her worry about Sally's foolhardiness, for he had met her at the party. She also exchanged letters with Gudrun, who kept her informed of Steffan's state of health and gave her news of happenings in Molde.

Winter began to ease its grip and there were snowdrops in Fru Dahl's garden where the snow had receded. Soon the little white wind-flowers, which Alex had told her about, began to spread their carpet throughout the forest. Anna was glad that she was able to see this lovely sight and began to think of a trip to the west coast to see the waterfall by the old house, which she thought of now as Ingrid's home.

Then at one of the war brides' gatherings Sally made a startling announcement. She was very white-faced, her eyes stark, and there was a hint of defiance in her voice as her words came in a rush.

'I'm going back to Canada, taking Tom with me. Arvid is going to leave the RNAF as soon as he is able and will join me there.'

A stunned silence followed. There had been rumours that Sally and Arvid were having problems in their marriage, but nobody had supposed that it would come to this state of affairs. Anna sat silent and at a loss for words. It was what she had feared. Then Jane spoke in a joking voice to ease the sadness and dismay that they all felt.

'Those Olympic medals that Tom is going to win will be for Canada now instead of Norway.'

Sally gave a tight smile. 'Yes, you're right.'

Rosemary spoke up in concern. 'But what will Arvid *do* in Canada?'

'My father will find him a good position in his company,' Sally answered.

'But will he care for that? Stuck in an office all day? He's like my Henrik and loves flying.'

Sally shrugged. 'Commercial airlines are starting to get underway. He could fly for one of those perhaps.'

'It would not be the same,' Pat insisted, wanting to have her say. 'The Squadron and the RNAF itself are part of his life.'

'Then he will have to adapt, won't he?' Sally answered coldly, no compassion in her voice.

'How do you feel about going home?' Rosemary wanted to know.

'I know my parents will be overjoyed. They have never seen Tom and they will love him. As for myself, I'll be glad to have life easier. At home we have very cold weather too, but I'll have my own car, which my Pa has promised me. There'll be no more waiting in freezing weather for a lift in a milk truck or standing in line with a ration book. Best of all, we'll have a house with everything we need.' Then her voice softened slightly. 'But I'll miss every one of you.'

All except Anna rose to their feet and gathered around her with reassuring words that she would be missed by them and that they could write and keep in touch. Then they parted to let Anna through to her. Sally looked at her in appeal.

'Don't be angry with me for going home, Anna. I have tried to do what's right, but this is the only way.'

None of the others knew what lay behind her words, but Anna understood. Unless Sally was half the world away from Jacques, her marriage, already in tatters, would not survive.

'I wish you all the best,' Anna said. 'At least Arvid knows and likes Canada from the time he spent training there, but he'll miss Norway and – as Pat said to me once – Norwegians are like homing pigeons, not just for Christmas as she mentioned, but for their beloved mountains and fjords. When Bjornstein, their greatest poet, died in France his last words were "I turn my face to Norway".'

For a matter of seconds there was an awed silence. Then Pat said, 'You're a marvel, Anna. I sometimes think that you, who were the last of us to come, know more about this country and its history than any of us.'

Anna smiled. 'After I met Johan I read everything about Norway that the local library could get for me, including a book of Bjornstein's translated poems and a wartime collection of Nordahl Grieg's too.' She had even read her way through all the sagas, but that she kept to

180

herself, not wanting them to feel even more neglectful of their new heritage.

Everybody wanted to give Sally a farewell party, while knowing instinctively that Arvid would prefer not to be included. Yet he came to every one of them, nothing in his face or manner to show that the departure of his son and his selfish wife was tearing him apart. Anna was sure that gossip about Sally and Jacques had reached his ears, or else he would have opposed her leaving and tried to sort out their marital problems here in Norway.

'Yes, I liked Canada very much when I was there,' he said to a query from Jane at the final party before Sally's departure. 'It's a beautiful country, and I found people to be very kind and generous to those of us in uniform. Yet,' he added wisely, 'I'm well aware that these are different times now. It will be starting a new life completely.'

'But Sally will have prepared the way when you arrive in a few months' time,' Jane said.

'I have no doubt about that,' he replied. Only Anna, standing nearby, caught the wry note in his voice. She was full of compassion for him.

Everybody missed Sally after she had left, but soon they became accustomed to her absence and, as only one letter was received, her name rarely came into the conversation.

Thirteen

Anna decided that now everything had settled down it was the ideal time for a second attempt to start reading Ingrid Harvik's journal. She would not be disturbed by any casual callers today or by a frantic Sally, now far away in Canada and enjoying all the advantages that she had missed so much in Gardermoen. As yet there was no sign of Arvid joining her, and Anna had become even more convinced that, if it were not for his son, it was unlikely that he would ever go.

She crossed the room to take the journal from the rosemaling cupboard, which had seemed to her to be the most appropriate place in which to store this aged testimonial. Then, as before, until Sally had burst in on her, she settled back in her chair against the cushion, aware of a certain excitement in her veins, and began to read:

July 17, 1878
Today, at the age of sixteen, I am free for the first time in my life. Just ten minutes ago I parted the lace curtains at the window, holding them aside with myself silhouetted against the evening light. From there I watched the last of

the mourners depart. Then I laughed, hysteri-
cally perhaps, but freedom is intoxicating when
it has never been experienced before.

I was fifteen when my widowed father,
although he was a cleric, virtually sold me as a
bride to Erik Berdal, a brute of a man and a
childless widower, who had buried two barren
wives and thought to have a son by a third,
hoping for better results from a younger one.
My father was not a heartless man, but his
weakness was gambling, and on the day of the
wedding Berdal settled his debts for him, which
saved my parent's livelihood and rescued him
from bankruptcy. If it had not been to prevent
my father from falling into disgrace, I would
have run from the church before taking the
vows, but I had to accept my fate. Sadly my
father is no longer here to start a new life with
me, for the winter sickness took him six months
ago.

Berdal has bequeathed nothing to me and
neither did I expect anything from his will,
which was read out by the lawyer today after
the funeral. In the end he hated me for failing to
become pregnant, not knowing I took every
precaution against it that was known to me, and
the fact that my chilly gaze unmanned him at
times. So all he owned has been left to his mistress, including this house. She was scuttling all
over it today after the reading of the will and
wants me out by the end of the week, but I
would never wish to stay where I have known
only beatings and cruelty. I'm leaving early

tomorrow morning for the house in the mountains that my late grandmother left me in her testimonial. It was where she spent her childhood, and although I have never seen it, I feel drawn to it as if it has long been beckoning to me.

Anna paused in her reading and lowered the book, thoughtful for a few minutes. Did she herself feel that the house was calling to her in any way? Was the summons in the few words that Johan had uttered when he said there was an old family house he hoped to restore at some time? Why else had she remembered that casually spoken comment in the midst of all the talk of Norway that he had shared with her? Perhaps something in his tone of voice had registered it with her. She returned her gaze to the book.

I have packed my belongings in my bridal chest. These include the bed linen and hand-woven blankets with the blue and white pattern that I brought to my marriage, but nothing that came from Berdal's purse. I have also taken my father's field gun, which he sold to Berdal once when he was desperate for money, and also a box of bullets. When sober, my father was a good shot at bringing down ptarmigan and other game birds in season. He was also a skilful angler and taught me to fish, and indeed sometimes it depended on our catch whether we had something for our supper. So I am taking my rod and line, which was a birthday gift from him and with which I caught my first salmon, and many more fish since that day.

I am not without money, although Berdal gave me nothing and every krone had to be accounted for in the household expenses, with a beating for anything he considered an unnecessary extravagance. But whenever my father had a win at cards, he would slip some of his winnings secretly into my hand or my pocket, knowing that otherwise Berdal would take it from me. As a result, I have become an expert in finding good hiding places and I never left my little hoard in one place for long. Poor Father! Sometimes he had to borrow back from me, but he always repaid his debt. I know my fate as a battered wife troubled his conscience until the end of his days. His best gift was a pony and a little red-painted wagonette, which Berdal could not deny me, although he would have used it himself if he had not thought it too old and shabby for him to be seen in, especially since he owned a fine carriage himself. Yet the most important thing my father did for me was when he inherited a deal of money from an elder brother, who had emigrated and done well in America. I was only ten years old at the time, but my father was in a sober period and, knowing his own weakness as far as money was concerned, he invested a share for me that ensured that I had a small income for the rest of my life. His own share went into higher stakes at the gambling tables and, after a few ups and downs, was finally totally lost in a single game of cards.

My pony, which I named Hans-Petter, is a fjording, one of the sturdy native breed that have been ridden and worked on this land since Viking times. Patient and gentle, they are a beautiful cream colour and have a characteristic black streak running through the mane and down the tail. Hans-Petter has been my only friend during my unhappy time, because Berdal disliked my having any female company with whom to laugh and gossip. He once took a whip to Hans-Petter and I think I went crazy, screaming and fighting for the whip only to have it turned on myself. But I suffered the beating gladly since it meant that Hans-Petter was spared.

I have some grand clothes in the closets here, silks and satins in a variety of lovely colours, most of them expensively lace-trimmed, for Berdal was one of the town's dignitaries and I had to accompany him to important functions. He guarded me closely, but liked showing me off, although I was never allowed to dance, since he considered dancing indecent – even our jolly national dances in which everyone has a good time. Without exception my gowns are high-necked and long-sleeved to ensure that my bruises from Berdal's brutal fists never showed in public. I am taking none of those garments. Instead, I have packed some cotton gowns and a couple of woollen ones that I made secretly for the time when I could make my escape and

186

run away. I never suspected that freedom would come to me through Berdal's demise. If I had anticipated it, I would have chosen much brighter colours for my secretly made clothes, but as it was I had not dared to risk his finding by chance a forgotten scarlet thread or a tiny frayed piece of yellow silk that would have made him suspicious. I truly believe that if he had made such a discovery, he would have guessed what I was plotting and probably murdered me in his erupting fury.

There followed a description of her setting off on her journey early next morning after a kindly neighbour had come with his son to load her bridal chest and all else she was taking into the wagonette, which included a basket of food to sustain her. They waved to her until she was out of sight.

She spent five nights in the open air on her journey, sleeping in the wagonette and washing in the crystal clear streams that were forever hurrying by on the way to the nearest river or fjord. Finally she came to a lush farming valley and to the track wandering up a steep slope that would lead her at last to her new home. She had seen its neighbouring waterfall from some distance away, a great cascading glory of water leaping and dancing from some source high in the mountains.

As she drove up higher, she was presented with a wonderful view of the valley that was a cul-de-sac of farmland and forest. Then, as if nature wished to treat her lavishly, there lay in the other direction the greatest of all views, the sparkling sun-diamond fjord that was as deep as the mountains were high. On its far shore stood the village of Molde. Even from here she could just see patches of red that denoted the presence of its lovely rose.

Ahead there were tantalizing glimpses of her new home through the trees. Then suddenly it came into full view, a two-storied house built of dark logs with its windows shuttered and padlocked. It was much larger than she had imagined it would be and she could scarcely believe her good fortune. Its roof was turf-covered and thick with harebells and buttercups and wild pansies as if it were wearing a floral crown in which to greet her. She felt her heart go out to it, this haven where she could live and breathe as a liberated woman at last.

Springing down from the wagonette, the keys in her hand, she set off on a tour of inspection around the house to see what else was there and was pleased to see redcurrant and blackcurrant bushes full of ripening fruit. She would be able to bottle juice for the winter and make jam. Close by was a *stabbur* that was surely as old as the house, built of the same dark timber. It had an outside staircase which led to a gallery where a door gave access to an upper room. At some time both the upper and lower doors had been painted white, a covering that had long since weathered away. Before long she would see that each had a new coat of paint and she would choose a sunny colour, which would always make her smile.

Nearby was a small barn with space enough for a cow or two if they had been wanted, as well as room for a few sheep to be kept out of the snow in winter. Hans-Petter could be comfortably stabled in the stall there. A privy located in the barn was entered from the rear of the building. It was set high and there were six steps up to it. She thought that she would feel like a queen on a throne whenever she sat there, which made her laugh out loud in her happiness. Skylarks, nesting under the eaves, twittered at this unexpected intrusion and some began to sweep in and out of the building.

'Don't be afraid, my dears,' she said to them, looking up with her back arched and her hands on her hips. 'You have been here longer than I, and I hope you always will be.'

Coming out into the open air again, she stood listening to the waterfall. It had a song on its own for her. She would hear it when she woke in the morning and it would be her lullaby at night. It fed the river that flowed by her land and she alone would have fishing rights to that section.

Well pleased with all she had seen, Ingrid turned her attention to unfastening the house's window-shutters, which had big hooks as well as padlocks keeping them closed. Behind one of the shutters some little bats had made their daytime habitat and they flew off in a flutter of wings as the sunshine fell on them. At last, her task finished, she set the house key in the lock and tried to turn it. It resisted her at first, but she was young and her wrists were strong and finally she conquered it, making a mental note to oil it at the first opportunity. Then she gave the door a thrust with the flat of her hand, sending it swinging wide, and her shadow fell inwards across the wide boards of the pine floor within.

Instantly, adding to the joy of her arrival and possession, she saw that the house was furnished, never having been told that its contents were still there from her late grandmother's time. She had fully expected to make do with a box or two for both table and chairs and also to sleep in her blankets on the floor until she could get some furniture. The windows, free of their shutters, allowed the sunshine to fill gloriously the large living room that was the width of the house from wall to wall.

She stood for several minutes just gazing around her. The warm breeze coming in through the door made the cobwebs dance where they hung from the ceiling and adorned the furniture that was decorated with the rich tints of rosemaling. This gave wonderfully subdued colours to the room and she clasped her hands together with delight at now being the owner of these beautiful things. The board of the long table at the far end was one to be scrubbed white, but its legs and a strengthening bar, much scuffed by countless feet, held the same traditional designs.

'This is my house of fjord and roses,' she whispered in awe of what had been given to her by a woman she had seen only once, and that had been at her mother's funeral. She had been five years old at the time, but was fully aware of the tragedy that had befallen her father and herself. She had the memory of a kindly old face and of being comforted in her tears. No doubt her grandmother would have taken care of her from that day onwards, but her father could not have borne to part with the adored child of the wife he had loved so much. She had had a happy if somewhat erratic time growing up with him, for he never stayed long in any parish, his gambling soon becoming talked about and considered a sin by most of his parishioners, especially when he tried to borrow money from them. There had been many times when she had wished that they did not have to move on, especially when she had made friends with local children and liked her present school, but she never complained to him, understanding that it was not by his choice that they had to leave.

Now, in a daze of joy, Ingrid went through to the kitchen where a great black stove spoke of many good meals served in the past. It had rings that could be lifted out to accommodate the size of the cooking pots that were stacked along a shelf, others hanging from a row of wooden pegs. She opened the door of a cupboard to find it full of crockery.

There was a neighbouring room of moderate

size that was empty, except for a table and chair, and it could have been a sewing room, although there was nothing to indicate its use. Then she went back into the living room to climb the flight of stairs that led to the upper floor. Here she found four rooms, each with a bed and one with a cot. All had mattresses and she could sleep on one of the beds tonight, for when these wooden houses were closed up it was as if they created a vacuum, for with nothing able to penetrate the stout wooden walls from outside they stayed dry as bone, as did everything in them.

I have chosen the largest room in which to sleep as mistress of the house. The bedhead there is magnificently carved with a design of a ship at sea and bare-breasted mermaids in abundance. I think that any woman would most surely welcome ecstatically a husband or lover into such a splendid bed.

Anna put a bookmark in its place and then closed the journal. Ingrid's description of the house and its setting had made her feel as if she were there too, seeing it all though that young woman's eyes. Now she had to think over what she had read and consider carefully whatever might come from it. As she left her chair to prepare a light lunch, she thought that Steffan had certainly known what he was doing when he had given her the journal to read. It was easy to hear Ingrid's voice coming out of the pages.

After her snack lunch Anna sat down again and took up the journal once more to continue reading. Ingrid's name for her new habitation seemed to ring in Anna's head – *House of Fjord and Roses*. How enticing it sounded and how beautiful! Now she was sure there would soon follow a description of the interior of the *stabbur* and she was eager to know what would be found in it.

This morning I postponed any further cleaning, having worked hard yesterday evening before bed, washing and scrubbing happily and to which the house responded with a smile, I am sure. Now it smells of fresh air and sunshine, its mellow wood aroma enhanced by my vigorous cleaning. There are only two of the bedrooms left to be done and I have already washed the floors there. So this morning I took my keys to the stabbur *that rests high on its four stone rat-proof supports. There I went up the well-worn steps to unfasten the shutters and to look inside its downstairs room. As was usual, this space had been used to store grain, hence the protection against vermin. A few empty barrels remained. Otherwise, the only object of interest was a butter-mould left on a shelf. It was like a small box, but was carved inside with a pretty pattern to shape butter for the table. I put it ready to take indoors and then mounted the staircase to the gallery. There I released the shutters and hooked them back against the walls before using my keys to unlock the door to*

193

the upper room.

It was like entering a setting of the Arabian nights after the austere furnishing in the house. I realized instantly that my grandmother's testimonial must have included very strict instructions that nothing was to be removed from the house or the stabbur, *for here was all the luxury that could be given in the old tradition that hospitality must ensure the best of everything for a guest. Hand-woven tapestries covered the walls and multicoloured rag-rugs lay across the floor, although there was one rug that looked to be Turkish. The grand bed had an ornately carved bedhead, much like the one that ornaments my bed in the house, and both were most surely made by the same woodcarver. The hand-woven spread covering the feather mattress was enhanced through being edged by a silky fringe. An iron washstand in the corner held a jug and basin, the cupboard beside it containing neatly folded towels. In all respects, except for a cleaning by me, it was ready to receive an honoured visitor. That caused me to wonder who would be the first guest to occupy this room that was now in my domain. I let my imagination run riot and I giggled when I considered that it should be a royal personage. After all, the room was grand enough. Maybe its first occupant would be a travelling story-teller, who would sit on the* stabbur *steps and transport me in my mind to far-off places with tales of the exciting times of long ago. I would hear the clash of Viking weapons and the cry of*

194

a woman taken in love. Perhaps he would be moved romantically to make up a poem about me that I could frame and hang on the wall. Maybe he would become lyrical about this valley too, for the scenery around this house is breathtaking enough to inspire any poet.

Then I smiled to myself at a fanciful thought that came into my head. Best of all possible guests would be a handsome suitor, eager for my favours. I eyed the bed speculatively. Enduring Berdal's rough usage of my body had not blinded me as to how it could be with a young man, loving and ardent with smooth muscled arms that would hold me close to his warm chest. I felt an ache pass through my body as if it were crying out for caresses. I had to press my clasped hands against myself to ease that sweet torment.

Anna paused momentarily in her reading. She recognized that yearning, although in her case she distrusted it, remembering how it had led her into Karl's arms. She hoped that the journal would not reveal a similarly unfortunate encounter for Ingrid, for already it was clear that she was a passionate young woman. She returned her gaze to the current page again.

I finished my inspection of the house by looking into the cellar. Some light comes through a tiny window, although in winter that will be covered with snow and there will be no illumination at all. There was nothing of interest there except a

195

spinning wheel, which I brought up into my kitchen and washed free of dust and dirt. I had been taught to spin and weave when I was young, part of most girls' practical education, and I was pleased with my discovery of it.

The last of the food I had brought with me had been finished at breakfast. Now I needed to replenish my larder. I made a list and took up an ancient basket that I had found in the barn. Then, wearing my most sober dress, which was a pale grey with a plain collar, and with my hair neatly arranged and tucked into a white frilled cap that fastened under my chin, I set off with the basket in my hand down the track that would lead me to the village. I had pegged out Hans-Petter where he could enjoy the lush grass and he whinnied, expecting to be ridden, but I had to tread cautiously in more ways than one to get myself accepted as a new neighbour in this community.

Anything ostentatious about me, such as riding luxuriously when I could walk, would startle these good, hard-working country people. They have a deep-rooted attitude, held by both sexes, that women should be modest in their ways and in their dress at all times – mostly daily wear of black garb for all but the very young – and not to draw vulgar attention to themselves at any time. On this day, my first in their community and suitably attired, they will not suspect that the newcomer in their midst is a rebel who has finally broken free and finished with all forms of subservience, for I

196

have no wish to offend from the start these neighbours that I want to become my friends. When they get to know me, I hope that they will accept that I have strong opinions about most things without ever wanting to hurt their feelings. They will also have to get used to the way I shall be dressing, because I have had enough of being ordered what to wear and intend to don myself in the brightest colours I can find.

I sang to myself as I went along, swinging my basket and loving the mingled scents of flowers, fern and grass, as well as the hay that was drying on lines stretched across the meadows like golden necklaces for giant trolls. As I reached level ground, I set out for the cluster of three little shops that I had glimpsed from a distance when I had arrived. The first one that I came to was a cobbler's and, peering through the window, I could see him handing over a pair of newly soled boots to a boy aged about six years old. I saw the cobbler laugh heartily at something the child had said, shaking his head. As I was about to move on, the boy came out and spoke to me, a worried frown on his round, pink-cheeked face.

'I told him three kroners were not enough for his work and wanted him to take more, but he wouldn't!'

I hid my smile. 'I'm sure he has charged you the right price.'

Then the boy, suddenly realizing that in his concern he had addressed a stranger, became confused by shyness, clutching the boots tightly to him. 'You're the new neighbour up at the old house!'

'That's right. My name is Ingrid. What is yours?'

'Arne Nilsgard,' he gulped before turning on his heel and bolting away in the direction of one of the farmhouses up the valley. Meeting him had been my first encounter with a local resident, but it was clear that word of my arrival had spread widely already.

The next shop was a little country store that sold almost everything from needles and thread to potatoes and home-made bread. The shopkeeper raised his bushy eyebrows in surprise as I entered and, by some signal that I did not notice, he summoned his wife, who appeared almost instantly with floury hands, to greet me breathlessly.

'Good morning,' she said eagerly. 'I am Helga Olsen and this is my husband, Andreas. We bid you welcome, Fru Berdal.'

So everybody knew my name too. 'Thank you,' I replied. Then I pointed to a shelf of various baked loaves.' Did you make that lovely-looking crusty bread?'

'Yes, I did. Mostly housewives around here make their own, but sometimes an unexpected guest or extra hungry farm workers brings someone in haste to restock from me. Do you think you will like living here?'

I recognized the beginning of some cross-questioning. The shopkeeper was serving somebody else who had come in, and I could feel the significant looks being exchanged.

'Yes, I'm sure of it,' I replied. 'Do you think there is anyone in the valley who would remember my grandmother?'

'Old Jacob is the most likely one. He is in his nineties and lives nearby.'

'I'll get his address from you another time. Now I have to stock my larder.'

I bought golden farm butter, two loaves, meat and various other items, including a little straw basket of strawberries and another of raspberries that were almost the size of young plums. When I left the shop, four or five women had gathered outside and stopped their conversation as I emerged. I guessed that the little boy had boasted that he had met me and they had hurried to have a good stare at the new arrival. I smiled, bidding them good morning. They all replied and I could feel their interested gaze following me as I set off for home again.

Home! What a beautiful word it is! If I could have run up the mountain track, I would have done it in my eagerness to see the old house again, but my basket was too heavy with all that I had purchased. I had to plod all the way, but the sight of my home became even more precious to me as it came into view. It was almost possible for me to believe that I could become a hermit here, needing nothing from the outside world, but I know my own nature too well. I would soon become restless, needing the company of others with the freedom to laugh and *even – if the right man happened to come along – to love.*

The next day I went down to the village again. This time I wore a brighter dress and no cap, drawing my hair back smoothly from my brow into a coil at the nape of my neck. The previous day I could not have carried anything extra, so this time I had an empty basket when I went into the dairy. This was where the local milk was brought in for distribution elsewhere, a proportion being made into a local cheese. There was a wonderful smell of cheese as I entered and a selection was displayed on a white cloth. A youth in a large white apron served me. I chose a brown goats' cheese, and another local cheese that was creamy in colour and in taste, both of which proved later at supper time to be extremely good.

I had not been long home again when I had my first visitor, whom I recognized as having been outside the shop the previous day. Young and pretty, with a round face enhanced by dimples and moon-fair curls escaping from her cap, she introduced herself as Marie Eikdal, wife of a local farmer. For me it was a great joy to chat with someone of my own age, and she had kindly brought me a little bunch of flowers from the garden of her home. I was quick to put them in water and placed them on the table in a vase that I had discovered the previous evening in one of the cupboards. We chatted over coffee and she told me much about the valley and the people who lived there.

'Do you like to dance?' Marie asked me when I was refilling her coffee cup.

'I would if I could,' I replied regretfully, 'but I was never allowed to try. My late husband would not permit it. He thought it was sinful for a woman to be held in the arms of a man not her husband and he was no dancer himself. But I'd love to learn! Could you teach me?'

'Yes, with pleasure! It will be fun!' Then Marie clapped her hand over her mouth and looked at me in sudden doubt and dismay. 'Perhaps I have spoken too soon! Are you still in mourning, even though you're not wearing black?'

'No, I'm at liberty to dance as much as I like,' I replied quickly. I could have added that I had not mourned Berdal for a single moment, only thankful for being liberated from his countless cruelties, but that period in my life and all it entailed was my own affair. I never wanted to speak of him or the bondage of my marriage ever again.

'Then let us start now!' Marie suggested enthusiastically, already clearing away the chair on which she had been sitting in order to gain more space. 'First of all, I'll teach you the basic steps of some of our old country dances. When you have mastered them, you will be able to skip through any dance just anywhere!'

So there began for me a good and lasting friendship, as well as learning at last a way to release my pent-up energies. At the same time I became proud as a little peacock that my feet

201

were light and nimble, each dance I learned a pleasure to me, and I earned praise from Marie because I was so quick to master whatever new steps she gave me.

When she judged I was ready, she asked her brother, Henrik, to come and play music for dancing on his fiddle for us, so that I could hear for myself the various tunes that she had hummed for me. He was a pleasant youth, yellow-haired and with a crooked front tooth that somehow only added to the charm of his merry grin. Soon I will be ready for the open-air dances that are held on Saturday evenings when the weather permits. So far there has been only lovely weather, but I know that the west coast with its mountains can have torrents of rain if its mood changes...

There followed two pages of how she made two new friends the following day. Their names were Sonja and Greta. Marie had brought them with her to help illustrate the exchange of partners in some of the dances. They were bright, happy girls, both betrothed to young men in the valley. They were like Marie in having come originally from other parts of Norway, it being the custom to send farmers' daughters for a year or more to other farming communities in the hope of marriage, and to bring fresh blood into families that had lived on their farms for generations. Ingrid enjoyed the prospect of their forthcoming weddings and had many discussions about what they would be wearing and how the celebrations should be. She thought how different her own wedding day had been, when tears had run down her face throughout the ceremony and then that night, innocent and terrified, she had been subjected to what had amounted to brutal rape.

Anna closed the book. There had followed some harrowing details that upset her and had brought the shine of tears to her eyes. Poor Ingrid! Yet, perhaps by writing about that night and other cruelties she had suffered, it had released her from the torment of those distressing memories once and for all.

During the days that followed Anna could not put the journal aside for any length of time. She was fascinated by this insight into another age and another time.

I could not understand, Ingrid had written at the end of her first week, *why Hans-Petter was so restless on Saturday afternoon, neighing and pulling on his tethering rope. Then I saw what it was! Since nobody works on Sundays, which is strictly observed by everybody, all the farmers in the valley release their* fjordings *into the mountains at the week's end. To my joy I could see these lovely horses galloping up the slopes to freedom, one after another, and I ran to release Hans-Petter to let him go with them. He snorted, reared up in his excitement and then went bolting off in the wake of the other horses, his mane and tail flying. I did wonder if I might have difficulty getting him home again on*

Sunday night, but he followed the other horses back to the valley and I fetched him from there. I was told that sometimes the horses played truant, ignoring the whistles and calls of their owners, but on the whole they were conditioned by routine to know when their period of rest was at an end...

Anna knew from farming talk she had heard in Molde that this custom was still in existence, and almost without exception farm horses were treated as if they were extended members of the family. Always beloved by the children, the horses showed the utmost tolerance towards them. It was this mutual affection and respect that had made it so hard for the animals and their owners alike when the Germans had commandeered the strongest of the *fjordings* to pull their loaded wagons and their guns. All these horses were abandoned when the enemy was defeated, and farmers from all over Norway had gone in search of their own animals, quite a number being successful. She had been told that one local farmer, having located his horse among hundreds, had tears of joy running down his face as he walked it up the valley, bringing it home again.

Already Ingrid's journal had had a profound effect on Anna. She found that she was identifying herself in quite a few ways with Ingrid, as if she had found a kindred spirit. Both of them had had traumatic experiences – Ingrid with her marriage and she herself with heart-tearing widowhood. She wished she could reach out and take Ingrid's hand into her own, linking them through the years and bringing them both into friendship. Would she experience that same wish to bond with the past when the time came for her to enter the old house, because by now she knew she would never rest until she had viewed Ingrid's home for herself.

The next time Anna settled to read, there was a description of the two weddings. As Sonja's parents were dead, the family with whom she lived had arranged for her and her betrothed, a pleasant young farmer's son, to be married from their home. Three hundred guests came for the occasion, which was quite customary, for a wedding was a grand occasion for merry-making in otherwise quiet lives, and everybody – even those that came from away – brought food to help feed the vast gatherings, and Ingrid was told that there was always more than enough. Many women were like the bride in wearing full national costume, the bridegroom among the men in their grand attire. Sonja also wore a borrowed, traditionally high golden crown, which had been handed down through generations of somebody's family. Both she and her bridegroom rode their *fjordings* to and from the church, with a fiddler playing merrily as he walked ahead of them. Everybody in the valley accommodated the guests and Ingrid had two of Sonja's cousins to sleep in her *stabbur*, while several children slept on the floor. The feasting and the dancing and the singing lasted three days before everybody departed and the valley was peaceful again.

Greta went home to marry, but, in contrast to Sonja's happy celebration, everything went disastrously wrong, including a change in the weather from warm sunshine to steady rain. Ingrid had been invited as an important guest, for she had helped Greta make a wedding gown trimmed with exquisite handmade lace and in which she looked beautiful. Then, a week before the marriage, an aged uncle in Greta's family died, which meant the unfortunate girl had to go into mourning. Although she was allowed her white bridal veil and flowers for her hair, she had to wear a black dress.

'I've never even met the horrible old man!' she sobbed bitterly on her wedding morning. 'How dare he spoil this day of all days for me!'

Ingrid tried to comfort her, wanting her to flout convention and wear the white dress as she would have done, but Greta did not dare face the shock and condemnation of both her own and her bridegroom's family at a lack of conventional respect.

'Take the gown, Ingrid!' she cried, waving it away. 'Keep it for your wedding day! You haven't any family to die at the wrong time!'

So when Ingrid returned home, she had the wedding gown with her and packed it away in her bridal chest.

Fourteen

Alex had become a frequent visitor, coming to see her whenever his work permitted, mostly at weekends. She had also discovered that when he had called on the day she had seen the concentration camp, it had not been at Steffan's instigation.

'I could not stay away from seeing you any longer,' he had told her, touching her face with his fingertips before bending his head to kiss her. 'I had only seen you for a matter of half an hour on the day of your arrival in my country, but I could not get you out of my mind.'

She was becoming very fond of him and looked forward to his visits, but whether it was the beginning of love in her case she could not be certain. Everything was so different from the time of the whirlwind romance she had experienced with Johan, when death was threatening everybody, civilians as well as those in the forces. This new experience was quiet and very calm, being taken with a careful approach, and she felt lost and unsure of herself in such different circumstances.

All her friends liked Alex and he was included in all their party invitations. The war brides eyed him appreciatively for his good looks and attractive presence, all beginning to hope that there would be a wedding before long, but Anna evaded answering their sometimes very probing questions.

On most of Alex's visits he took her into Oslo where they ate at interesting places. She liked very much the artists' restaurant where the walls were covered with sketches and drawings by Scandinavian artists who had eaten there in their time. After seeing a splendidly acted production of Ibsen's *Hedda Gabler*, she particularly liked dining at the Grand Hotel where Johan made sure they sat at a corner table by the window, for it was there, many years before, that the playwright had always seated himself, coming to his favourite table every day at noon as regular as clockwork. Before the snow melted away, they went up many times to the Holmenkollen ski jump to view competitions there. The height of the jump dazzled Anna as she watched the breathtaking events. She joined in with the rest of the spectators in cheering the skiers who soared through the air like eagles, reaching incredible lengths when they landed, and she waved a national flag as enthusiastically as if she were as Norwegian as the rest of the spectators. Alex often glanced sideways at her and smiled at her enthusiasm.

They went to plays and concerts as well as to the movies, holding hands. He always drove her home afterwards, and although he stayed for a coffee, he never put pressure on her, seemingly content to wait. Yet his kisses had become more deeply passionate and his caresses lingering. Privately she yearned for greater intimacy between them, but was held back by the ties of the past when Johan had filled her life. She remembered Gudrun's advice to her, but she did not know yet if she had permanent room in her heart for another love. Alex most surely understood her state of mind; otherwise, he would not have been so patient.

One of the trips they made was south of Oslo to the east of the fjord. By now he knew how almost anything antique fascinated her.

'I guarantee that what I'm going to show you will be the oldest thing that you'll ever see,' he had said before they set out.

'Whatever can it be?' she had asked. 'Give me a clue.'

'How about four thousand years?'

She laughed. 'It is an old pot in some museum!'

He shook his head, laughing. 'No, you're far out with that idea.'

She was intrigued, and on the drive, which turned out to be much longer than she had expected, he would not give away what she was to see, although she kept guessing in vain. It was in the countryside when they came at last to a national sign indicating the presence of an historic site. There he parked the car. Then he took her by her hand to guide her along a path that wandered on until they came to a large rock. Incised into it were the Stone Age carvings of the first inhabitants of this northern land. Depicted as if they were pin-men, all of the male figures well-endowed, they were sailing on Viking-shaped boats as well as fishing and using bows and arrows, and – most astonishing of all – many were on skis. She had seen ancient skis in the ski museum at Holmenkollen, but none as old as these. A very human touch, which linked the present with that ancient time, was the shape of a little child's outspread hand that a prehistoric father must have chiselled out of the rock after outlining the shape of it.

Anna put her own hand over it. 'I'm touching the past,' she said wonderingly.

Alex put his arm about her waist and drew her close to him. 'Come back to the present,' he said and then kissed her. Caught up in the atmosphere of the moment, she responded warmly and he kissed her again, his hand finding her breast beneath her silk blouse and fondling her lovingly. If they had not been in a place where some other sightseer might appear without warning, she thought afterwards, it would have been the moment they became lovers in the true sense of the word.

In the city's National Gallery he took her to see two paintings by Magnus Harvik. As with the artist's other paintings, such as the one in Johan's room and those in the hall of her father-in-law's home, she was enthralled by the artist's brilliant use of colour. Both paintings were mountain views and blazed across the canvas.

Then they moved on to another section of the gallery where Alex introduced her to the work of Edvard Munch, which he much admired, and she was in full agreement with him as she viewed Munch's *Girls on the Bridge* and another of little children holding hands. His painting entitled *The Scream* chilled her with its torment while filling her with admiration at the power of this artist's work.

Before they left the gallery, Alex bought her a book about Munch, and not long afterwards, on a fine spring day, he took her to the little town of Asgardstrand by the Oslo fjord to view Munch's home, with everything just as it was in his time. While there in Asgardstrand, they went on to the bridge reaching out into the fjord, where they leaned their arms on the railings.

'I feel as if I stepped into a Munch painting,' she said happily, thinking of the paintings the artist had done in this location, and having recognized a white house and the lush green tree that had featured in the background of more than one of his works.

Alex was amused. 'Yes, there are girls on the bridge in his paintings, but not a solitary pair of lovers.'

She turned her head to meet his eyes. 'Are you sure that is what we are?' she asked quietly.

He nodded, his gaze serious. 'Yes, even though I have yet to make love to you as I wish to do.' He took both her hands into his. 'Marry me, Anna.'

211

A kind of panic gripped her and she seized the first excuse that came into her head. 'I can't decide anything until I've seen Ingrid's house!' Then, in her agitation, she gave away what had been on her mind for a considerable time. 'I feel as if in some strange way my life is tied up with it.'

He misunderstood her meaning. 'As it will be if you accept ownership of it.'

'No, that's not the reason.' She wished again that she could tell him about the journal, but she could not break the trust that commanded her silence, not even for Alex. 'I still need time.'

'Then how long is it to be before you come back to Molde?' he persisted. 'There will be easy access to the old house now that the snow has gone. Your father-in-law told me that he has already had the obstructive bushes cleared away and a tree felled.'

'I'll come soon,' she promised wildly, momentarily feeling trapped.

He was not to be deterred. 'Pack a suitcase and I'll take you back with me tomorrow.'

'No,' she declared firmly. 'I'm not ready yet. Not even to give an answer to what you have just asked me.'

'Then I'll fetch you as soon as you let me know that you feel the time is right for you to return to Molde. And,' he added softly, 'to me.'

'The other day you mentioned that you had a court case coming up that you expect to last three weeks,' she said thoughtfully. 'When you have finished with that case, I think I'll be ready to return.'

That evening, after they had supper together, he set off to drive back overnight in the everlasting daylight to Molde. As she prepared for bed, she wished she could explain to him that the reason for her procrastination was that she needed to read more of Ingrid's journal before she visited the old house. Somehow she could not hurry her reading of it, almost as if every tiny incident, however mundane, had to be retained in her memory. A new paragraph in the journal had particularly caught her high interest.

Today I made a strange discovery! Quite by chance I found an old bridal chest that at some time had been dumped in this secret place! It was most skilfully hidden away and I would defy anybody to find it. I only found it myself because I was curious to explore every part of my property. The chest has a great lock on it, but any key that it had once possessed was missing. I think somebody had stored it for future possible use and it had just been forgotten. Although I managed to lift the heavy lid, I found nothing inside. It was empty. Not as much as a hairpin in it. Then I could not hold the lid up any longer and it crashed down with a noise like thunder. I could not read the bridal name on the front of it, because the chest had been so ill-used, but if ever I gain some treasures I shall hide them in it. No thief would ever discover them in such a secret hiding place...

The entry had been made when Ingrid had been living in the house for almost two years. By now she had bought two sheep, but only for their wool, for she knew that even if she were starving, she could never eat them. She called them individually Ida and Klara and had wept for their moment of pain when one of the farmers had obliging clipped their ears to distinguish them as her property, for she let them wander with other flocks and grazing herds of cows on the high mountain pastures during the summer months.

She sometimes went to check that her sheep had come to no harm, fearful of them being whipped away by the claws of a great eagle, for they were often sighted wheeling high against the sky, and once one swooped low over her head with thundering wings when she was fishing in the river. Sometimes she went higher up in the mountains to a lake in the rocky terrain that was full of speckled trout. There she would catch two or three and fry them over a little fire before eating them with crusty buttered bread.

At other times she enjoyed going up to the mountain pastures where there was a little cluster of cabins forming what was known as a *saeter*, one of many on the mountainous west coast. It was where the daughters of the local farmers stayed all summer on the high pastures, their duty being to milk the cows allowed to graze there at that time of year and then send the daily output in large churns down wires every morning to the valley below. Then turns were taken by the girls every evening to bring the cans up again. They all loved the freedom away from parental supervision, and on Saturday nights the lads from the valley came to join them for parties, bringing bottles in their pockets. Ingrid had been invited to these gatherings, but she had no interest in the local lads.

When the wool from her sheep was cleaned and washed, she dyed it in colours of her choice – red and orange and mountain green – and spun it on her spinning wheel before weaving it into cloth on a loom, which she had purchased and had installed in the room off the large living room. She described, with the aid of little illustrations, the new winter cloak, pretty blouses and simply styled gowns that she made for herself. She had glued beside the entries tiny scraps of the material used for the garments that she had mentioned, which pleased Anna immensely, for it gave her such an insight into Ingrid's wardrobe.

I know myself to be the best-dressed woman in the district, Ingrid declared, causing Anna to smile at her unabashed conceit. It was clear that Ingrid would have been the focus of attention wherever she went, for she must have been as bright as a parrot in her colourful garments compared with the sombre everyday clothes usual to country women.

Ingrid had had a number of suitors, some

local and others who had heard about her and came to try their luck. But she had sent them all away and her description of some of them made highly amusing reading, causing Anna to give a gasp of laughter. Yet Ingrid also wrote openly of what pleased her about some of them, such as noting that a particular suitor had a firm bottom or good legs in tight trousers, as well as observing under her lashes that some of the young men were greatly blessed in the right quarters. Others who were included as being pleasing to the eye had broad chests against which Ingrid thought any woman would like to lay her head. Strong muscled arms also attracted her as she thought how easily she could be lifted up and swept off to bed. She never minced her words, but wrote as freely as if she were talking to an intimate confidante, which indeed she was, as in reality the journal was meant entirely for her eyes alone. More and more, Anna understood why her staid father-in-law had not wanted the journal to be read by other than family eyes.

Anna wondered what Ingrid would have thought of Alex with his intelligent good looks and very male attractiveness. It was almost certain that she would have approved of him, perhaps even marrying him if the decades between them had not existed.

There was another happening of interest that Ingrid had recorded and which Anna read eagerly. It was Ingrid's account of a visit she made to see an old man named Jacob, who remembered her grandmother and told what he had heard of her great-grandmother too. He was stone deaf and so he did most of the talking, for he could not hear Ingrid at all in spite of his ear trumpet, which he thrust in her direction whenever he saw her lips move. But he had been told why she had come and was like many old people in being able to remember the past vividly, while not being able to recall anything he had done the previous day. Ingrid had recorded the interview in detail, saying how they had sat outside in the sunshine, he with a battered old hat on his head and his feet in plaid slippers. She had held a fringed, brightly patterned parasol over herself that she had bought at a market.

'You're a pretty one,' he said, complimenting me in his reedy old voice, 'and so was your grandmother. I have heard tell that your great-grandmother was a comely wench too, but I was not born when she lived in your house during her widowhood. Her Christian name was Ragnhild and her daughter, who was your grandmother, was Solveig. She was a happy child and was grown into a young woman at fourteen when her parents took her off to America. She did not want to leave here, but her father thought he could make his fortune there. He died on-board ship before he had even reached American shores, but Solveig and her mother worked hard and did well. They kept a boarding house, sold it and bought a bigger one

and then another, until eventually they had a small hotel. By this time Solveig was married and had a daughter. Then after she was widowed and her mother died, Solveig waited until her daughter was married and then came back to Norway. It was the best move that she could have made, because it was said she had lost her smile the day she left here and never regained it until she was home again.'

'Did she move back into my house as soon as she returned?'

'Yes, she did and I have heard say that she sang like a songbird out of her joy at being home. Not long after she had moved in, she married again – a childhood sweetheart living in the valley – and she made him leave his farmhouse and move in with her as she refused to live anywhere else. She was in her mid-forties when she gave birth to your mother.'

Then Ingrid had written: *How my poor dear homesick grandmother must have suffered until she was back where she belonged! I shall never leave my dear home, which she loved as much as I. Not even if a king or an Indian potentate or any other rich man should propose to me and want me to live in his grand mansion! My own mama most surely had yearned for the old house too, but had loved my father so much that she had let him take her away to live in one town after another, his being always on the move. I recall his saying once that my mother used to talk of her childhood home as if it had been paradise.*

At that point Anna had closed the journal for the time being. Now she understood the strong female hold on the house and also its link with America. It must be one of Ragnhild's female descendants who was now entitled to the house if she herself did not claim it. The more she read of the house in Ingrid's journal, the more she became fascinated by it.

Anna was still involved in all the activities enjoyed by the war brides. At their coffee mornings they chatted about letters they had received from family and friends in England, where life was still far from easy and some food rationing was still in progress. In spite of rebuilding in London and other cities, there were still gaping holes everywhere from the bombing. Then one day Anna received a letter from her aunt that surprised her immensely.

'My aunt in England,' she told the others, 'who has been a widow for years, is going to marry a lodger who came to live at her house not long after I arrived in Norway. He is manager of a fun palace on the pier.'

'Shall you go to the wedding?'

Anna shook her head. 'No, it was notification only and not an invitation. Most importantly, if I went to England now, there would be people on this side of the North Sea who would be afraid that I'd never come back. I don't want to cause them any distress.'

Including, she added silently to herself, Ingrid, who had been calling her to the old house ever since she had first opened the journal, even though she had not realized it at the time.

Anna hoped that Ingrid would give a clue as to where she had found the secret place with the old bridal chest in it, but it seemed as if Ingrid was not going to refer to it again, ensuring even more that it would never be discovered by others. Much of what she wrote was mundane, such as how many logs she had ordered for the winter, the higher price of flour, the cost of a clock for the kitchen and the recipe for what she called a sunset pudding, which consisted of egg whites and sugar whipped until peaks formed and then ripe cranberries were folded into it, turning it palest pink.

Whenever the snows came, Ingrid would see in the morning light a *fjording* plunging its legs into the white depths as it came up the slope, dragging behind a wooden snowplough to clear a way for her. A farmer's son followed it and was in charge. Once or twice, when the snow lay extra thick, the boy would get up on the roof of the house and clear it, for roofs sometimes fell in if the weight of the snow was too heavy to be sustained. Then the boy would urge the horse down the slope again, clearing the way even more, but not before she had given him a mug of hot chocolate to drink and some cake. She always found a titbit for the horse too.

Once Ingrid was ill and had to stay in bed, developing a high fever. She was cared for by Marie, who had never left the valley, living with her husband on his father's farm. In the neighbourly custom that prevailed, local people came with offerings to help Ingrid recover from her illness, such as eggnog or a nourishing broth and sometimes a specially cooked invalid dish, all in the hope of aiding a speedy recovery. It made Ingrid aware how much she was missed by the local community and she knew that although many thought her strange with her bright clothes and outspoken manner, they all – except the most straight-laced – liked her, the men always following her with their gaze whenever she walked by with her swift step and a sway of her hips that was natural to her.

When Ingrid was well enough to sit out of bed with a shawl over her knees, she raged against her physical weakness, causing Marie to be thankful that her role as a nurse was almost at an end. Yet all she had done had been deeply appreciated by the invalid and she knew it.

It was while I was still convalescing, Ingrid wrote, *that I saw at last the man whom I knew instantly to be my soul mate...* She had come down to the valley on horseback, lacking the strength yet to walk down and up again. In the shop she waited to be served and heard the shopkeeper telling another customer that there was an artist at work nearby.

'Who is he, Andreas?' she asked as soon as she was being served, being long since on Christian name terms with most people in the valley. 'Why is he here?'

'He's from Bergen and just now he is painting a scene that includes old Jacob's house,' the shopkeeper replied. 'Says it's picturesque, although since the old man died last year, his son doesn't take much care of it and it stands there empty.'

She tried to think what would have appealed to the artist about the house, for in her opinion it was a blot on the landscape and should be demolished. Outside the shop again she put her purchases into Hans-Petter's saddlebags. She decided that she had just enough strength to walk the short distance to Jacob's house to see the artist at work and judge his talent, for she needed a picture or two for her house, and then she would walk back again. She set off at a slow pace that was all she could manage, much to her annoyance, and came to where she had a good view of the artist. He sat on a portable stool with his back towards her, concentrating on the canvas set up on an easel in front of him.

The painting looked extremely good from a distance, highlighting the colours in bold strokes unlike anything she had seen before. Then, as he turned his head slightly to gaze at some aspect of the scene he was capturing in his particularly bold style, she saw his face. It seemed to her that her heart stopped for a few golden moments. This was he! The very one whom she had always hoped to meet one day. He had the most beautiful face she had ever seen, framed by a mass of tousled dark hair, his strong well-shaped nose balanced by a determined chin, his mouth wide with a full lower lip that hinted at a passionate and sensuous nature that would match her own entirely. She could not see the exact colour of his eyes, but they were dark and shadowed by thick black lashes. She was almost overcome by a longing to rest her arm along his broad shoulders and to feel those hands with the long nimble fingers on her naked body. Dazedly, she realized that for the first and only time in her life she had plunged deeply into love.

If she had been her normal exuberant self, she would have gone to him across the grass and used every one of her wiles to hold his attention, instilling a first attraction to her beauty, which her mirror normally reflected. But she had to face the bitter truth. She was not as she had been before her illness, for she was as physically weak as an old crone, and she had lost so much weight that her face was gaunt and her whole body was thin, her seductive curves no more. She could have wept in her frustration. Immediately, she returned to the shop and borrowed a carrying-can that Andreas filled with cream for her. Then she doubled up on the same measure of milk and purchased another slab of butter, some fat bacon and extra loaves. She was going to fatten herself up to her normal weight and regain her figure as quickly as possible. There was a sack of potatoes stored in her cellar and she must eat plenty of those too.

'How long is the artist going to be here in the valley, Andreas?' she asked casually as she paid for her additional purchases.

'About four or five weeks, I think,' was his

reply, filling her with relief. 'He's staying with us as we have a spare room.'

'What's his name?'

'Magnus Harvik.'

'That's a good old Norsk name,' she remarked. 'Does he have his wife with him?'

'He is not married. He told me he values his freedom too highly. He is much taken with our valley, which he says inspires him, and he has had a couple of portraits commissioned.' Then Andreas gave her a conspiratorial wink. 'All you womenfolk seem to like him. Even my wife blushes every time he speaks to her.'

As Ingrid rode Hans-Petter back up the slope, she tried to estimate how long it would take her to get back to her normal weight on a heavier diet. Until now she had had no appetite, but now she must force herself to eat well, which was something she had neglected to do in spite of Marie's constant admonishing whenever she came to the house. But it should not be difficult to gain enough weight to recapture her looks and her figure in the time that the artist would be here. There was one thing of which she was certain: no other woman should have the man that she was certain fate meant for her. She also resolved to avoid seeing him before she was her true self again.

Regaining her strength and her looks did not take as long as she had feared, although sometimes she was afraid that she would choke on the food that she forced into her mouth. She kept a constant check on the artist's whereabouts and the work he had in hand, gaining her information from either Marie or the shop-keeper. She was concerned when she heard he was painting the portraits, for both sitters were good-looking women and married to boring husbands. Then he was back on to landscapes again and Ingrid became a little less anxious, eating now for pleasure instead of just sustenance. When Marie remarked one day that if Ingrid put on any more weight she would soon be fat as a barrel, it was clearly time for a return to moderate portions.

She became less tense, satisfied that she had achieved her aim. Best of all, apart from regaining her figure, a bloom had returned to her cheeks and her hair had regained its lustre, which she encouraged by brushing it many times every night. Finally, the day came when she ready to ensnare with her charms the un-suspecting and unprepared Magnus Harvik. She planned to discuss whatever he was paint-ing and say she would like to buy it when it was finished, for that meant he would have to deliver it to her house. There she would serve him coffee and a cognac, having already pur-chased a bottle in readiness from Andreas, even though he was not officially allowed to sell spirits. What happened after that had to be left to fate, but she intended to tantalize Magnus Harvik during the rest of his time in the valley until he was unable to keep from asking her to marry him.

Well pleased with her restored bosom, she

chose to wear a blouse with a round neck that gave a seductive glimpse of her cleavage and the ankle-length skirt she chose to wear was bright orange. With a ribbon of the same vivid colour holding her blond tresses back from her face, she strode strongly down the track and set along up the valley, looking to one side and then the other for Magnus Harvik, or just his easel, which would show his whereabouts. Yet there was no sign of him anywhere.

She returned to the shop, hiding her rising anxiety as she pretended to examine some fruit in a tray on the counter. 'Where is Magnus Harvik painting today, Andreas? I've a mind to buy one of his pictures.'

'He's gone.'

For a second or two she thought she might die from shock. She felt the colour drain from her face with a force that made her cheeks sting and her heart began to hammer like a drum. 'I had made up my mind to buy one of his paintings,' she managed to stammer, trying to hide her reaction to the information she had received so unexpectedly. Fortunately, Andreas was not very observant.

'He has left a couple with me in case anyone should still want to purchase. I'll fetch them—'

'No! Not now! Did he say where he was going?'

'He was undecided whether to move on to Alesund, where he could do some sea scenes with the ships and the fishing boats there, or else he could make his way up to Geiranger.'

She clenched her fists. 'What did he decide?' she demanded, beyond caring now whether or not Andreas thought her attitude strange.

'He did not say. Maybe he told my wife. I'll ask her.'

He was gone no more than a few minutes, but Ingrid stood tapping her foot impatiently. 'Well?' she asked sharply when he returned. 'What did he decide?'

'He did not say for certain, although my wife thinks she persuaded him to go to Geiranger, because that's a sight that would inspire any artist's brush.'

Within the next hour, Ingrid had packed all her essential needs into a bundle and had strapped it to her back. She could not take Hans-Petter, because she had studied an old map very closely and saw that her route would go over high mountains where perhaps some slopes would be too steep for a horse to gain a foothold. Leaving him in the care of Marie, whom she had taken into her confidence, she ignored her friend's persuasion not to go on what could be a pointless expedition. Then Marie, seeing that nothing would persuade Ingrid to change her mind, came with her own pony and trap to take Ingrid as far as she could on what was little more than a rutted track along the way. Then, when they came to a signpost pointing to Geiranger, Ingrid jumped down excitedly from the trap.

'I've left a list on the table of everything needed for my wedding,' she said happily.

'Please iron the lace wedding gown for me and make sure it does not have any creases. Invitations can go out by word of mouth when the date is settled.'

Marie looked down at her from the trap's driving seat, her expression serious and concerned. 'I'm not doing anything until I see you return with Magnus Harvik. If that should happen, then I'll move heaven and earth to do all I can for you. But I beg you not be too disappointed if you fail to find him.'

'I shall find him wherever he is and bring him home with me forever!'

Waving cheerfully, Ingrid turned to follow the direction the signpost had indicated. With the aid of the map, she walked to Linge where she paid a boatman to row her across to the other side of a fjord that flowed there. Then she continued along her route for several days, once taking a turn in a wrong direction that proved to be hazardous. Sometimes she had to struggle to find a foothold and had her skirt tied up about her waist as she hauled herself along from one vantage point to another. Once she slipped, hitting her head, and she lay dazed for a few minutes, only moving when she felt a trickle of blood down the side of her face. Panic-stricken that she had harmed her looks, she studied her reflection in her little hand-mirror and was thankful to find it was a small graze at her hairline, which she could easily disguise with a curl.

Once, when her food had almost run out, she

came to a *saeter* where the girls gave her something to eat in the timeless tradition of mountain hospitality. She left with her food supplies replenished. Drinking water was always on hand from the mountain streams, where she also washed and bathed herself. There were some dreadful days when the rain was unceasing and she would huddle under the shelter of a rock, thinking that surely there was nowhere in the world that became as cold as Norway in the rain. Yet never once did her resolve weaken, and her spirits always soared once more when the sun came out again, warming her before making her sweat as its August heat increased throughout the day.

Finally, she came to Geiranger on a glorious day, but before she was in sight of its fjord she bathed in a stream, shivering deliciously in the icy water. She also washed her hair, and then brushed it until it floated down her back, the graze on her forehead now healed. Her orange skirt had been amazingly resilient to all she had done and she had had it hitched up most of the way. She smoothed it down, glad to see that its creases were minimal. Then she put on the fresh cotton blouse that she had kept for this moment. She had trouble with a herd of goats that from higher up had sighted her eating the last waffle of the *saeter* package of food, and they came swiftly down to see what they could scrounge from her. They would not be driven off, even trying to chew her skirt hems, and so she had her first glimpse of Geiranger fjord while

229

escorted by a cluster of goats.

She thought it a fjord beyond belief. It was as if a giant troll had brought down the side of his hand in a blow of such force that he had split the mountain range in two, allowing the sapphire sea to pour into the enormous gap and releasing great waterfalls to cascade down the walls of rock. Such beauty caught her by the throat and she stretched out her arms towards the fjord's magnificence. She could see a cluster of houses that formed the small village at the inner end of the fjord, but as yet there was no sign of her quarry.

She set off and the goats turned back, having found her unrewarding prey, although they had eaten the paper that had covered the last of her food. Then she saw him. A tiny speck in this vast arena, he was painting at the edge of the water.

Although she did not know if Magnus had seen her, he had glanced up from his easel and caught sight of what he thought was a young female goatherd. Her orange skirt was exactly what was needed in his painting, and by mixing a swirl of red and yellow paint he added her with a satisfying splodge of vivid colour. Then he took another brush and, concentrating on his painting, he did not see her start running down the long zigzag track toward him. It was not until the rattle of small stones warned him that he was about to be interrupted in his work that he looked up and saw her.

It was at that point he lowered his brush and

stared in surprise, seeing that she was coming at a run towards him. Her lovely features were radiant and her hair streamed out behind her in a golden flow.

'I've found you!' she exclaimed, casting aside the bundle she was carrying and holding out both hands to him.

He put aside his palette and brushes, rising from his stool to clasp her fingers lightly and automatically, supposing her to have come with some urgent message. 'Yes? What is it?'

'I'm Ingrid and I have come to claim you as my husband!'

He laughed, throwing back his head and showing his white teeth. His guess was that this must be some game the local girls were playing. 'I'm a little too busy to husband you today,' he said wickedly, 'pleasurable though it would be. I'm sorry to say you must look for somebody else.'

'There isn't anybody else!' she declared triumphantly. 'I've followed you all the way from my valley to take you home with me. I need a husband! I want babies! I already love you with my whole heart!'

To his astonishment, she flung herself against him, clasping him close, and suddenly the scent of her was in his nostrils and her lovely young body had moulded itself into his, making his desire soar. Then, for a few moments, he held her face between his hands, looking into her eyes as if into the depths of the fjord. All he could see was love. Almost as if she had cast a

231

spell on him, he bore her down on to the soft grass beside a rock that would hide them from view. She had loosened her blouse and her lovely breasts spilled into his clasp. His lips bore down on them and tears of happiness trickled from the corners of her eyes. Then his exploring hands found their way beneath her skirt and she cried out in joy as he caressed her with his long fingers, which she had so admired.

When he entered her, her response was so ecstatic that he was totally swept away himself, amazed in some distant part of his brain that she could stir such depths of feeling in him. But this was no ordinary young woman, and although she was not a virgin, he had seen a kind of starry innocence in her lovely eyes. Maybe he had sensed her uniqueness when she had approached from a distance, which was why he had needed to record and capture her in his painting just in case she tried to fly from him like a will-o'-the-wisp.

'I don't even know your name,' he said softly, brushing a strand of her hair away from her eyes. He was still lying across her and she did not want him to move.

'I'm Ingrid.' She did not really want to talk, for she was full of bliss at what had taken place between them and did not want these moments of intimacy to end. 'I was married at fifteen, and now I'm a widow. But,' she added, 'soon I'll be a bride again with you as my bridegroom.'

He smiled, wondering why he did not shy away at her talk of matrimony. 'Are you a hex?' he asked teasingly, referring to the mythical female creatures that took the form of beautiful young women with one aim, which was always to joyfully ensnare a mortal man into marriage with them. The only giveaway was that they always had a tail.

She replied indignantly. 'No, I'm not! You should know that already!'

'That's true enough. You're not a hex,' he added with amusement, sliding a hand to and fro under her buttocks. 'You are a beautiful young woman with a body that deserves to be painted.' Then he propped himself on his elbows to smile down into her face. 'So what happens now?'

'You may make love to me again.'

He needed no prompting and held her in his arms as if he could never let her go. They dozed afterwards, for the sun was high and they lay in satisfied bliss together.

She was the first to move, sitting up and becoming practical as she tidied her hair and put her clothes to rights. 'You shall come back to the valley with me now and we'll be married without delay. I have a good, weatherproof house on the mountain slopes and you can paint all day and every day. How often do you sell a painting?'

'Quite often. I have an agent that sells my pictures here and abroad. I'm not just a drifter. I have a studio in Bergen and accommodation there.'

She looked at him in horror. 'I couldn't live in a city! We should have to come to some arrangement. You can live most of the time with me and visit Bergen when necessary.'

'I suppose that is possible.' He was regarding her with amusement, totally fascinated by her and accepting in his heart that he had met his nemesis, for this fey creature would never let him go. He had had plenty of women in his time, but never one like her. Even if she was not a hex, she had him under her spell and there was no escaping the fact.

Afterwards, he thought he must have been in a trance to pack up his belongings at her orders and go with her as he did. They took a far less arduous route back to the valley than the one she had taken, for her map was much out of date. When they came to the signpost that she had followed to Geiranger, he hired a *fjording* for her to ride the last lap home, for she had a sore heel where her worn-out shoe had rubbed it and he could see she was in pain. So his thoughtfulness enabled her to return on horseback to the valley with pride and in triumph, as if she were a Viking queen with her captive walking beside her.

Word of her return spread quickly and Marie was the only one that was not wholly surprised to hear that the artist was with her.

Fifteen

Anna had read a great deal more of the journal by the time Alex came to take her to Molde. She was quite dazed to realize that the painting that had been Johan's, and was now hers in the bedroom at Steffan's house, was surely the most important of all Magnus Harvik's work since it depicted the meeting between two very remarkable people.

Alex had won his case and she had read details about the trial in *Aftenposten*. She congratulated him when he arrived to spend an evening with her before they set off for Molde the following morning. She had cooked dinner and they had a quiet evening with music from the radio making a background to their conversation. He was interested in everything and they had lively discussions as well as laughing a lot, for he had a dry sense of humour that appealed to her. She was very aware of being intensely attracted to him physically, not only for his good looks but by the athletic strength of him in the breadth of his shoulders and the overall maleness of him.

As they sat talking together, his arm around her, his conversation took a serious turn. 'I do love you, Anna,' he said softly, his arms tightening about her as he bent his head to brush his lips in a kiss on her throat. 'I know there will never be anyone else for me.'

She knew he wanted to make love to her and she wished she could respond and speak of her own feelings for him, but she did not want their first intimate moments to happen here. She had never managed to clear from her mind her experience with Karl. When she made love with Alex – and she knew it to be inevitable some time soon – it would have to be in a different location altogether. She straightened her spine away from him and he sensed her present rejection.

He spoke reassuringly. 'I understand.'

She knew he had drawn the wrong conclusion, thinking it was still Johan holding her back. Yet she was coming to terms with her memories. Johan would always occupy part of her heart and nothing could ever dislodge him. Yet she was learning to love Alex too. She thought of Ingrid, abandoning herself with such joy, and she wished she could be similarly unrestrained, but that was not possible under this roof.

He glanced at his watch. 'It's getting late and you have to be up early tomorrow morning. I'll be here at six o'clock to pick you up. The weather forecast promises a fine day.'

At the door he kissed her long and hard. She watched him go off down the stairs and wished she could have called him back, but it was all too soon, even though he had come to mean a great deal in her life.

They set off just before six o'clock the next morning. It was a perfect day, and the countryside everywhere was fresh and sweet and green with orchards in full bloom, everything being a little later here than it had been for Anna in the south of England. Over ten days before, she had let Steffan and Gudrun know that she was returning and had received the promise that a warm welcome would await her. It gave her the feeling of being part of a family at last, something she had always wanted so much as a child. As they drove along, she told Alex how she felt and he listened with understanding and compassion. Although his parents had gone, they had given him and Ivar, his brother, a happy childhood with a united family background. At present Ivar, an architect, was working in northern Norway where the Germans had burned down whole towns and villages, but Alex was looking forward to introducing Anna to him.

Anna had brought a picnic with her as she always did for these journeys, for as yet public places to eat were still far apart in the countryside, although there were plenty of picnic areas with wooden tables and benches, almost always set by a picturesque view. Today Alex stopped the car by a spot from which they could look down into a lush valley. It was on a grassy promontory that was almost circular in shape.

'Do you think we are sitting on the flat top of

a troll's head?' she asked on a laugh as she set the food out on the picnic table. 'He has his back against the cliff below us.'

'Most certainly,' Alex replied in the same vein, his grin wide, and he looked over the edge. 'Yes, I can see his feet. He has chosen this spot to sit with his knees drawn up to admire the view. But he will not object to us being here. Trolls like to be friendly when they get the chance.'

She laughed again, her eyes dancing. 'Then let's hope he does not decide to move before we have finished our picnic or else everything on this table will fly all over the place and us as well!'

She loved the Norse legends and had said one day to Alex that there were times when she had seen the faces of trolls in the mountains, for the crags and hollows and sharp precipices often gave the look of grotesque faces. He agreed that it was most surely how the legend had first come into being. Yet, although the trolls were always spoken of with a grin or an amused twinkle in the eye, she had never heard a Norwegian deny that they existed and that sense of fun pleased her.

Their picnic was peaceful. Nobody else came to share their quiet spot, and almost reluctantly she packed up again when they were ready to leave.

When they reached Molde, she could see that much progress had been made since her last visit. Then, as promised, Gudrun greeted her with warm words of welcome when they arrived at the Vartdal home. 'How good to have you back again! I know Steffan has been counting the days ever since we received your letter.'

'Where is he?' she asked, slipping off her coat. Alex had taken her suitcase upstairs and then departed, giving her a wave as he went out of the house and back to the car.

'Steffan is still in the garden, making the most of this lovely evening.'

Anna went through to him. He was dozing in a basket chair, one hand resting on the head of his cane. He had not heard her arrive and she was aware for the first time that a deep fondness for him had formed in her, making her glad that she was bringing him good news. She spoke his name and his eyes opened instantly. She saw such pleasure come into his face that she was deeply touched.

'What is it to be?' he questioned instantly without any preamble.

'I'm here to view the house,' she said.

'It was what I had hoped you would say! I'm very glad!'

'Ingrid in her own way can be very persuasive. She is so exuberant that she has made me want to know her better by seeing where she lived. Is any of her furniture still there?'

'Just a few items.' He gestured for her to take the basket chair beside him, and she brought it nearer him as she sat down. 'As soon as we knew you were coming, Gudrun wanted to take her domestic help with her and scrub the whole place clean for you, chasing away all the spiders that have probably taken up residence there. But I stopped her. I said I thought it best that you see it much as Ingrid saw it the first time.'

'It was kind of Gudrun to think of cleaning it for me, but you were right. I want to see it the first time from Ingrid's viewpoint.'

'Do not expect it all to be just as Ingrid described, because I happen to know that after her death her children naturally shared out the items that they wanted from their childhood home.'

'I have to admit that I haven't quite finished reading the journal yet.'

He looked surprised. 'You're taking your time over it.'

'I did not want to rush a single word. By taking the journal slowly, I've been giving myself time to think over all that Ingrid has written and in that way I believe I have really come to know her.'

'What do you think of her?'

'I think Johan's description of her was extremely apt. A formidable character and yet able to love generously.'

He nodded. 'Indeed she was! How do you judge Magnus?'

'I think he was exactly right for her. Whether he was always faithful to her when he was away from her on his painting trips, I do not know.'

'I like to give him the benefit of doubt.'

'So do I. Did Ingrid and Magnus have a

240

wedding photograph taken?'

'Yes. It hangs in her house where it belongs. Her children would have had copies.'

Anna felt she could hardly wait to see it, but she also had another matter on her mind. 'There is something I want so much to ask you. Why are you so against the American relative claiming Ingrid's house?'

He smiled, shaking his head. 'I have nothing against her personally. She is a very pleasant woman – indeed, she visited me with her husband and sister-in-law before the war – but I could tell that having viewed her roots she would not be interested in returning for any purpose linked to the house. After all, she had been born in the United States and she enthused about all that was new there. Her husband had Italian roots and so there would be no call on him to encourage her links with Norway. In any case, she's now too unwell to travel any distance and has no daughters to whom she could pass on such an inheritance.'

'How soon may I see the house now that I am here?'

'I would say tomorrow, but Harry is on another business trip to Sweden at the present time. He can take you next week when he is home again.'

She did not want Harry anywhere near her when she visited the house. She felt he had downgraded it too often to be in harmony with her links to it. Although he had had the journal printed for Steffan and had therefore read its contents, it was clear that Ingrid herself had made little or no impression on him.

'That's very obliging of Harry,' she said as tactfully as possible, 'but there is no need for him to give up time for me. Alex has offered to take me.'

'But Harry has been insistent about wanting to be your guide. He asked me to give my word that nobody else should escort you.'

'Did you? Give your word?' she questioned swiftly.

Steffan frowned. 'I cannot recall exactly how I answered him, but I believe I said that I could safely accept his offer on your behalf.'

'I'm afraid that was a misjudgement. In fact, I've become too impatient to await his return. I'd like to go tomorrow morning.' Her voice was firm, showing that her mind was made up and she would not be deterred.

'I recognize your tone,' he answered drily. 'It is one that Gudrun uses on occasions, as did my dear wife, and so I'll not try to persuade you otherwise, especially since you will be fulfilling my long-held wish for you to visit the house.'

'Then I should like to phone Alex and fix a time for meeting.' She had discussed a visit to the house with him on the journey. He had given her an outline of his work for the next few days and so she knew he could get away from his office after ten o'clock the next morning.

'Then make the phone call now,' Steffan said, pleased that the house was to be viewed so soon, it not being important to him as to whether it was Harry or Alex who took her there. He was so impatient to know what her ultimate decision would be.

The phone call settled that Alex would be with her as soon after ten as he could make it. She went early to bed that night, both Steffan and Gudrun believing that she was tired from the journey. But that was not the reason. She wanted to read more of the journal before the next day, when at last she would enter Ingrid's home.

Before leaving Gardermoen she had read Ingrid's description of the wedding and the feasting, all of which had been blessed by wonderful weather. Magnus's bedding of Ingrid on their wedding night was the only entry over which she had drawn a veil.

Our first night as a married couple was so joyously passionate and intimate that I cannot share those ecstatic memories even with these pages or with my pen. Yet what is not written will stay in my heart and mind forever. It is enough to say that ever since that night I have felt as if I am floating in happiness, my feet scarcely touching the ground. Today Magnus is starting a portrait of me before he puts his painting brushes to anything else. I wanted to wear my best silk dress, but he insists that I put on the blouse that I was wearing when I went running down the path to him at Geiranger and even the same skirt, although that will not be shown. He has framed the painting he was working on that day of our meeting and it is hanging in our living room. I am only an orange blob of paint, which does not please me. I wanted him to paint in more of me, but he says that would change the whole balance of his picture.

I know he is annoyed with himself for not having insisted at the time that we stay longer in Geiranger, where we could have enjoyed ourselves just as fully, but I have promised him that we shall make a return trip before long and then he will be able to paint the views that still linger in his mind. This time I am determined that I shall appear in more detail. Meanwhile, he has had a studio built that stands a little higher up the mountainside where he can paint undisturbed.

It had soon become clear to Anna in the next few pages that the marriage, although a love match, was a stormy relationship. They quarrelled over many things and made peace again by making love wherever they happened to be, whether it was in the mountains or at the house, and once in the snow, making an indentation that remained until the next snowfall.

Ingrid was to become Magnus's model for many of his paintings. He painted her both nude and clothed, at work in the house or in some local terrain, and once when she was tending her two beloved sheep. One day he made her sit so near the waterfall, wanting to capture the mist of spray around her, that inevitably her garments became damp and cold.

It was probably due in some part to her earlier illness having left her with a weakness in her chest that she caught a chill from sitting so near the waterfall and an inflammation went to her lungs, which then developed into pneumonia. She was seriously ill and Magnus was in a panic that he would lose her. Marie came forward to care for her again, with the aid of a retired nurse from the valley. Eventually, Ingrid began to recover, although her convalescence was likely to take some time. Privately, Marie believed that she and the nurse had saved Ingrid's life by sponging her down with cool water and constantly changing cold compresses on her forehead when the fever was at its height.

'Ingrid is going to take much longer to recover her strength than last time she was ill,' Marie said coldly to Magnus. 'So when she is well again, you'll not make her sit by the waterfall or anywhere else that could be dangerous to her health.'

'No, I promise you!' he vowed, his eyes still stark.

In the days that followed, when Ingrid was still lying weakly in bed, Magnus tried to think what he could do to make amends for being the cause of her illness. Then he remembered her love of rosemaling and immediately knew what he would do. A carpenter made him an easily erected platform on trestles and, lying on it, he began a great task, which was to cover the whole ceiling of the large living room with the old traditional designs. He thought to himself that he was like Michelangelo painting the Sistine Chapel, except that he did not put himself in the same category.

On the day that he carried Ingrid downstairs at the beginning of her convalescence, she looked up in amazement at the ceiling, and tears of joy trickled down her cheeks at what he had done for her. She put the palm of her hand against his face as he lowered her into a chair before tucking a rug over her knees.

'Now this is truly a house of beauty!' she said quietly, her weakened voice catching emotionally in her throat. 'I'm going to live the rest of my life under a bower of roses!'

When she was fully recovered and Magnus felt able to leave her again, he selected some of his paintings and took them with him to Bergen, travelling from the nearby port of Alesund on the *hurtigruten*, which was the coastal steamer service that plied the length of the west coast. He had given the first of the many paintings in which Ingrid featured the title *The Quiet Woman*, which was the very reverse of her nature. It was a private joke, which they both shared, she being only too aware that her exuberance was overwhelming at times. He kept to this secret joke in all subsequent paintings of her, never anticipating that over the years these *Quiet Woman* works of art would become extremely collectable and eventually fetch astronomically high prices at the world's auction houses, even when she was sometimes reduced again to a speck of oil paint.

She never did get back to Geiranger with him. When a trip was all arranged for them to travel by coastal steamer to the port of call at the village, she found that she was pregnant for the first time and so she sent him off to paint on his own. When he had captured on canvas all he wanted from Geiranger, he had gone direct to Bergen and the gallery that sold his work, making it a long time before he returned home.

Ingrid soon began to hate the times when he was away. Early in their marriage, she had made two trips to Bergen with him, mainly to see his rooms and his studio, but he was so busy during their stay that she hardly saw him while she was there. Although she walked all over Bergen, lingered in the fish market, went to a service in the ancient Stav Church and managed to get tickets for herself and Magnus to hear Ole Bull give a violin recital, she was soon impatient to be home again. What finally made her decide never to go to Bergen again was that she was horribly seasick on both voyages almost as soon as she stepped on to the coastal steamer's deck.

She gave birth to a fine son in the summer when she was nineteen. It took place the day before Magnus returned from one of his Bergen visits. She had been attended in her labour by Marie, who was always on hand in any kind of crisis, and also the local midwife. Before the birth, Ingrid had tried to talk to Magnus about a choice of names for their child, but when he had a project on his mind, or a painting that was not going exactly as he wished, he scarcely listened to what others were saying, completely preoccupied. Ingrid finally made the decision by herself. If the baby should be a boy, he would be called Haakon after her late father, and also this had been the name of a brave Viking king, which she thought was also in its favour.

When Marie heard Magnus dismounting from his horse upon his arrival home, she hurried to tell him the good news.

'Your son has arrived!' she announced happily.

He gave a shout of joy and rushed upstairs to kiss Ingrid heartily, and then went to the cradle and pick up his child. He loved his son on sight, carrying him around the room while she sat back against her pillow and watched him contentedly. She knew him so well that after telling him her choice of the baby's name she could see that he would have liked his firstborn to be named after him. So on the day of the christening their first offspring became Magnus-Haakon.

In order not to create any confusion, the child was always addressed or spoken of by his full name. He grew strong and fearless, climbing the mountains at an early age with or without his parents, and becoming a fast skier of champion potential on the slopes before he was twelve years old. By then he had a sister, named

Liv, who was born a year after him. Emma arrived a little too soon and spent her first three months in hospital, but she thrived and Ingrid always had an especially soft spot for her. Nils, unexpectedly copperhaired, was next to arrive and brought his own sense of fun into the family. Following him was Anders, who was to become a keen sportsman. Then came the twins, Christofer and Erik, who had arrived just eighteen months later. Then came Kurt, who even as a toddler hero-worshipped the twins, always following after them whenever possible.

Ingrid had always ignored the discomfort of her pregnancies, thinking only of the new baby she would love as she loved the others she had borne, but now it seemed as if her family was complete. Yet a surprise was still in store for her, and out of the most difficult birth of all she had endured another daughter came into the family, who was named Sonja. She loved music from an early age, attemtping to sing when she was still very little.

Magnus-Haakon, as the eldest, always felt himself to be in charge of his siblings and intervened swiftly if any one of them was in trouble. He was particularly good with the twins, who would never have been parted in their play or on any expedition if he had not made them carry out separate tasks.

'Now listen to me, Christofer and Erik,' he said sternly to them when they were still very young. 'We are a family and we all belong to one another. You two must share yourselves

249

with the rest of us and not go off on your own to play.'

His death in a terrible fall, trying to save one of the twins stuck behind a high crag, shocked the whole valley and devastated his parents. At times of joy and sorrow, all of the farming families in the valley became as one family. So many came to the funeral that not all could be accommodated in the little church and the crowd of mourners in their best black clothes gathered outside in the rain. They parted to allow an avenue to form when the casket was borne from the church to its resting place. Anna felt tears come into her eyes as she read the account of the tragedy, and Ingrid's own grief was marked on the page in tear stains that had smudged her ink. She had also drawn a little diagram, showing where in the churchyard her seventeen-year-old son was lying at peace.

By this time, art dealers had long since dis-covered where Magnus lived and frequently toiled up the slope to his studio, hoping to get the next *Quiet Woman* painting before anyone else. Norwegians were drawn strongly to the new school of painting created by the French Impressionists, many buyers already influenced by the work of their own Norwegian artists, Munch and the sculptor Gustav Vigeland. Mag-nus's paintings became even more in demand. Always the art dealers took away whatever paintings he had done, not knowing there were a good number that he kept out of their sight. These were mostly of his children, as well as his own favourite paintings of Ingrid, which were displayed in rooms where the dealers never entered, for he always received them in his studio.

As Magnus became more and more prosperous, he began to talk of buying a fine house in Bergen and keeping the old house for holidays. It led to a quarrel with Ingrid of such magnitude that it almost tore them apart. He went off to Bergen in a fury and did not reappear for eleven weeks, during which time she felt she must surely die of heartache. When she saw him coming up the slope again, she ran to meet him. Then they fell into each other's arms.

While Magnus had been away, he had purchased a fine house, mainly as an investment, and had transferred his Bergen studio there, but he was never to live in it beyond a few weeks at a time and then it was entirely for business. He and Ingrid were both satisfied with the compromise.

Ingrid had recorded meticulously the names of her children, their weight at birth, their following accomplishments, as well as their scholarly progress at the little school run by a retired clergyman and his wife in their own home, before they went on to a bigger school nearby. She had also sketched the faces of each of her children. It was clear to Anna that these drawings portrayed a distinct likeness of each child and she wondered if Magnus had ever known that his wife had considerable talent.

Most of what followed in the journal were accounts of family events, including mountain trips and skiing outings, picnics and other social activities, a highlight being when all the Harvik children were in a group photograph taken outside the house by a friend who was a professional photographer. It was taken shortly before Magnus-Haakon's fatal fall, and after the tragedy Ingrid mentioned in her journal that the photograph had been hung in the living room where Magnus-Haakon would always be within the family circle.

Magnus was away when, during the school summer holiday, the children talked about a bear they had named Erik the Red after a Viking king, because although he was dark-brown the bright summer sun gave his fur a reddish tinge. Ingrid paid little attention to their chatter about the bear as they sat for their meals, for they were imaginative children and were always thinking up new games. There had not been bears in the local forests for some years. It was more of a concern to her that a wolf had slain several sheep. She was keeping Klara and Ida safely penned in for the time being and the children had been instructed to keep near the house.

Then one day, when the children were out playing and the front door stood open for a cooling breeze, Ingrid came from the kitchen to see a brown bear on the threshold, looking into the room. She went cold with horror to think that the children had been at the animal's mercy and their talk of a bear had not sprung from their imagination. It was a young bear, but this was the slayer of the unfortunate sheep. Clearly it was making up its mind about entering, probably lured by the aroma of food, and Ingrid backed slowly away into the kitchen until she could just reach out to where a tin tray lay on a cupboard by the door. Seizing it, she sprang back into the living room and with her fist she banged the tray and shouted as she ran forward to confront the bear.

Startled, it backed away and turned tail, but at the same time there came a distant clamour from the valley. The bear was to face a still more bewildering noise as all but the old and infirm were coming to chase it back over the mountains, hopefully over the border into the forests of Sweden from which it had probably come. Cooking-pot lids were being crashed together, tin trays banged and whistles blown, and the local musicians were thundering drums and playing trumpets. Some field guns were fired, but only into the air to add to the noise. Nobody aimed at the fleeing bear. There was an inborn respect for wild life and unnecessary killing was not to be considered except in an emergency.

Ingrid gathered in her children and told them they must always report to her if they saw any more bears in the future, as well as wolves or wolverines.

It was at that point sleep began to overtake Anna. She put aside the journal and it seemed as if it was only a moment before she opened her eyes to a brilliant day, the very one during which she would enter Ingrid's domain for the first time.

Sixteen

Alex arrived at Steffan's house in good time to catch the ferry. Anna was waiting in the porch and went lightly down the steps to slide into the car.

'I'm excited,' she said as they drove away, while Gudrun waved good wishes for their outing from the window. 'But I'm full of trepidation too. Suppose Ingrid does not like me?'

He laughed, shaking his head. 'Are you expecting to meet her there?'

It was a relief to her that Steffan, seeing how close she and Alex had become, had given her leave to tell him about the journal, which she had done the previous evening in preparation for this visit.

'No,' she replied seriously, 'but she comes through as such a powerful presence from the pages of her journal that I feel something of her aura must surely linger on in the house she loved so much. I'm so glad that Steffan has agreed that you should read it after me.'

On the south side of the fjord, Alex drove into the valley and up the slope that would take them to Ingrid's house. At some time the track had been widened and, although it was still steep, Alex was able to drive all the way up and park at the side of the house.

Getting out of the car, Anna could not take her gaze from Ingrid's home and she went forward slowly to stand facing it. Heavy shutters covered the windows and Alex went at once to unhook them and fasten them back against the walls. Immediately, the old glass of the windows sparkled where it caught the sunlight. Anna breathed a sigh of quiet anticipation, for she would soon see the interior in much the same state as when Ingrid had first entered there on her day of arrival. Even the turf roof was the same, although she knew it had been returfed since Ingrid's time. But, just as Ingrid had noted in her journal, there was an additional covering of wild flowers. She could see tiny wild pansies and my lady's slipper growing in abundance, even some wild orchids and dancing buttercups, as well as numerous harebells, some of which were dipping down in a fringe over the top windows.

Alex had unlocked the door and was standing back to let her enter first, but she reached out her hand for his and they went linked into the house, he brushing aside a festoon of cobwebs. Then she stood to look around her with a deep and quiet pleasure. There was dust, but nothing excessive, and no sign of mice. Then she looked up at the rosemaling ceiling, the painting of which had been a true labour of love, the design extending down to border the pale wood of the walls. It was beautiful. She found it easy to imagine Ingrid's joy when she saw it for the first time, most especially since she had such a great love of colour. Here in the intricate design was a canopy of rust-red, various blues in deep shades, greens, flashes of yellow and orange, as well as white swirls in fan-shapes around roses and even a little bird here and there. She thought how Ingrid must have loved the way her two sheep had been incorporated into one small section full of blossoms. Time had barely faded any of it, but the wood itself had matured the lovely shades, as if they had been part of the great logs themselves when the trees had been felled to build this mountain haven. Ingrid had mentioned once that she never allowed anyone, not even Magnus, to smoke indoors, for nothing yellowed the wood more than tobacco smoke.

A floor-to-ceiling black iron stove, ornamented with elaborately fashioned ironwork, stood in a corner, and under the window nearby was a long white scrubbed table with a bench on either side, where the children would have sat for family meals. A large chair with a carved back stood at the head of it, Ingrid having wanted Magnus's presence to still be felt at family meals and nobody since then had ever removed it. There was an ordinary chair at the opposite end, as if Ingrid took whatever chair was nearest for herself, or else someone had felt that a chair should mark her place too. Maybe Steffan had done that or even Johan.

Still looking around at everything, Anna went across to sit down on what she now thought of

257

as Ingrid's chair. She tried to imagine the family scene at mealtimes and supposed there would always have been a high chair for the latest baby at Ingrid's right hand.

Then Anna's gaze went to a family photograph on the wall above and behind Magnus's place. Swiftly she stood up and went to it. There were the children altogether, grouped outside the house, and only Sonja, who was yet to be born, was missing, for it was the photograph including Magnus-Haakon that Ingrid had wanted always to be in the centre of family activities. He was easy to pick out, for he was the tallest with a mop of fair hair and an impish grin in contrast to his siblings, some having clamped their lips with the effort of keeping still for the photographer. One boy had turned his head and smudged his likeness.

Moving away, Anna gazed around again. It was a warmly welcoming room, although only the table and chairs remained in it, as well as a tall rosemaling cupboard that was built into the wall. She went through into the kitchen with its ancient cooking stove, the shelves and hooks no longer holding pots and pans. Opening the door that led to the cellar, she went down a few steps and could just discern in the darkness that were was some furniture stored there under dust sheets. Alex had handed her his torch, which he had brought with him from the car, but although its bright ray swept over the items in storage, she could not see in any detail what was there.

'We'll look at all these things next time we

come here,' she said before they went back up the steps to the kitchen. Then she looked into the side room where Ingrid had kept her spinning wheel and the loom, but it was empty. No doubt those two items had been taken away by her children. There was also a complete lack of ornaments and any kind of knick-knack, which suggested that the same had happened to those items. It would also explain why there were no paintings by Magnus on the walls.

All the time, Alex had been watching her, noting the serene pleasure in her face. When she began climbing the stairs, he followed her, not wanting to miss any of her reactions to this old house. On the upper floor, all three of the smaller bedrooms were devoid of any furniture. Another room, little more than a cupboard, had a hip-bath in it. Then she entered Ingrid's room. It was empty and Anna wondered what had happened to the great bed with its carved headboard that Ingrid had described vividly in her journal. On the wall was the wedding photograph. Anna went at once to study it.

There was Ingrid in her lace-trimmed wedding gown, seated on a high-backed chair with Magnus standing beside her in well-cut clothes, and there was a backcloth of classical pillars behind them. Ingrid was exactly how she appeared in the painting on Steffan's hall wall, beautiful with an impish look in her wide eyes, which tilted slightly at the corners. She looked triumphant and she had every reason to be, for the man she had captured was exceedingly handsome with a virile look about him. What was more, judging by her journal, he had proved to be a passionate husband and a devoted father.

'Just look at this handsome couple!' Anna said to Alex, who had come to stand by her side and put an arm about her waist as he studied the photograph with her. 'Ingrid and Magnus. I feel I have known them all my life. I think they have left happiness in this house for all to share.'

'How would that be for us?' he questioned softly.

She turned within the circle of his arm and their gaze met as she considered her answer carefully, for she recognized the fact that she had reached the point of no return.

'I believe that we could enjoy life together and I know that I have come to love you, Alex. I never want us to be apart ever again.'

He was very serious. 'Then you will marry me, Anna?'

She nodded, inwardly amazed by the ocean of love for him that had engulfed her. It must most surely be Ingrid who had brought her face to face with the truth. 'Yes! I believe I began to love you months ago, but so much blocked the way for me.'

He kissed her long and passionately, crushing her to him and almost lifting her off her feet. She knew such intense happiness that she responded as eagerly, locking her arms about his neck.

When they came downstairs, Alex locked up

and they wandered hand in hand around the house to see the layout of what had once been a herb garden, with nearby flowerbeds and a vegetable patch all vastly overgrown. Black-currant and redcurrant bushes had spread their growth enormously and were in great need of pruning. There was also a cherry tree and an apple tree. Anna could picture Ingrid's boys climbing these trees for the fruit. She did not look for Magnus's studio, for Steffan had told her that Liv, Ingrid's daughter, had had it demolished after her mother's demise. Nobody knew why, although he thought it came from some long-held resentment against Magnus for dying too soon and never being there for her.

It was as Anna and Alex were turning towards the *stabbur* that they heard a car coming up the track. Then it drove into sight.

'It is Harry,' Anna said in quiet exasperation that he should intrude at this special time.

Harry drew up and sprang out, looking flushed and agitated. 'I told that old fool uncle of mine that I would bring you here on your first visit, Anna,' he exclaimed in irritable tones. 'I returned early from my Swedish trip to be on hand as your guide.'

Anna regarded him coldly. 'I'm grateful that my father-in-law let me come here today with-out any delays and it was kind of Alex to bring me.' Then to appease him, since she wanted to prevent any backlash of his temper against Steffan, she added, 'I have yet to view the barn and the *stabbur.* You can be my guide there.'

He failed to catch the coolness in her voice, although his tone modified. 'Yes, of course. Do you have the key? Good.' He took the ring of keys from her, selecting one as they turned for the *stabbur*.

'The house isn't much, is it?' he was saying conversationally. 'Nothing of any value in it.'

'It is just how I expected it to be,' she replied casually.

'Good. I did not want you to have high hopes of the place and then be disappointed.'

Alex had moved across to his car. 'I'll wait for you here, Anna.'

Harry turned with a dismissive wave to him. 'There's no need for you to hang about. I'll take Anna home.'

Anna spoke up quickly. 'No, I'll go with Alex. Gudrun has invited him back with me for *middag*.'

'Oh, in that case...' Harry's voice trailed off. Then he turned back to her with a retrieved smile. 'We'll do the barn first.'

Again, all was exactly as Ingrid had described. There were the broken remains of the sheep-pen to show where Klara and Ida had spent their winter days, and the stall where once Hans-Petter had been stabled. Anna wondered if she had been alone at that moment, would she have sensed Ingrid looking over her shoulder and maybe have heard her cooing to Klara and Ida long since gone?

'The first thing to do is to demolish this old stable before it falls down,' Harry said, waving his hands about dismissively. 'It's a real eyesore and unsafe.'

Anna smiled to herself. Did she hear Ingrid hiss disapproval in her ear? No matter what Harry said, she was determined that everything should be restored to just how it was in Ingrid's day.

The outside stairs up to the *stabbur* were bow-shaped by wear over many years, the handrail smoothed by many hands. To oblige Harry, she looked into the storeroom, which had nothing in it, and then they went outside again to go up the outer staircase to the upper room. This was also completely empty. Anna recalled how Ingrid had described the room at her first viewing, declaring it was like a setting from the *Arabian Nights*. Anna looked around for some sign of its former grandeur. There was nothing. All she could see that was probably left from that time were a few wooden curtain rings on a rod above one of the windows. Harry, bored by waiting for her to finish looking around, made a play of testing the floorboards, although to Anna they looked sound enough for the next hundred years. She saw him give a nod of satisfaction that showed he had drawn the same conclusion.

Then abruptly she shivered as if a cold hand had brushed by her. It was a strong feeling and yet there was nothing here to mar the pleasing appearance of the room, with its mellow walls and the pale ceiling that hid the rafters supporting the roof.

Harry broke into her thoughts. 'What are you going to do to this place? Make it a guest room again? If you need any work doing, I'll gladly take it on. Although I say it myself, I am considered an expert in the restoration of historic and other buildings.'

'So Steffan has told me. As for the future role of this *stabbur*, I haven't decided.'

She would have turned to leave, but he barred her way. 'I have something I must ask you, Anna,' he said, his expression intensely serious. 'When the house is yours, all papers signed, would you rent or sell it to me before you make any changes or alterations? Steffan need never know. He is an old man in poor health. He cannot last much longer and you never wanted this house, I know. I would be glad to take it off your hands.'

She stared at him for a few moments in angry disbelief that he should imagine she could be so devious. 'I would never accept this house under false pretences! I shall give my decision to Steffan this evening.'

He shrugged carelessly. 'I thought I was doing you a good turn.'

'You were much mistaken!'

She left the room and led the way back down the stairs to where Alex was waiting for her. Harry locked up the *stabbur* again and returned the keys to her. Goodbyes were exchanged and Anna felt enormous relief to be free of him as they drove away. It was as if a sinister cloud had fallen over the day when he had appeared.

She had also experienced a brief moment of unease when she was alone with Harry that she could not define. Maybe it was just her growing dislike of him that was bothering her. She decided that whatever it was would soon become clear to her if it was of any importance.

On the ferry, Alex bought coffee and waffles from the little counter, and they sat a table by a window, not looking at the passing waters of the fjord, only at each othcr. They did not talk very much, but were content. When they had arrived off the ferry at Molde, Alex drove on through the town until he drew up outside a jewellers' shop. He looked at Anna with a smile.

'We have rings to buy,' he said, leaning across to kiss her.

She smiled happily, knowing that this man was truly the one to fill the lonely gap in her life and whom she was destined to love until the end of her days.

In the jewellers' shop they were given a choice of plain gold rings that also acted as wedding rings, an engagement considered as binding as a marriage, and there was no exchange of rings during the marriage cere-mony. She selected the rings, which were placed in little boxes, charmingly wrapped with a bow and then handed to Anna while Alex wrote out a cheque.

They came out of the shop together and paused to look smilingly into each others' eyes. 'Where would you like us to exchange our gold rings?' he asked.

Without a moment's hesitation, she pointed to a spot in the mountains rising above the town. 'Could we drive up there?'

He looked in the direction she was pointing. 'To Varden? Yes, we can. But why have you chosen that spot?'

'I haven't been there yet and I was once told that it is the best place to view the eighty-seven mountain peaks. That makes it a very special place at all times and particularly for us today.'

'Today is also a perfect day for viewing. Not a cloud in the sky.'

The zigzag road they travelled left a few neat houses behind on the lower slopes, and then it was little more than a rough track that took them through thick forest up and up until they reached a green sward where they parked. She sprang out of the car and went forward as at last the full panorama of the range of the Romsdal mountains was revealed to her. Everything here was so still and quiet, not even a breeze. The reflection of the great peaks was held in the mirror water of the fjord, which was only disturbed where a ferry-steamer was leaving ripples in its wake. Eighty-seven peaks! Who could begin to count them?

Alex, seeming to understand that she wanted to view alone, rested his weight against the car with his arms folded as he watched her.

Her thoughts were full of Johan. It was here that he had wanted to bring her and it was here that she had to put him away into her memory

266

where he would always be loved. Slowly she removed her wedding ring, which had been on her finger since the day he had placed it there. She put it to her lips in a private kiss and then slipped it into her purse. Only then did she turn to Alex. He came to her at once.

'Is it to be now?' he asked her fondly.

She nodded. They opened their own ring boxes. Then, holding their rings firmly, they slid them on to the third finger of each other's right hand. She was glad that this was fresh and new to her, sparing her any comparison with the past. With a shout of joy, Alex picked her up and swung her around before setting her down in a kiss that seemed to last forever.

'You do realize what this means,' she said as they drove down the mountain slope again. 'I'll be telling Steffan that I'll be accepting the house now that I'm going to marry you.'

'I think the matter was settled as soon as you set eyes on the place. You looked as if you were in a trance.'

'I think I was.'

'How soon shall we marry? Tomorrow?'

She laughed. 'Not quite so soon. I know Gudrun will have a wonderful time helping to arrange everything. I cannot deny her that pleasure, but I should like it to be a quiet wedding. I don't want a crowd of people.'

'That suits me too. I'll invite my brother. That's the end of my wedding list.'

'Mine is almost as short. I should just like to invite Molly and Olav, also Aunt Christina. She

267

has been so hospitable and kind to me. She could travel with them. I know they would look after her.' She paused thoughtfully. 'I'll ask Steffan to escort me to church if that should please him.'

'I'm sure it would.'

'I'd like us to be married in the museum church.' She needed everything to be unique with Alex. There were too many poignant reminders of Johan's young days in the little Tresfjord church and she did not want cherished memories of her wedding to him disturbed in any way.

'That can be arranged,' Alex was saying.

She gave a sigh of satisfaction. 'Let us promise ourselves that we will try always to overcome whatever hurdles we meet just as smoothly as we've arranged everything for our marriage.' Then she laughed. 'Maybe that is too much to expect. You have a stubborn streak and I can be very obstinate.'

He grinned and took his hand from the wheel to put it over hers. 'Now you tell me!' he joked. 'But we will do our best.'

She was never to forget the pleasure that suffused Steffan's eyes when she broke the news to him and put out her hand to display her ring.

'Today I have made two of the most important decisions in my life,' she said. 'Alex and I are to be married and I accept the house most gratefully. It is a very special house in one of the most beautiful settings in the world, and I promise you that I will always take care of it and ensure that it will go to the right person after me.' Her next words echoed what Alex had said when first meeting her on the day of her arrival in Norway. 'Perhaps to my own daughter.'

Steffan took both of her hands in his, nodding his satisfaction and momentarily beyond speech. After a few minutes he did manage to congratulate Alex and wish Anna joy, but his quiet acceptance of their great news was in contrast to Gudrun's exuberant reception of it.

'It was what Steffan and I hoped would happen!' she declared, throwing up her hands in delight.

Later, when Anna was on her own with Gudrun, discussing the weddings arrangements, she said with a tremor in her voice, 'It was not an easy decision.'

Gudrun nodded in understanding. 'Just remember that Johan did not have a selfish bone in his body. He would rejoice that you have found happiness again.'

'I'll never, never forget him.'

'I know you never will and so does Steffan.'

'There is something I must ask you. Why is Harry so determined to find fault with the house. He has tried to put me against it whenever he has had the chance. The same happened when we saw him there today.'

Gudrun did not hesitate in her reply. 'He has always wanted it for himself. That's the reason! It is a perfect holiday home for the mountains.

Many people have cabins from which to ski in winter and climb and walk in summer, but none can compare with the house that you have now.'

Anna was staring at her in surprise. 'How can Harry ever have hoped to have it? Ingrid's house has to be passed on to a woman!'

'He would have managed that by marrying. He has had a lot of girlfriends and there is one he seems to prefer to all the rest. She lives not far away in Kristiansund. He brought her here once, but Steffan did not like her superior airs. If you feel that Harry is trying to destroy your pleasure in your newly acquired property, you should remember that after the loss of Johan it was natural that Harry should expect to be Steffan's heir. Harry had not counted on your appearing on the scene, especially when you did not come to Norway when the other war brides began arriving. He thought you were never going to show up. I must admit that although you had written to Steffan, I had begun to have doubts that we should ever meet you.'

'Yet in spite of what you say, Harry has always been very pleasant to me.'

'Yes, of course, but privately he will be bitterly disappointed by your decision to accept the house.'

'Have I taken a property that should be more rightfully his if he married?'

Gudrun shook her head. 'Not at all,' she answered vehemently. 'Never suppose that! As Johan's widow all that would have been his inheritance has becomes yours. In fact, Harry has been falling out of favour with Steffan for some time. In my opinion, it began when Harry lost the ring.'

'What ring was that?'

Gudrun frowned. 'Of course, you do not know anything about it. It was during the occupation. Steffan gave him an unusual gold ring that had belonged to Magnus Harvik. It was very old and fashioned with a Viking cipher. It had been given to the artist by Ingrid. It was hard for Steffan to part with it, but he had wanted to reward Harry for his many kindnesses. Naturally, he had thought that Harry would value it highly.' Gudrun gave a sigh. 'Perhaps he did, but he was careless with it. Then one day he came to confess to Steffan that he had lost it.'

'However did that happen?' Anna asked, dismayed.

'He said it had been slightly on the large size for him and declared that it must have slipped off his finger, but Steffan suspected that he had sold it. Anything made of gold was in high demand during the occupation, and Harry always seemed to be in need of money. Steffan has been generous to him many times. But let's not talk of that any more. We have a happier subject to discuss.' Gudrun steered the conversation back to the wedding day, and Harry was not mentioned again.

Anna wrote to her aunt, saying that she was to marry and extending a direct invitation, but it

271

was frostily declined. In contrast, Molly in Gardermoen accepted with enthusiasm. She and Olav arrived on the eve of the wedding, bringing Aunt Christina with them, and also accompanied by Pat and Rolf. Both couples had left their children with Helen, who was going to look after them. The war brides had clubbed together in a joint gift of an elegant coffee set, for at last some beautiful things were appearing in the shops. Molly had also packed up Anna's belongings at her Gardermoen rooms, having offered to do it, and these were handed over in Anna's own suitcases.

'Everybody sends love and they are all so pleased for you,' Molly said happily. 'Alex is extremely dishy and you deserve the best.' Then a serious look passed between them as she added, 'You had the best of men last time and he would be glad for you.'

Anna nodded wordlessly and then turned to Aunt Christina, whom she had hugged fondly on arrival and who was now awaiting her turn to speak to the bride-to-be. She was delighted to be a wedding guest and the gift she brought with her was to be a total surprise. She handed Anna an envelope. 'Inside is a picture of my gift,' she said. 'You will have to wait a little while to receive it, but you will soon understand why.'

Anna opened the envelope and inside was a picture postcard of a young woman in the national costume of Romsdal, just like the girl on the painted plaque that she had bought on

272

her first shopping trip in Oslo. 'Does this mean...?' she began uncertainly.

'It does indeed,' Christina endorsed. 'Since you are marrying here and are becoming a Norwegian citizen, you have every right to wear the national costume of this region, and it is my pleasure to give it to you.'

Anna gasped and hugged her joyfully. 'It's the most wonderful gift!' It was something she had hoped to have in the future, but these costumes were expensive, being made of home-woven cloth and hand-embroidered, which amounted to many hours of work.

'You are to have the costume made locally and, thanks to your father-in-law, everything has been arranged,' Christina said with satisfaction. The cost of her generous gift was unimportant to her, for she only felt thankful that she was able to give a lasting gift to the girl that had given her beloved nephew some true happiness in his short life.

After refreshment, the three arrivals went off to check in at the Alexandra Hotel where rooms had been booked for them. Next morning they would take a taxi to the museum church for the marriage ceremony.

Word of the marriage had spread and many people turned up to see the bride. Alex was well-liked in the community, being active in town affairs, and Anna had already made friends in the town. The gift that gave Anna the greatest pleasure was a painting by Magnus that Steffan had been keeping out of Anna's sight until she should accept the house. It showed Ingrid and Magnus together. He was seated on the steps of the *stabbur* as he watched her, brightly dressed in her orange skirt and a yellow blouse, absorbed in picking blackcurrants from the bush by their house.

After Anna had thanked him, her whole face showing her pleasure in the gift, she said, 'I feel that I have become very close to Ingrid through her journal.'

'That's a good beginning to becoming the owner of her house,' Steffan said approvingly. 'There will be some papers you will have to sign, but Alex will take care of that for us.'

Alex's brother, Ivar, had also arrived the day before the wedding. He was as tall as Alex, good-looking and friendly. He and Anna liked each other on sight.

'I wish both of you every happiness,' he said warmly. His gift was a crystal decanter and glasses.

Gudrun had made sure that the ancient church was full of flowers on the wedding day and the air was scented by the blooms. Anna wore a new cream silk dress with a wide-brimmed 'halo' hat, as the style was called, for it set off the wearer's face, and she carried a small bouquet of mountain flowers. Steffan escorted her up the aisle, and when Alex turned his head and smiled at her, she knew beyond any shadow of a doubt that he was why fate had eventually brought her to stay in these northern climes.

They went to a hotel in Geiranger for their

honeymoon and the windows of their room gave a view of the great fjord. Yet it was not the incomparable view that held their attention, for they saw only each other. As soon as he had locked the door, they moved into each other's arms. A few minutes later his nakedness met hers as passion possessed them. Without conceit, she knew that she had a beautiful body, and when he drew back to explore still more of her, she felt the rays of the sun through the windows fall warmly across her like a welcome back to love. When at last he entered her, she cried out in joy as their mutual ecstasy engulfed them. Afterwards they dozed in blissful exhaustion until they woke to make love again, and gradually the night with its deceptive daylight slipped away.

Before the wedding, Steffan had agreed to Anna's request that when she had reached the last page of the journal, then Alex should read it too. Already Alex was keenly interested in all Anna had to tell him about Ingrid. One morning on their honeymoon they tried to find the place where Magnus had been sitting at his easel when Ingrid had burst into his life, but there were so many great rocks and so many possible places that they just made a guess at one.

Anna had moved her belongings into Alex's apartment the day before the wedding and, after they returned from their honeymoon, she went to see Steffan and Gudrun while Alex caught up with work in his office. They welcomed her back and naturally their conversation soon turned to Ingrid's house. Steffan had some furniture of the period under covers in his *stabbur* and whatever was stored in Ingrid's cellar could be brought up and repaired if necessary. During Anna's absence, Gudrun had taken two women to scrub and wash and clean every inch of the house. She had also put some crockery and cutlery into cupboards and drawers, as well as hanging three saucepans and a frying pan on pegs in the kitchen.

'I hope that I have not overdone getting basic things ready for you,' she said uncertainly, not sure whether Anna would consider what she had done as interference.

'Of course not,' Anna assured her, relieved to know the hard work of cleaning the house had been done. 'I'm most grateful. I had realized that there would be a great deal of work ahead of me to make Ingrid's house into a home again.' She had been surprised and pleased to be told that the fund available for restoring the house had originated with Ingrid, who had left a sum for the continued care of it, and would more than cover whatever needed to be done.

Anna was getting near the end of Ingrid's journal. As her family had increased, the entries in it had become spaced out, mostly recording matters concerned with the children such as first steps, first teeth, illnesses and school successes. Magnus had become renowned both in his own country and abroad. Ingrid never accompanied him when his presence was wanted elsewhere, partly because she would not leave

276

the children in the care of others and there were too many now to hand them over to Marie, who had an increasing family of her own. Yet the main reason why Ingrid would not leave home was that she could not endure the thought of being anywhere other than her beloved haven.

She wrote with pleasure that Magnus had bought a sailing boat large enough to take the children and some of their friends.

Sometimes we fish from it, she wrote, *Young Anders is the true fisherman. Whenever he puts his line down the fish seem to be jostling one another to take his bait. 'Another one, Mama!' he will shout. Often we sail to a little island in the middle of the fjord where I set out a picnic and the children all love it.*

Then Ingrid reverted to her description of the little island: *The grassy mound there is said locally to be the site of a Viking king's burial, although it has never been excavated. Strangely, I did find an ancient gold ring in the grass one day and a jeweller friend confirmed it was very old and probably dated from that time. I gave it to Magnus and he would wear it sometimes, but he never cared much for it. He likes best the one inset with a diamond, which I gave him on our first wedding anniversary, and it has never has left his finger. I often wear the diamond and ruby brooch that he gave me at the same time. We had made love all night as if we were only just wed.*

Ingrid then went on to write about Magnus's departures. 'Be faithful to me!' she admonished him every time. 'Because if you are not, I shall know and kill you when you return.'

He had always laughed. 'I would not dare to disobey the only woman in the world for me!'

Meawhile, Liv was gainfully employed as a dressmaker' assistant in Molde and she wrote to Ingrid to update her on her new life.

It is work she enjoys, having always loved new clothes, and she made some of her own garments when she was still quite young. Thankfully, she has done nothing so far to upset the friend of mine with whom she is living. She has to obey the very strict rules that I laid down, for I am aware how foolish and flighty she can be. Although I love her, as I have loved all my children, perhaps my particular indulgence towards her has stemmed – although I should not even think it – from never quite liking her. It was a jubilant letter that Liv had written this time, all because a little while ago she had met Martin Vartdal, son of the late shipping magnate, who built that grand mansion just outside Molde not long before he died. Martin is now head of the company, owning a large mercantile fleet that sails all over the world. I cannot begin to estimate how rich he might be. Liv brought Martin home to meet me and I could see he was besotted with her. He is a fine-looking young man, very charming and

278

with the kind of superb manners that I always tried to instil – not very successfully – into my boys. It will suit Liv very well to marry into money, for she has always spent on fripperies and from an early age was forever prancing about in front of mirrors and admiring herself.

'I just want to look pretty,' she had said. 'It is all very well for you to criticize others, because you have always been beautiful and never had any need to make yourself look better.'

I saw that she meant what she said – I can read her like a book and can always tell if she is being false.

Ingrid was outraged when Liv became discontented with her comfortable life and, more alarmingly, with her husband. Ingrid recorded a meeting with her daughter when the matter was discussed.

'Martin is so dull,' Liv grumbled to me on one of her rare visits home. 'There's no fun in him. All he thinks about is work, work, and more work.'

I gave a sigh and paused in beating a cake mixture. I still have a baking day, as I always like to have a selection of cakes and biscuits to serve with coffee when people call in, which happens frequently. I always serve it in the traditional way, with a best cloth on the table and a lighted candle of welcome whatever the time of day.

'I know what ails you,' I said. 'Now that you

279

can have anything you want in the way of jewellery and finery, you have become bored. I've always known that under your silly ways you have a brain as bright as a button. Now is the time to use it. You have said that you like going to the company's offices to see where the vessels are plotted on the map and what cargo they are carrying and so forth. You told me also of your idea that one of the company's vessels should be togged up to take foreigners on cruises up the fjords, just as the German Kaiser does every summer with guests on his yacht.'

'Yes!' Liv snorted indignantly. 'And what happened to my good idea? Martin was not interested.'

'That is because he lacks the drive and ambition that made his father a rich man. Make him listen. Get yourself a seat in the boardroom. You may face difficulties getting there, but you always have managed to get whatever you have wanted in one way or another.'

Liv had been watching me and listening attentively. 'Yes, I have,' she agreed reflectively. 'You are a wise woman, Mama.'

'Yes, I am,' I agreed. 'Now you go home and – for once in your life – do as I have told you.'

It took six months, but by that time Liv was fully established in the company. Although her idea of a cruise ship has never been taken up she has become influential in other ways, particularly in the welfare of the crews and their families.

A later entry described a much happier meeting.

Liv and Martin came to visit and she told me she was expecting her first child. She wanted me to be with her when the baby was born. So when the time came, I held her hand and rubbed her back. Then finally her son arrived with some difficulty, but he is healthy and strong and has been baptized with the name of Steffan...

Anna closed the journal with a smile. So Liv was Steffan's mother.

She asked him about Liv the next time she was at his house and they were on their own. 'Did she have time for you when she was so deeply involved in company business?'

'I did not see much of her when I was young, except that we always had family meals together. My father was the greatest influence in my life, teaching me to ski and climb and generally encouraging me in all sports. He was a splendid tennis player himself, a sport not much played in Norway at that time, and so he often went abroad to take part in contests.' He paused. 'It was through those trips abroad that my mother almost lost him to another woman. I don't think adults realize how quickly a child senses trouble – the charged atmosphere, the angry looks exchanged, the door quickly closed to keep an argument from being overheard.' He shrugged. 'It was all there in my childhood.'

'But their marriage held together?'

'Yes. It was probably because my mother never wanted to lose anything that was hers and so, to her, divorce was out of the question. They settled down again after a while when I was about fourteen and I think my grandmother had a lot to do with it. I heard her say once that one affair was not worth breaking up a marriage. We know from Ingrid's journal that she herself had had her moments of anxiety when my handsome grandfather was being fêted far away from her.'

'But, in their case, love prevailed.'

Steffan gave a smiling nod. 'It did indeed.'

When Anna returned to the journal she saw that Ingrid's next entry was some time later and recorded a momentous day for the country in 1904, for which Magnus had had a flagpole erected by the house, as had most other people in the valley, and the national flag flew every-where throughout the land.

This week has seen a great day for Norway. After we had thrown off Swedish rule nearly a hundred years ago, we have had our own Norwegian government, but no figurehead. So a young Danish Prince, named Haakon, and his wife, Maud, who is an English princess, were recently invited to be our King and Queen and they accepted. They stepped ashore a few days ago, our new King holding high his young son in his arms, and he announced in a strong

282

voice, 'All for Norway!' In those three words he dedicated his life and his service to his new country. I think we shall be pleased with him...

Anna, reading this paragraph, smiled. Ingrid's foresight had been correct. He had become the bedrock of the resistance, a courageous man who had defied the Germans from the first day with his defiant 'No!' to their demand for surrender.

Ingrid continued to record her doubts about Magnus in her journal, only too aware that his looks had matured handsomely and how attractive he would still be to women. But he was also still her ardent lover, and she knew in her heart that no matter what happened he would always come back to her. Then the terrible day came when he was brought home to her in a pine casket. It had been a traffic accident in Bergen. His carriage had collided with another and he had been thrown into the street, hitting his head against a post. At the sight of the casket, Ingrid had uttered a terrible cry as if her heart had burst. Then, for the sake of the children, she regained control of herself and went about all she had to do while consoling them as best she could.

At the funeral, even though local people had become used to her often eccentric ways, she made everyone stare by not being in deep mourning black with a veil to cover her stricken face as when she had lost her first-born, Magnus-Haakon. Instead, she startled them all by wearing one of her most vividly hued gowns and had trimmed her bright yellow hat with real flowers. Her daughters in party dresses also had blossoms on their hats and her sons had their own choice of flowers in their buttonholes.

'We are dressing up for Papa,' she had said to them. 'Black was a colour he never liked, not even on his palette, and so we must be as colourful as we can.'

After the service he was buried in the little churchyard next to Magnus-Haakon. It was exactly thirty-two years since she had married him in that same church. She did not shed a tear, remaining calm and dignified, and afterwards poured the coffee herself for all the many mourners who gathered in the village hall for the *smorrebrod* and cakes that had been prepared. Yet that night, in the everlasting summer daylight, she went alone up into the mountains where no one could hear her and howled her grief from where she had flung herself down on the grass under a tree.

She thought often afterwards that Magnus had gone from her at a time when she had never needed his support more. It was not just to comfort Sonja, who would hammer her fists on the studio door, unable to believe that her father was not going to reappear. The crisis had arisen because the twins, Christofer and Erik, had finished their education at eighteen and were restless, reluctant to take up training for the future. They had heard travellers' tales about how wonderful it was in America and how fortunes could be made overnight there. Ingrid shook her head wearily at this renewed wave of enthusiasm for emigrating that was sweeping the land. Both of the boys had shown every sign that they would do well here in their own country, but a sense of adventure was high in them. Ingrid was baffled as to why it should seem so marvellous to them. Yet she could not forbid them their dream. They were grown men, even though they were still children in her eyes and always would be.

'I wish I could come with you,' Kurt said enviously to them. He had always trailed along with the twins in their adventures and he felt bereft now that they were going away. How could fishing and sailing and climbing and skiing be fun anymore without his two older brothers, even though they would not take him with them whenever they went out to meet girls?

Ingrid saw the yearning in his eyes and quickly put her arm about his shoulders. 'We'll always be a family, and when Christofer and Erik have made their fortunes, they will come home and visit us. Maybe they will even discover that Norway is the best land in the world in which to live after all.'

She did everything possible for the two emigrants, making sure, with the aid of the bank manager, that they would not be without money in an emergency and also having them measured for new clothes at the best tailors' in the district, which would then be packed in fine new leather suitcases. They were like all Norwegian emigrants in having to sail first to Newcastle in England, as there were no ships as yet going directly to the United States from Norway, and then they would travel by train either to the port of Liverpool or Southampton where they would embark. They had chosen the southern port as then they would see more of England on the way. It was their hope that they would catch a glimpse of the great English shire horses working in the fields, having heard that they were three times the size of *fjordings*. In the midst of their excited planning, all Ingrid had asked of them was that they should write home regularly.

'Yes, Mama! Of course we will!' Christofer answered gladly, his freckled face earnest in the strength of his promise.

'We'll take turns,' Erik promised with equal enthusiasm, holding her by the shoulders as he looked down into her anxious face from his fine, straight-backed height. 'Then, as soon as we have an address, you must send us all the news from here! We shall want to know all that happens.'

On the day of their departure, Ingrid and her other children stood together outside the house and waved the boys on their way. They were both so excited, and she thought how smart they looked in their new suits as they stepped jauntily down the slope, pausing to wave back again and again until they were out of sight. Only then, with a deep sigh, did Ingrid turn back indoors, her arm around Emma, who was very close to her. The other children still lingered where they stood, privately wishing for their brothers to change their minds and turn back home again.

Indoors, Ingrid noticed a leaflet that had been left on the table with a picture of the ship on which her sons would be sailing. She picked it up and looked at it again, although the boys had shown it and others to her many times. She noted the name of the ship again. It was SS *Titanic*.

Seventeen

Anna received Christina's gift of the national costume in time for Steffan's fiftieth birthday celebrations. It was a deep blue, finely embroidered on the bodice and around the hem, as was the little cap worn at the back of the head. She twirled around for him and he applauded her appearance.

'You look very fine! But your attire is not complete without some traditional jewellery.' He took a velvet-covered box from the table beside him and handed it to her. 'This is what my dear Rosa wore with her costume, and both she and Johan would wish for you to have it now.'

It was a very handsome gift. In the box was a magnificent gold brooch, the size of a small saucer, from which hung tiny pendants that swung and glittered. There were also gold earrings, as well as cufflinks for the white blouse worn under the blue sleeveless bodice, the whole set including a gold link belt. Gudrun helped Anna put it all on before standing back and giving a nod of smiling approval.

When Alex arrived for the party, he was wearing the scarlet jacket and cream-coloured knee breeches, with high white socks from the Bergen district where he had been born. 'I had to compete with you, Anna,' he joked, but he was not the only man similarly clad in national costume that evening, and a number of women were in costume too, all as a compliment to their host.

Alex was a help to Anna in putting Ingrid's house in order. He added shelves and repaired some of the furniture they had salvaged from the cellar, all of it dating back to Ingrid's time. A plumber came with his apprentice to change the smallest bedroom into a bathroom, Anna welcoming the installation of modern plumbing. She had not cared for the loo in the barn any more than the one at Gardermoen with the old magazine pictures on the walls.

They were doing nothing to the *stabbur* for a while, needing to decide whether to take it back to its origins as guest quarters or to make a library of it, for Alex had a great number of books in their apartment and Anna had had some of her favourite books sent by her aunt from England, which were still in a crate.

Alex was only free at the weekends, but sometimes on a midweek summer evening they would go to the house with every intention of fulfilling some small task on her list. Then, instead, they would just sit outside in the sunchairs they had bought and enjoy a drink together, having installed some bottles in one of Ingrid's cupboards. Anna loved the peace of the surroundings. Sometimes the only sound was that of cowbells somewhere on the mountain pastures, although these days new tractors and other agricultural machinery had taken over on several farms and could be heard in the distance like the hum of a bee.

They often spent Saturday nights at the house, for a bed in Ingrid's bedroom was now fully made up with a duvet cover in the orange colour that the *Quiet Woman* had liked so much. It was the morning after a night they had spent there when Anna had her first spell of morning sickness. She was astonished that she had become pregnant so quickly when she had hoped in vain so often during her previous marriage. Alex was as delighted as she that they were starting a family, even though it was happening sooner than planned. Steffan received the news with deep and quiet pleasure, while Gudrun was as excited as Anna had anticipated.

It was clear to Anna from the start that Alex had his heart set on the baby being a boy. He was so certain of the baby's sex that whenever they had a discussion about names it was only ever a boy's name that he put forward.

Often, Anna's thoughts would turn to Ingrid at this time. After the loss of her husband and her two sons, Ingrid had not written in her journal for a long time. It was as if something had died in her too and she had lost all interest in life. Then, when she did make a new entry, it was to record the forthcoming birth of the first of her grandchildren to be born in Norway. Her beloved daughter, Emma, who had married a local doctor, was heavily pregnant. It was clear that Ingrid was looking forward with great joy to the event and the news of it had released her from a long and agonizing mourning period into a more tranquil frame of mind. As a result, there was life in her pen again and she entered all that had happened to her other children in the meantime.

At this time of writing, Nils is at sea as a lieutenant in the Royal Norwegian Navy. I have a hatred of oceans, which anyone would understand, but he was always keen on sailing, even more than the other children. I take comfort from knowing that at least on a navy ship there will always be plenty of lifeboats unlike that other unfortunate ship that I remember with great sadness. Anders, who was once the family's top fisherman, is also in the service of his country, having joined the Army, and he has recently become a royal guard in a very smart dark blue uniform worn with a bowler-shaped hat that has a splendid plume.

It was always a disappointment to Magnus that none of his children had inherited his artistic talent, but I cheered him by saying that sometimes these gifts reappear in grandchildren, and he hoped that would happen. Sonja was the most talented of his offspring with her art work, but he had been too critical in his judgement of her efforts to give her the right encouragement.

'Papa does not like anything I do,' she sob-

bed, coming from his studio.

I stooped down to put my arms around her. 'He is proud of what you can do, but he wants you to be an even better artist than himself. You and I know that is impossible, because there is no other artist in the world that can paint better then Papa. I'll suggest to him that you have more violin lessons instead.'

Her eyes shone with hope as I dried her tears with a corner of my apron, for she loves music. 'Could I?'

'I'm sure he will agree.'

That seems a long time ago now, but it was the right move to make and now she plays in an orchestra of repute in Trondheim. She comes home to see me whenever she can. Although she is quite plain in her looks, she has a lovely serenity in her expression and never more so than when she is playing her violin.

My dear Emma calls in most days, arriving in a smart blue-painted trap drawn by a fjording named Rasmus. Normally she likes to walk from where she and her doctor husband live, but it has become too much for her to take the slope on foot as she gets nearer her time.

Olav, who has always enjoyed farm work, has recently married Marie's daughter, Jenny, and since the girl will eventually inherit her father's family farm, he can look to a settled future.

'I've always loved Jenny,' he had said when they first stood hand in hand before me, not realizing how long I had been aware of it.

I gave them my blessing and watched them

running off down the slope, laughing and kiss-
ing as they went. It is comforting to know they
will always be in the valley now that I have
other children so far away. Kurt is another of
my dear children who turned his eyes to
America. His early thoughts about emigration
became firmly set in that direction after news
came of the loss of his twin brothers. It was as
if he wished to take up their dream and bring it
to fruition, healing the grief of his bereavement
at the same time. Now he is living in a little
town called Seattle on the west coast. He start-
ed in salmon fishing and now has a small
canning factory that is about to be enlarged on
a grand scale, such is the demand for Harvik
salmon. Now and again he sends me some cans
of his salmon in a parcel. It is good, but it
cannot compare with the more delicate flavour
and finer texture of our Norwegian salmon.

I still take my rod down to the river in late
summer when the salmon come up to spawn.
One of my good neighbours in the valley
smokes my catch for me in his smokehouse. As
I always get a good number of salmon before
the season ends, it means I have plenty of this
delicacy to enjoy on my own or with guests.
Sometimes I make gravidlaks *out of the fresh*
*salmon – '*gravid*' is the Norwegian word for the*
wooden dish in which the fish marinates in
*alcohol and '*laks*' is the Norsk word for salmon.*
I explain this only because recently two English
travellers here in Norway for the salmon fishing
were puzzling Andreas, the shopkeeper, with

questions about 'gravidlaks' when I came into the shop. I managed to get understanding into their thick heads and also corrected their terrible pronunciation of the word, which I thought was an insult to my country's culinary masterpiece.

According to what I have been told by Kurt in his letters and from what I have read elsewhere, Seattle has become quite a Norwegian-American settlement, as in addition to being by the ocean, it has mountains around it that remind Norwegians of their homeland. I do not have to record my anguish waiting for a first letter from Kurt after his departure, for I do not trust any ship after what happened to the one that had purported to be unsinkable, all of which adds to my concern for Nils on those horrible waves. Kurt, knowing how anxious I would be after he left, had a postcard ready written that he put into a mailbox as soon as he stepped ashore in New York after interrogation on Ellis Island. I hear from him regularly. He has married a young woman named Helga of Swedish descent and they recently had a son whom they have baptized with the name of Irving.

Then, as if that great country had not cruelly taken enough away from me, my lovely Sonja married a Norwegian-American clergyman, named Stein Thursen, who was visiting his own relations and delivering messages from those in his parish who came from this area. Sonja was at home at the time and it was love at first sight. I saw it happening right before my eyes. She

294

writes regularly to me and seems to be happily settled in Minnesota with the good man she married, and they have two daughters, Ingrid – named after me – and Christine, and there is another baby on the way. I have received studio photographs of all my children and grand-children, which are framed in a group arrange-ment on the wall of the living room. I look at them every day, but it is not enough. I have a great yearning to see my American grand-children for myself, but they are living such an impossibly great distance from me that it can never be.

Meanwhile, I have had a suitor! A very attrac-tive man! I had plenty after I lost Magnus and sent them all away, but this was one of the art dealers who still come hoping to persuade me to part with the last of Magnus's paintings, which I will never do, for all are earmarked for the family after I am gone. These dealers, with their smooth talk and greedy eyes, cannot begin to understand why I reject out of hand the large amounts of money that they offer. They try to entice me to sell with talk of a grand house in Oslo with furs and jewels and the chance to travel in luxury to foreign places. They are too foolish to see I have all the riches I want here in my home, with the love of my children and the joy of good friends, as well the beautiful vistas I have from every window. They know the num-ber of paintings I have in my possession from a list of Magnus's works somewhere and they sometimes look as if they are ready to tear down the walls to get hold of them. This particular dealer, whose name is Henrik Heggedal, is a good-looking man with a pleasing smile, and he had a very different approach.

After our first meeting, during which I had rejected his enormous offer for a particular 'Quiet Woman' painting, he came with flowers and chocolates, paid me lavish compliments and then took his leave again without any reference to Magnus's work. As I had expected, he expressed the hope that he might call again as if I were the attraction instead of a work of art.

After that I did look a little longer in the mirror and reassessed myself. I have done the same again today out of curiosity. My complexion is still free of blemishes and my lips are full and have a good rosy colour. My eyes have some crinkles at the corners, but they are as greenish-blue as they have ever been, and my lashes are still long and dark. Unfortunately, there is no mistaking the strands of grey in my golden hair, which these days I still wear drawn back from my forehead and coiled at the nape of my neck.

Magnus always loved the moment when I released the pins from my tresses and shook them free to cascade about my bare shoulders, as I stood eager and waiting, my arms held out to him. How often we made love with laughter, he tossing me on to the bed, throwing up my nightgown and taking me with him up to the heights of passion. At other times he treated me

296

as gently as if I might crumble away under his touch, while I lay naked and trembling with delight, scarcely able to bear such exquisite torment. But I must not think any more of those wonderful nights of loving, because then my whole self will start crying out for his arms to hold me again and I have other things to write about just now.

It amused me to play Henrik Heggedal along. I have not forgotten how to intrigue a man, and although I am no longer in my prime, my figure is still shapely, and I would have enjoyed being kissed again as much as when I was young, except that it would not have been like kissing Magnus. On his third or fourth visit, he began to talk of his being a lonely bachelor and that it was time he found a good wife – as if I would be tempted! He did not wear a wedding ring, but it was my guess that he slipped it in his pocket before coming to the house.

I did seriously consider letting him make love to me, for my desires have only been lying dormant, but I thought better of it. If he had come up into the bedroom, he would have probably have been so distracted by the number of Magnus's paintings on the walls that he would have given a poor performance. I joked with myself that he might forget all about bedding me and instead snatch a painting off the wall and scatter shoals of golden kroner in his wake while making a speedy exit. So I began to keep the door shut and locked whenever I saw him coming. I happened to be up the mountains when he hammered on the door for the last time. I watched his frustration through my binoculars when, getting no answer again to his hammering, he threw down yet another bouquet in a temper and stalked away. I have not seen him since.

I told Magnus about it, because I talk to him all the time. I feel his presence here and I know he is waiting for me. When the children were still at home, their cheerful noise kept him silent, because he knew that although I missed him every minute of the day and night, I was not lonely. Before I get old and forgetful, I must decide where I am going to hide my journal, because I want it to stay here forever, and then I will always be part of this house that has given me both deep sorrow and great joy, which I realize is probably the pattern of most people's lives. If any descendants of mine should discover my journal's secret hiding place, I would have no objection to their reading it or their handing it over to those whom they truly love, allowing them to read it too. All I ask of them is that afterwards they return my journal to where they found it or else into an even better hiding place...

Anna closed the journal and looked across at Alex. 'I've come to a reference Ingrid makes about a possible hiding place for her journal. It's quite a heart-touching entry as you will read for yourself. It has reminded me that earlier in her journal she wrote about an old wedding

298

chest she had found in a hidden place and where treasures could be safely stored. Can you think where such a spot could be? Some of Magnus's paintings might still be in it.'

Alex lowered the book he was reading and frowned thoughtfully. 'Nothing comes to mind. After all, we have been all over the house in one way or another with various small repairs and there is nothing left in the cellar. I can't think of anywhere a large chest could be hidden, not even in the *stabbur*.'

'I'll ask Steffan if it was ever found.'

They called in on Steffan before returning home. He shook his head. 'I have wondered about that myself many times. I can only conclude it was found in a section of the cellar and that it was thrown out at some time. Yet it is strange that Ingrid never mentioned it when she recorded so much. I asked Harry about it long ago, hoping he would be able to think of some solution to the mystery. He searched the house for me without result.'

'When did he do this investigating?' she asked.

'It was during the Nazi occupation. I believe I told you that German soldiers had broken into the house when searching for a resistance fighter, whom Harry had helped to escape.'

'Maybe as time goes by I'll find something to give me a clue to the whereabouts of the chest, if it is still there in a hidden place,' Anna said hopefully. 'I like to think that Ingrid hid away some of Magnus's paintings in it when she was being bothered by art dealers wanting to buy them.'

'Then it would prove to be a treasure chest indeed!'

The next time Anna was at the house with Alex, they searched every inch of the cellar, even feeling the walls in case there should be any evidence of a space being bricked up, but they found nothing. None of the furniture originally seen under sheets in the cellar was there anymore, for all of it had been carried up into the daylight and examined. The only truly good find had been a little school desk that had once been painted green. It now stood against the wall in the living room as part of the decor; two old school books dated 1889 had come to light at the same time and were neatly arranged on it.

When the whole house was fully furnished, with antique pieces from Steffan's *stabbur* filling in the gaps, Anna felt that Ingrid would have approved of everything. The final touch was the framing of several good prints of Magnus's paintings, which blazed forth their beautiful colours from the white pine walls just below the canopy of rosemaling.

Those same rich hues covered the valley as autumn came, even the cranberry leaves turning crimson to compliment the rich colours of the trees. Anna and Alex walked in the mountains and took shelter under a rock whenever the rains came. They were both always well clad against the weather, and Anna joked that she thought there was no other rain in the world that managed to fall in such heavy sheets as from Norwegian skies. Then, towards Christmas, the snow began to float down again.

It was easy to tell from Ingrid's journal that she had always loved Christmas. There were various accounts of decorating the house with greenery, and the fun the children had had going into the forest with Magnus to find the perfect tree and then bringing it home on a sled.

Anna would have liked to spend Christmas in the old house, certain that she would have caught the echo of children's long-ago laughter and maybe had a fanciful image of Ingrid reading the Bible story to her family as she had done every Christmas Eve. But Anna said nothing of this private wish, not even to Alex, because it was the time of the year to be spent with Steffan and Gudrun, who were her family now.

Early in the New Year, the time came for Anna to make a trip back to Gardermoen to fulfil a promise made to Molly on her first day in Norway. In conversation, Molly had said she would always want Anna to be with her whenever she should give birth as she would have no family near at hand. Now that time had come and Anna, who was in the fifth month of her own pregnancy, planned to spend just two weeks with Molly after her baby was born. Alex drove Anna to Andalsnes railway station. It was the first time they had been apart since their marriage and he was anxious about her.

'Come back as soon as you can,' he urged as she stepped into the train.

'I will,' she promised.

She took a seat by the window and their gaze held as the train began to move. Then she waved until he was lost from sight.

He had bought her a newspaper from a newsstand to supplement her reading matter, for she had brought a book with her. Unfolding *Afterposten* she began to read. Half an hour later, a white-jacketed waiter came to take her order for lunch in the restaurant car. Then, as he moved on to other passengers, she put away the newspaper and looked out at the passing scene. There was said to be more snow than ever this winter. Roofs of buildings everywhere had had to be cleared of snow two and even three times. Alex had cleared the roof of the old house twice. Recently there had been an unusual number of avalanches. In the valleys, people always built in safe areas, the knowledge garnered over centuries as to where rocks would fall or snow cascade in great force. The scenery today was spectacular.

Although Norwegians always seemed to go well-provisioned on any journey, she noticed that every time the train stopped at a station it seemed as if the train was emptied of passengers as they all streamed off into the buffet restaurant. They would emerge with mugs of hot soup or coffee and often sandwiches too. It was the same on the ferries, for as soon as people came aboard they would line up at the snacks bar for nourishment. Anna smiled. She was the same now. She and Alex always had coffee and waffles whenever they crossed the fjord. It must mean that she was becoming as much Norwegian as she was English. At least she would not get overweight. Sport in both summer and winter kept her new fellow countrymen on the whole a slim and healthy race. Naturally there were exceptions, but she did not intend to be among their number.

She was looking forward to seeing Molly and her other war-bride friends who were still at Gardermoen. She received news of them quite regularly from Molly, either by phone or letter. Somebody had heard that Sally and Arvid were divorced, which was no surprise to anyone. As the waiter appeared, banging a small dinner gong to announce the first sitting for *middag* in the restaurant car, Anna was pleasantly hungry and looking forward to what she had chosen from the menu.

She had just settled herself at a table, the napkin spread across her lap, when the avalanche struck. Out of the corner of her eye she saw it coming in the last seconds before it crashed against the train, shutting out all daylight. There was no time even to scream. She was tossed from her seat as the carriage was thrown on to its side and she knew nothing more as the avalanche thundered on.

Out of the darkness she heard Ingrid speaking to her and coaxing her to answer. How had it happened that they were together? They must be in the house and somehow there was no longer any time span between them.

'Are you wearing your orange skirt, Ingrid?' she whispered.

There was a slight pause. 'Open your eyes, Anna. Then you will see for yourself.'

She tried, but it was difficult. Her lids seemed to be swollen. 'We can't find the old wedding chest that is hidden somewhere.'

'Keep looking, Anna. You'll find it one day when you're well again.'

'Am I ill?'

'You've had a few knocks and bruises, but you're on the mend.'

'You must be confused, Ingrid. It was your first husband that gave you knocks and bruises. Alex has only given me love.'

Then she heard Alex's voice. 'As I always will, *elskede*.'

Beloved. She liked that word both in English and in Norwegian. It meant so much. Somehow she managed to lift her eyelids enough to see a nurse looking down at her and Alex seated by her bed. He was clasping her limp right hand in both his own. Then memory returned in a painful spasm and she cried out.

'My baby?'

Alex drew her hand up to his lips and kissed it. 'We lost our little one,' he said quietly.

She gave a hoarse strangled cry. 'No! No!'

The nurse answered her. 'It was too late for anything to be done by the time you arrived here. It was over an hour before they found you in the wreckage.'

Then the nurse left them on their own, with a nod to Alex that she would be within call.

Tears had begun rolling down Anna's cheeks. 'Our baby,' she said brokenly. 'I loved her from the first moment I knew she was coming.'

He slid his arms about her. 'I'm sure she knew that,' he said. It was his first acknowledgement that the baby could have been a girl instead of a boy, and in the midst of her overwhelming sorrow she loved him anew for it. Then her eyelids became so heavy again that she could not keep them open any longer and she slept.

Later, she was able to ask him questions about the train disaster. She knew now that she had suffered a broken leg, but was assured that it had been well set and she should make a full recovery.

'Were there many casualties?' she asked.

'No, I'm thankful to say. Fortunately, it was a minor avalanche that hit only part of the train, but its impact threw two carriages off the rails while the rest went helter-skelter, although they remained remarkably upright. Yet passengers were hurled about like die in a box, including you, Anna.'

'Where are we?'

'In a hospital at Eidsvold. It was the nearest for the casualties.'

She managed a wry little smile. 'Eidsvold? That's where I had to wait four hours for a train that Christmas, when I know you had to wait all night to meet me. I'm not very fortunate at

Eidsvold.'

He gathered her hand close to him. 'But you are! You caught the train that night in spite of the delay, and here you are alive and well when I could have so easily lost you. There is nothing wrong with Eidsvold.'

She smiled acknowledgement. 'I suppose you are right.'

After three days Anna was able to leave the hospital with crutches to help her master walking again. She sat in the back of Alex's car with her injured leg resting on the seat. She was comforted to a degree by a doctor's reassurance that there was nothing to prevent her becoming pregnant again after a while. Molly's husband, Olav, who would have met her off the train at Jessheim, phoned several times at Molly's instigation to check on Anna's recovery. In the meantime Molly had given birth to a healthy baby girl. Anna was very glad for her. As for herself, it had been a girl that she had miscarried.

Eighteen

Anna suffered deeply from depression after her miscarriage. Somehow she could not break free of it. Whenever she was shopping, or had some other reason for being in town, she always went past the toddlers' play area. Even though it was like salt in a wound, she would pause to watch them for a minute or two. Whatever the weather, they would come outside suitably dressed to stamp in puddles, roll in the snow or attempt to make castles in the sandpit, all according to the season. Sometimes she would turn away to blink tears from her eyes. She had even lost interest for the time being in the old house and also in Ingrid's journal, which had lain untouched in a drawer for quite a while.

Alex was very concerned about her, even though the doctor had said that it was not un-usual for women to suffer from post-natal depression after a miscarriage. He wanted her to recapture the lively interest in life that was normal to her. He had tried to lift her spirits by taking her on holiday to Sweden and Denmark, but although she seemed to enjoy the trip, there was little change in her. He was at a loss to know how to divert her in some way from the sorrow that continued to engulf her.

'Why not reconsider that offer to teach that you told me about once,' he suggested one evening. 'It was when you first came to Molde, wasn't it? You could do some part-time teaching. Even just an hour or two a day could be interesting for you.'

'I have thought about that,' she said, being desperate herself to try to find some way out of the dark mood that encompassed her. 'But whether I should still be wanted I don't know.'

'Give the headmaster a phone call at home. Just say you would like to visit his school tomorrow morning.'

She glanced at the clock. 'It's late. Nine o'clock.'

'He'll not be in bed yet.' He had seen the way she had lifted her chin as she considered the prospect of teaching, almost as if seeing it as a challenge, which he took to be a good sign.

She fetched the telephone book and found Daniel Andersen's name. The call was soon over. Anna turned with something close to excitement in her eyes.

'I'm going to see him tomorrow morning at ten o'clock!'

'Good! Let's have a drink to celebrate.'

'I haven't been accepted yet!'

'You will be.' He had moved from his chair to the drinks cupboard. 'What are you going to have?'

They both had a cognac.

The school was not in Molde, but was linked

308

to a village some little distance away, but she had the car, for Alex always walked the short distance to work. As she drove, she timed the length of the journey, which turned out to be a little under half an hour. When she arrived, a senior pupil showed her to the headmaster's study. As she entered, Daniel Andersen, tall and thin with horn-rimmed spectacles, rose from behind his desk to shake her hand and invite her to a chair. She could tell she would be accepted almost before they had exchanged a word.

'It is some time since we last met,' he said, 'and I still cannot emphasize too much what it would mean for us to have a qualified English teacher on our staff.' He was seated again with his hands clasped before him on his desk. 'The English language has long been universal, but I believe that it will soon become of utmost importance for all those of other nationalities to be able to speak the language as well as their own. That is what I want for my pupils here. During the occupation we were only allowed to teach German, but those days have gone.'

He went on to explain that she would have her own class of first-year pupils, seven being the age of entry into schools. All his pupils were having English lessons already, since he believed the younger the child, the easier it was to learn a foreign language, and Anna agreed with him. She would also be taking English language classes with all the older children.

'But whom should I be replacing?' she asked with concern, not wanting to be the cause of any disruption and ill feeling.

Daniel Andersen put her mind at rest. 'A teacher who will be glad to surrender the task as his subject is mathematics.'

After they had discussed her salary and the part-time hours of her teaching, he took her to meet the youngest class of her future pupils, both boys and girls. They had been rehearsed, for although standing for the teacher's entry was customary, this morning they spoke in unison and in English.

'Good morning, Mrs Ringstad. Welcome to our school.'

She replied, smiling at them. All the little girls had bows in their hair. After a few words with the teacher, Anna and Daniel Andersen left again. Then he showed her over the rest of the school and introduced her to the other teachers on the way. He shook her hand again when they parted. She was to start teaching the following Monday.

On her first day she began to get to know the children in her class. They were the same as the pupils in England that she had met in her teacher training classes when days were spent in schools. There were the talkers and the daydreamers, the workers and the lazy, the ones who wanted to please her and others out to play tricks. Yet on the whole they were remarkably well-behaved, coming from a country community that had always had its standards with regard to honesty, politeness and working hard.

As the weeks went by, Anna began to enjoy

her new routine and, although she still mourned the child she had lost, she began to look ahead with hope and to enjoy again the good times that life was giving her. She opened Ingrid's journal again.

Ingrid had had much the same attitude as Anna in her later years, appreciating all blessings that came her way. Yet there were still troubles too.

Anders comes home periodically on leave. He has become quite the gentleman, for the guards are taught to behave in a correct manner at all times.

'Come, Mama,' he says when a meal is ready, the old mischief in his eyes, 'I'm holding your chair for you.'

I sit down very grandly at the end of the table where I have always sat, which pleases him, and then, as he takes his place next to me, I smile my approval of his good manners and he gives me a cheeky grin.

I was thankful he was still at home when I received an official letter informing me that Nils had been injured in an explosion on board ship and was presently in a hospital in Oslo. A letter arrived from Nils at the same time, telling me that his injury was slight and not to visit as he would be home very soon. Yet it was six weeks before Nils was ready to leave hospital, and Anders was given special leave to escort his brother home. I watched constantly for their arrival. They came ten days later in a hired

311

pony and trap from the fjord steamer. I gave a sharp cry of anguish, clapping my hand to my mouth, for the driver had taken charge of a pair of crutches and Anders was lifting his brother out of the vehicle. Nils adjusted his crutches and then looked up to give me a reassuring grin. Half his left leg was missing, his trouser leg pinned up neatly.

'Don't get upset, Mama,' he said. 'I'm all right, but my days in the Navy are over.'

I kept my good sense in spite of the inner distress tearing at me and managed to stop myself from running to him. I knew better than anyone that he would never want to be treated as an invalid. 'It will be good to have you home for a while,' I said casually from where I stood in the doorway. 'I need some logs cut.'

He gave a quiet laugh as he came forward to where I stood and looked down into my eyes. 'You and I know, Mama, that we Harviks are never defeated by anything. I'll start on those logs tomorrow.' Then he gave me a fond kiss on the cheek. 'It's good to be home.'

As soon as word spread of his arrival, old friends came to visit and I was forever serving coffee and cakes. Emma and her husband were his first visitors, and she hugged her brother while behaving as if this homecoming was no different from any other. Liv and Martin came the next day after receiving a message from me telling that them that he was at home and the reason why. Most sensibly, Martin came with an offer of employment for him. It was soon

312

arranged that Nils should join the shipping company since there was plenty of work that he could handle and he would have his own office. Liv gave me a sideways glance with the hint of a smile to show that it was at her instigation this arrangement had been made so quickly. Nils was enthusiastic. The prospect of being unemployed had haunted him throughout his convalescence, but now to be able to deal with vessels at sea was some compensation for not being aboard one of them.

It was Midsummer Eve when Anna and Alex, who had been earlier to the lighting of a Molde bonfire, were awakened when their telephone rang in the early hours of the morning. Alex was swift to answer it; concern for Steffan, who had not been well recently, was instantly uppermost in his mind, as it was with Anna sitting up in alarm. But the caller was not Gudrun with worrying news as they both had feared. Instead, it was Rune, Ingrid's great-grandson, who had taken over his late father's farm in the valley. He gave his reason for calling in the calm unhurried way of country folk.

'Your *stabbur* has been on fire, Alex, but don't worry. The fire brigade is here and they soon had it under control. There's not much damage, because some of us at a late bonfire party spotted the flames and ran to start dousing them with water from the river. It is the outside staircase that has suffered most. You'll have to replace that and a small part of the roof has

313

gone.'

'I'll get there as soon I can,' Alex said urgently.

'Well, you can't get here before the first ferry unless you tip somebody out of bed to bring you in a motorboat. You go back to bed. I'm in charge and everything is under control here. I'll be around when you come.'

Anna was already in her dressing gown, wide awake and declaring she could not sleep peacefully again until she had seen the *stabbur* for herself. 'Thank goodness the flames were not mistaken from a distance as just another bonfire!'

'That could easily have happened,' Alex agreed, getting back into bed, and he was asleep again almost instantly. She marvelled at the way men always seemed to be able to sleep whatever the circumstances. She lay awake until at last it was time to get up and have an early breakfast.

They caught the first ferry of the day. Anna was full of anxiety as to what she would see when they arrived at the house. When the *stabbur* came into view, it was a sorry sight. The whole west end of it was blackened and scorched, the staircase reduced to charred pieces of wood, some dangling over the ashes below. A section of the roof had also fallen in.

All that day people came either to view the result of the fire or to offer helpful advice. Harry also arrived. 'I'll deal with the fire damage for you,' he said, his attitude one of being completely in charge. 'A replacement staircase must be in the same weathered antique wood as the original. I know where to get that and everything else I would need. The roof will need returfing too.'

'I want it to be exactly as it was before,' Anna said anxiously. She did not like the thought of him restoring her property, but there was no way she could refuse him.

'It will be. I can get my men working on it by tomorrow.' Then he gave her a reassuring smile. 'It is as important to me as it is to you that our country's heritage should always be preserved.'

She thought to herself that he had not spoken in that way previously, when he had tried to divert her interest away from the house for his own ends. Alex had already shown that he would approve of Harry carrying out the work, but he turned to her for a final decision.

'Is it agreed then, Anna? We do have a restoration expert here.'

She nodded. 'Yes, of course. I'm sure it could not be in better hands than yours, Harry,' she said genuinely. 'Perhaps you would restore the old barn at the same time?'

He raised his eyebrows. 'Are you sure? It does not add anything to the other two buildings here and was a much later addition to the property.'

'Maybe, but there is a good reason. Alex and I would like the old stall widened to garage our car whenever we are here.' She did not add that she thought Ingrid would have approved that alteration.

Harry nodded. 'Yes, that's a good idea. I'll see to it for you. In the meantime, keep well away from the *stabbur*. We don't want any accidents.'

He was so emphatic that she could see he seemed genuinely concerned for their safety. 'We'll keep our distance,' she promised.

Before she and Alex left, she took a long look at the scorched and damaged *stabbur,* thankful that good neighbours had been in time to save it from total destruction. But how had the fire started? After all, it was too far from any other bonfire for a drifting spark to have ignited it. Some rockets had been fired that night and she could only conclude that one had landed on the *stabbur*'s staircase. On the dry old wood it would have acted like a match to tinder.

Alex was away on the evening when she felt compelled to go and take a look at the damage to the *stabbur* once again. She left a note as to her whereabouts in case he happened to return much earlier than expected. Then she slipped on her coat, took her purse, and by walking briskly she was in time to catch a late evening ferry as it was about to leave. She had made up her mind to spend the night at Ingrid's house. There was everything she and Alex needed there, and she did not even have to take a toothbrush with her. Alex had been insisting recently that it should now be called Anna's house, but she felt that would be ousting Ingrid's goodwill from it before the time was right.

'When will it be right?' he had questioned, puzzled by her answer.

'I can't tell you that now, but I'll know when the time comes.'

Crossing the fjord in the moonlight gave her another angle on its beauty as she sat by one of the windows in the ferry's saloon. When she came ashore, there were no taxis to be seen and as it was such a perfect autumn night she decided to walk to her mountain home. The night was full of little sounds and once, startling her, a deer dashed across her path.

'Good night, Bambi!' she called after it.

It was as the house came into sight that she saw in the moonlight that a car was parked by it. She was momentarily alarmed until she recognized Harry's number plate. Yet there were no lights anywhere. Ladders and other workmen's gear showed that work on the site had been started that day. The burnt staircase had been cleared away and everything looked set for the more advanced work to begin.

She was about to call out to Harry, but a sudden wariness silenced her. It was all so odd that he should be here at this hour with only the moonlight to illuminate everything for him. Then, when she would have used her key to open the front door of her house, she saw that there was a duplicate key in the lock. As she touched it, the door swung inwards. Instantly, it angered her that Harry should feel free to come and go in the house – even in the night – without ever asking if it was OK. How many other

317

times had he been here without her knowledge?

Normally, she would have lighted one of the oil lamps, but instead she stood listening in the moonlit room for the creak of a floorboard to give her some hint as to where in the house he might be. The total silence soon told her that he was not anywhere indoors. Puzzled, she went across to a side window and looked out in the direction of the *stabbur*. Almost at once there was the momentary flash of a torch through the roof damage and then it was extinguished. Even as she watched, she saw a figure descend by a tall ladder that had been set against the end of the building. The moonlight caught the top rungs as it was swung away and replaced almost silently with some other ladders lying on the ground. Then he stood to brush off the ash and debris from his sweater and trousers, which he must have gathered somewhere under the eaves. Then he turned towards the house.

Increasingly convinced that there was something very strange about Harry's midnight activity, Anna went silently into the room where Ingrid had kept her weaving-loom and stood waiting. When he came back into the house, she would step forward and take him by surprise, demanding to know why he was there. But he did not re-enter the house. Instead, he simply closed the front door from outside and turned the key in the lock.

Emerging from her hiding place, Anna ran across to a front window and watched him drive away. Then, using her own key, she unlocked the door again and went outside to where he had come down the ladder. Gazing upwards, she tried to see if there was anything that would give her a clue as to his purpose in risking such a dangerous entry at such a height, but there was nothing. It was not the upper floor of the *stabbur* that he had entered, but incredibly he had managed to get through the damaged end into the space between the ceiling boards of the upper room and the roof to which there was normally no access. In English, she would have called that space an aperture, for it would not be high enough in there for anyone to stand at full height. She supposed there was a square door, much like a trap door, allowing access to the aperture, but it had passed unnoticed in the weathering of the timber over many years. Harry, being an expert, would have seen it or, with his experience, looked for it, knowing that the room on the upper floor of these buildings was usually open to the rafters.

She decided to say nothing to Harry about his night-time visit, but would wait to see if he should tell her about it and thus disperse the mystery.

Nineteen

Anna awoke to the early arrival of the work-men. When she was dressed and ready for the day she went outside to see what work was already in progress. There were two men and a youth on the site and their van was parked nearby. Both the men were in their fifties. As she approached them, they greeted her. The man on a ladder said his name was Per, and the other man paused in sawing wood to extend a sawdust-covered hand to shake hers. He just said his surname.

'Larsen.' Then he introduced the strong-look-ing youth, who was their apprentice, as Bjorn.

'Have you found anything of interest up in the rafters, Per?' she asked casually, as she looked up at him on the ladder, although he was only level with the lower floor.

'We haven't been up there yet,' he replied. 'There's a lot of preliminary work to be done before we start to put the roof to rights. But we do find forgotten or lost things from time to time. The best item I have ever found was an old sword – that's in a museum somewhere now.' Then he gave a nod down to her. 'Harry Holmsen will take charge of anything found.

No treasure will escape his eye.'

'I should like to take a look into that top space under the eaves. Could you put a longer ladder up for me?'

He did not query her request, well used to his fellow countrywomen climbing mountains and having a head for heights. He descended his own ladder and then he and Bjorn swung a longer one into place for her. She mounted swiftly in her eagerness, but when she reached a viewpoint she could see only a little way into the aperture, for scorched and fallen turf made a screen that Harry must have pushed through, which was why he had taken his time brushing himself down when he was back on the ground again. Had he gone the whole length of the aperture and rearranged the fallen turf again to keep something hidden in the darkness at the far end?

'I see you will have a lot of work to do with the roof, Per,' she said when she had come down again. 'It is more than I realized.'

'Yes, but when we have finished here, it will be as if the fire had never been.'

Harry arrived early in the afternoon and went first to discuss some matter with his workmen before he came to give a knock on Anna's door and enter the house. Anna, who had been expecting him, put aside a letter she was writing to her aunt and looked up.

'Hi, Anna,' he said cheerfully. 'I've just been told that you were here. You have two of my best workmen on site now and the *stabbur* could not be in better hands.'

'Yes, I'm sure of it.'

'Any chance of a coffee?'

'Yes,' she said, getting up from her chair. Normally, coffee was offered almost as soon as a visitor had arrived, but she had not felt like being hospitable to Harry.

He followed her out into the kitchen where he looked around. 'You have made it look very nice here. Have you cooked on the old stove yet?'

'No. I use this primus for heating things up,' she said, placing the kettle on it. 'We're hoping to get electricity laid on any day now. I have an electric cooker and a washing machine on order too.'

'I'll see what influence I have with the local electricity board to get you some priority.'

'No,' she said firmly, wanting no favours from him. 'Our order is in and we have been told it will be fulfilled next week. Until then, if we stay the night, we still have to carry hot water upstairs to the bath.' She knew from the journal that Ingrid had used a tin bath for herself and her children in the kitchen on bath nights. There had been one paragraph in the journal about the enjoyment of sharing it with Magnus and how most of the water had ended up on the kitchen floor.

Harry took the coffee that she handed to him, eyeing her speculatively under lowered lids. 'You really have taken to this house in spite of a lack of facilities, haven't you? But I don't want you to forget that if ever your circum-stances change, my offer to buy or rent from you still stands.'

She glanced at him sharply. 'Are you suggest-ing that my marriage might not last?'

He shrugged. 'Who knows what can happen in these unsettled times? Alex played the field extensively before he met you.'

She felt too angry to answer him and went back into the living room. Again he sauntered after her, and, with his mug of coffee in his hand, he went to study one of the framed prints of Magnus's paintings. She sat down at the table where she had been writing and took up her pen in what she hoped would be a hint to him not to stop long.

'Magnus really could paint,' he commented admiringly, still regarding the print. 'It's a pity the family did not overlook some of his work when this house was cleared. Then you would have had a nice little nest-egg. One of his mountain scenes went for the highest price his work has ever fetched at a recent New York auction.'

Her interest sharpened. Did he think that there still might be a painting or two somewhere in the house? Was that why he had gone secretly into the attic in the hope of finding a painting to take for himself? At an auction, a seller could have his identity withheld and nobody would have been any the wiser. Another question came into her mind. Had he been using the door key to search this house when she and Alex were absent, even though he had had ample opportunity to look everywhere when he repaired the house after the Germans had crashed their way into it? He had read Ingrid's journal and would know that she had written about a special hiding place that nobody could ever find.

Anna felt anger blaze in her at his deviousness, but she kept it under control. At least she knew now that there was nothing in the aperture or else he would have brought it down with him.

He chatted until he had finished his coffee, not seeming to notice her lack of response since he clearly enjoyed the sound of his own voice. 'I'll be going now,' he said finally, putting down his emptied mug on the nearest ledge. 'Shall you be staying long this time?'

'I'm not sure. Probably until Alex comes home on Friday evening.' Then, as Harry reached the door, she added, 'I believe you have my other key to the house, Harry. May I have it?'

'Yes!' he said willingly. 'I'm glad you reminded me! I have meant to hand it over to you several times, but have forgotten to do it.'

He had already taken it out of his pocket and he placed it within her reach on the table. Then he bade her goodbye and off he went. She wondered if he had had a duplicate key made since he had surrendered it so willingly. Then she let her gaze drift slowly around the room. Had Ingrid hidden a painting or two in that secret hiding place she had mentioned? She had written about the avaricious dealers ready to snatch Magnus's work off the walls, although that was just her humorous way of describing their greed. And yet? Maybe she had been afraid of having a certain painting stolen from her, one that she liked more than the rest of them. At least it was not the one where Magnus had included her as a blob of orange paint, which Anna treasured.

When Alex came home, Anna told him about Harry's nocturnal visit. 'It was so odd! He could go up in that aperture any time during the day, but instead he chose to go there by night with a torch! Yet he can't have found anything or else I would have seen that he was carrying something when he came down again.'

'I'll take a look there myself at the weekend,' he said. 'I had no idea there was access to that space under the rafters.'

'It is likely that we should never have known about it if it had not been for the damage to the roof in the fire.'

'The *stabbur* could have burned like a torch if nobody had spotted the fire in time. Then, if there is something of value up there, it would have been lost forever.'

The following Sunday morning, with the workmen absent, Alex went up the ladder and climbed through into the aperture. Anna, standing below, watched his long legs disappear. After about ten minutes he reappeared.

'I need some tools. There is a false wall partitioning off the far end and I'm going to knock through it.'

He went into the house and found what he wanted from tools he had brought there when putting up shelves and doing other small chores. This time he was so long in the aperture that Anna guessed the partition must be very solid, for there was a great deal of banging before finally there was silence. She waited impatiently and then anxiously for him to re-appear. When he did, his expression told her that something was seriously wrong. He was looking shocked and saddened.

'What is it?' she cried as he descended. 'What did you find?'

He dropped his tools on to the ground and took hold of her by the shoulders. 'I found an old wedding chest up there.'

She gasped. 'That was Ingrid's secret hiding place! She said nobody would ever find it!'

He shook his head. 'This is nothing to do with Ingrid or anything she ever thought of hiding there. Its contents are far more recent and must have been there for the past six or seven years.'

'Dating back to the occupation?' she whisper-ed in mounting horror, for he looked so grave.

'I believe I have found the remains of the resistance fighter whose death has remained a mystery ever since he disappeared. I must get to the nearest phone and call the police.'

She thought of the following few hours as a nightmare when she looked back afterwards on that hideous time. A police car arrived very quickly and the two young policemen who sprang out looked stern and important, neither having come in contact with such a serious crime before. One hastened up the ladder to investigate. Soon afterwards he emerged to give a grim nod to confirm what he had found. He made immediate contact with the police station at Molde, while his companion began to cordon off the *stabbur*. Then senior officers came by launch across the fjord, and both Alex and Anna made clear and precise statements to them. They were informed that two detectives were already flying up from Oslo and would question them again. In the meantime, the house had to be vacated as it was located in the crime scene and was about to be cordoned off too.

Anna, intensely protective of Ingrid's house, left it reluctantly. Later she heard that there had been great difficulty in getting the heavy chest brought down from the aperture, and Anna thought how light-heartedly Ingrid had thought of it as a perfect hiding place for treasures, never suspecting that one day long after her time it would be used to conceal a grisly murder.

Several weeks of investigation passed before Harry was arrested and charged. His nocturnal visit had been to check that the chest was still well hidden behind the stout partition he had built himself at the time of committing the crime. He had also needed to know that there was no danger of the hiding place being revealed during repairs from the fire damage. It was not Anna's evidence of witnessing his nocturnal coming and going that settled Harry's guilt, but the discovery amid the skeletal remains and rotted clothing of a gold ring that had slipped from his finger as he had struggled to lift the body into the chest in such cramped quarters. Steffan identified it as the one that had belonged to Magnus and which he had given to Harry.

Alex and Anna both went to the funeral of the resistance fighter, which was held at the little church of his country birthplace, and he was laid to rest in its churchyard. The service was attended by many people, including the Crown Prince, who came to pay his personal respects to a man of great courage.

It had all come out at Harry's trial that throughout the occupation his loyalty had been to Hitler and the Nazi regime, his own advancement being his prime concern. The meagre help he had given secretly to his fellow countrymen had been to ensure that the resistance did not suspect his duplicity, especially when it was beginning to look as if the Allies might win the war after all. He had convinced the local Nazi commander that he had shot and buried in the forest the resistance fighter they had been hunting, but in reality he had not dared to risk firing a gun where people in the area might come to investigate. He had stabbed his victim in a confrontation, and the hiding place in the *stabbur* had seemed ideal for concealment, since it was too risky to start digging a grave when he could be sighted by a local person in the mountains at any time. The old chest in the *stabbur* near at hand, which he believed destined never to be found again, seemed the perfect solution.

At his trial he also admitted setting fire to the *stabbur* in the intention of finally destroying forever all trace of his crime. He had not expected one bonfire too many to be noticed that night, when almost everybody was celebrating Midsummer Eve. Now, many such nights would pass and he would be a great deal older before he ever saw these celebrations again.

When the restoration work on the *stabbur* was finished and the aperture blocked up forever, the doors were painted the same mellow tawny colour that must have been Ingrid's choice in days gone by, and which was in harmony with the surroundings of fir and pine, particularly in autumn when many trees took on blazing colours and even the cranberry leaves turned crimson. It was a fresh beginning for the *stabbur* and it became both a library and guest quarters, with a few comfortable and traditional pieces of furniture, as well as some very fine hand-woven wall hangings, which, with the bright rag-rugs, had been bought at a handicraft shop.

A year later Anna gave birth to a son, whom they named David. Steffan delighted in the child, but not long after David's first birthday Steffan died quietly in his sleep. He had bequeathed the house to Gudrun for her lifetime and an income that would keep her in comfort till the end of her days. But, after Steffan's demise, her health deteriorated and she moved into a home for elderly people. She lived long enough to see Anna's daughter, who was born two years after little David and was named Julie. Although Anna, as well as Steffan's grandchildren, received generous bequests, a large portion of Steffan's fortune went to secure the future of a school for orphaned children in Africa that he had supported for many years. The four paintings that had hung in the hall of his home were bequeathed to a Bergen art gallery.

Anna felt the time had come now to decide where Ingrid's original journal should be hidden away again, but as yet she had not decided where that should be.

Twenty

To Anna's great joy, her children grew to love Ingrid's old house from which they went climbing or skiing or walking. It was also a place for them to take friends and hold parties, both in childhood and throughout their teens. David and Julie grew up with stories of Ingrid, for Anna wanted them to know what a remarkable woman Ingrid had been and how proud they should be of the magnificent paintings by the man she had married. They liked all they heard of Ingrid, admiring her for being so unconventional, which held a particular appeal for them in their tumultuous teenage years.

Julie had started early to keep a journal herself. She had always wanted to write, even as a child she had made up stories and written them down. She was presently a reporter with an Oslo newspaper and working on a novel at the same time. Her brother had become an engineer and was on one of the rich oil rigs in Norwegian waters. Anna had retired from teaching a while ago, which gave her the chance to travel with Alex whenever he had to go far afield.

Molde had spread out widely over past years and was again as charming a town as it had been in the past, with its new church and grand town hall and fine shops. A German horticulturalist, visiting the town on holiday, heard of the lost Molde rose through the wartime bombing and went home to propagate a red rose as like the original one as it was possible to be. So this rose now bloomed in the town's many flowerbeds. Although the magical scent of the original rose had proved impossible to recapture, this generous German gift had been a wonderful act of reconciliation. Anna always made sure that the new Molde rose flourished profusely in the garden of the fine house that she and Alex had built with a superb view of the fjord.

The roses had finished blooming and snow covered everything once again when Anna answered the telephone one afternoon. It was Molly on the line. Over the years, Anna had seen her and Pat frequently, for the three of them had remained good friends and always enjoyed one another's company.

'Pat and I are arranging a girls' weekend in Paris!' Molly exclaimed. 'It will be a reunion only for those who were in our circle of war brides at Gardermoen. So far everyone we have phoned has agreed to come. We have decided on a date in December, when all the tourists will have gone home and Paris looks more beautiful than ever in its tasteful Christmas illuminations. So can I include you? And don't you dare say no!'

'I'd love it!' Anna replied, laughing. 'Give me

the date.'

When Molly had told her, she looked in her diary and saw she had no commitments that weekend.

'Who will be coming?' she asked after giving her acceptance.

'Only I know that! You and everybody else will have to wait and see. We're all going to just turn up at the excellent hotel where Olav and I have stayed a couple of times. But on this occasion no husbands are to be in tow. Or grown-up children either. This reunion is just for mature war brides!'

After the call ended, Anna wondered whom she would be seeing again. Nobody lived in those old Gardermoen houses any more, for they had been swept away long since in an enlargement of the airfield and the extension of all the runways, but there was a memorial where the concentration camp had been. Not all the husbands had remained in the RNAF, but those who were still serving had soared in rank, their wartime experience invaluable in the expansion of the country's forces under NATO. Molly's Olav was now a wing commander and they had a large and pleasant home in the Oslo suburb of Grefsen. Anna and Alex had visited many times. Along with everything else, much had changed throughout the country, old customs gone, and the *saeter* huts and high mountain farms had become weekend holiday retreats for the families that still owned them.

Anna arrived in Paris as arranged on Friday

afternoon. After leaving the snow in Norway, the air seemed surprisingly mild, and as the taxi took her along the Champs Élysées, she thought how right Molly had been in praising Paris in December. The trees were hung with tiny golden lights that made them look as if they were magically gilded.

Molly was waiting in the hotel lobby and with a cry of pleasure came forward to give her an exuberant hug.

'Isn't this fun!' she exclaimed joyfully. 'You're the last to arrive. The others are already here.'

She led Anna into one of the lounges. For a few seconds, Anna was reminded of the first time she had met these women. All were looking towards her with beaming smiles just as they done all those years ago. They had become her friends and had endured with her all the domestic ups and downs of difficult housing, rationed food, the lingering presence of enemy prisoners and – above all else – had faced up with her in an unfamiliar northern clime to the coldest winter in living memory, when even Oslo fjord froze. Here was Jane, the one-time Wren and baker of cakes, now twice her original size, coming to give her a welcoming hug.

'Anna! How good to see you again!'

Then Pat, whom Anna saw quite often, gave her a welcoming wave as Vanessa, who had once almost died of homesickness, embraced Anna fondly. She still had her shy and gentle expression, but her hair was tinted a challenging bronze, which suggested she now took everything in her stride. 'You look as young as ever, Anna,' she said admiringly.

'Not quite!' Anna contradicted in amusement. 'Although I can feel the years falling away from all of us in this reunion.'

Now Helen had sprung to her feet and did a Scottish twirl. 'I hope you've remembered all I taught you? I have a successful dancing school these days and Kristan is a football manager. He was always crazy about sport.'

Anna almost did not recognize Rosemary, who had been such a clever dressmaker, for her red-gold Rita Hayworth hair had turned a silvery white. Yet somehow it did not age her, for it had been expertly cut in a short, fashionable style that suited her, and she was wearing large sapphire earrings.

'I hear from Molly that your marriage to your handsome Alex has worked out well,' she said to Anna after they had embraced. 'Unfortunately, mine fell apart after five years when by chance Henrik met the girlfriend he had been in love with before he had escaped to England. Everything flared up between them as if the time apart had never been.' She made a little grimace. 'The hardest to bear was the realization that I had always been second best.'

'I'm so sorry to hear that,' Anna said sincerely. 'But you decided to stay in Norway?'

'Yes, it had become home to me more than England by then, because I had no family there any more, whereas my in-laws continued to be very kind to me. By then I had a little dress shop that was doing well and so I saw no reason to leave Norway. It was a decision I have never regretted. My business has expanded into much larger premises.' Then she added with a twinkling look, 'I also have a lover and he is very good to me. So life can have its compensations.'

Last of all to exchange a hug with Anna was Wendy Misund, who had retained her shy, old-fashioned look. 'Edvard and I are living now in Bodo beyond the Arctic Circle. He is a group captain these days. Our son followed him into the service and is an experienced pilot now.'

'That must make you both very proud of him,' Anna said warmly, remembering when she had first seen Terry asleep in his pram at Gardermoen.

It was then that a waiter came with the champagne that Pat had ordered. They drank a toast to friendship. Then, dressed up and in high spirits, they went out to dine and afterwards to pre-booked seats at the Opera House. Next morning, they went for a tour of the Palace of Versailles. As Molly had foretold, there was almost nobody else there and they were often alone in the great rooms, except for an occasional caterpillar of schoolchildren going through, giggling and whispering with one another and not looking at anything.

When the war brides came to the Hall of Mirrors, it was to find its glorious length filled with a golden blaze of winter sunshine, which was pouring through the windows only to be held captive by its reflection in the opposite multi-mirrored wall. With nobody else there, Molly and Pat removed their shoes and merrily waltzed the length of it where once tragic Marie Antoinette had danced and dazzled with her beauty.

Back in the city, and after some serious shopping in the Champs Élysées, they dumped their purchases at the hotel and spent the rest of the afternoon in the Louvre. It was a tired but satisfied group that emerged later to sit down thankfully around one of the outside café tables, under a green and white striped awning. They did not notice that a woman in a taxi, caught in a traffic hold-up, had sighted them in surprise. Thrusting her fare at the driver, she seized the moment to alight and dodged across the busy street.

'I've always wanted to see the Mona Lisa,' Helen was saying on a sigh of satisfaction, 'and now I have done it at last.'

'When I first saw her on a trip here in the fifties,' Pat said, 'she was hanging on the wall in one of the galleries, but now she is enclosed in bulletproof glass.'

'A sign of the times,' Anna said on a sigh.

They had all been served with the variety of drinks that they had ordered when the elegant woman from the taxi, wearing a Chanel suit and a fashionably tiny hat, began threading her way through the tables towards them. None of them

337

noticed her until she reached them.

'Hello, girls! How are you all? Are you having a reunion without me?'

It was Sally. They all gazed at her in astonishment.

'What are you doing here in Paris?' Molly gasped, while Anna pulled an extra chair forward for Sally to sit down.

'I live here,' she answered blithely, taking the seat. 'Surely you have guessed why? I'm married to Jacques. I found that I could not settle back in Canada when I was so in love with him. So after Arvid and I were divorced, I came to Paris. I let Arvid have custody of Tom, whom I used to see whenever I went back to visit my parents. He is a geologist working somewhere in the wilds of South America and so I haven't seen him for ages.'

'And Arvid?' Vanessa asked. 'What has happened to him?'

'He married again and has a family. He is now chairman on the board of a very successful commercial airline.' She gave an airy wave of her hand. 'That's all I know, so don't ask me any more questions about him. I've told you about myself and now I want to hear all about every one of you.'

Anna thought to herself that Sally was just as self-centred as ever, but she did seem to be genuinely pleased to see them all again. There followed plenty of chatter.

Before they left the café, Sally invited them all to dine with her that evening at Jacques's

338

restaurant. 'It's one of the highest-rated in Paris. My late father financed it for him, which gave Jacques the chance he had always wanted – to own his own place and show the world what a master chef he has become.'

Anna had been pleased to know there had been a happy ending for Arvid, although she wondered if, in the depths of his heart, he had ever managed to erase his memories of Sally, with her beauty and maddening selfishness and thoughtless disregard for the feelings of others, for he had loved her so much.

Jacques's restaurant proved to be extremely plush with glittering chandeliers, crimson drapery and gilt-framed mirrors reflecting the snow-white linen and sparkling wine glasses, and orchids on every table. An orchestra was playing soft music on a raised dais. Sally made her entrance just as the friends were settled at the best table in the extravagantly decorated room. She was wearing a black silk sheath that shrieked money and a diamond necklace and earrings that were even more dazzling than the surroundings.

'Jacques is coming to greet you,' she said, taking her place at the head of the table. 'He is overjoyed that you are here.'

He appeared a few minutes later, wearing his chef's attire and waving his arms about in delight at the sight of his guests. He looked older and uglier, as well as having become quite rotund, but Sally gazed at him with still loving eyes.

'Dear ladies!' he enthused. 'Welcome to my domain! I remember you all so well. What happy days we shared at Gardermoen! I trust you will enjoy all that is to be served to you this evening, which will be under my personal supervision!'

It was a splendid meal and the wines superb. The friends were all very merry, and when back at the hotel, they said goodnight to one another and went into their own rooms. The weekend was over and friendships had been renewed, although Anna thought it doubtful that Sally would hold to her promise not to lose touch again. She was not very reliable when it came to keeping her word.

In the months that followed, and with the exception of Sally, they all telephoned one another or met up whenever they could, but gradually those who lived farthest apart dwindled in their meetings, until, with some, it became only the exchange of a Christmas card with some snapshots and a short summary of what had happened during the year. These were the times when they saw Norway, which had been so stricken when they had first stepped ashore, become rich and strong with its oil wells discovered offshore and other important business interests. There were also the cruise ships and coach tours that were bringing an influx of tourists, who seemed to be responding to an echo of the words of a long ago tractor-dealer, who had said that, in his opinion, Norway was the most beautiful country in the world.

Twenty-one

It was a warm sunny afternoon when Anna went into the garden with a basket and trowel. She found gardening therapeutic and hoped to keep her troubled thoughts at bay for a while. She and Alex had had their ups and downs like every married couple, but nothing had ever come seriously between them or threatened their love for each other until yesterday evening when everything had changed in a single hour.

Now, with retirement looming on the not too distant horizon, Alex had made up his mind that they should move to Spain when the time came and enjoy the rest of their years in a kinder climate. Many of his fellow countrymen and women in their age group had been doing the same for some time. Anna thought that this exodus was comparable on a smaller scale to the wave of emigration of younger folk to the States in Ingrid's time and she had her misgivings about it. Then yesterday evening Alex had produced an architect's plan for a house he wanted to build on the Spanish coast in readiness. It had resulted in the fiercest and most distressful quarrel in their whole marriage.

'I'll not go!' she declared, her hands clenched.

'I'll not leave my home and my country.'

He refrained from saying that Norway was only hers by adoption. 'But you've always enjoyed the holidays we have spent there.'

'Holidays are entirely different from pulling up roots forever!'

'You did it once before.'

'When I came from England, it had not been my intention to stay in Norway, but I met you.'

'We can always come back for visits, just as we have returned from trips to England and Italy and elsewhere.'

She answered with a fierceness that surprised him. 'No, this is a different matter altogether. I will not become a visitor in the land where my heart lies!'

'You sound like Ingrid!' he taunted in exasperation. 'Is it the old house that is causing a barrier?'

She threw up her hands impatiently. 'No! You know that I have bequeathed it to Julie in my will and she will always take care of it. If you move to Spain, you go alone.' Then she added bitterly, 'There will be plenty of widows there to console you in my absence.'

She regretted her words as soon as she had uttered them, for he had turned livid with rage, having always been faithful to her. 'Yes, there will be! Settling in Spain is what I intend to do, and it will be up to you whether you come with me or stay here on your own.'

Tears clouded her gaze as she knelt down on a mat and began to use her trowel. It would tear

342

Alex apart to leave her behind, but if his mind was set on it, he would go. Norwegians always held to what they believed to be right. She had once said to Alex that if Hitler had studied the Norsk character, he would not have invaded, for he would have known ahead that he could never break their resolve.

'Mama, there you are!'

Julie had come into the garden, a local newspaper in her hand. She was home from Oslo for a few days, a tall, willowy and lovely-looking girl with honey-fair hair and blue eyes. She had already been twice to the old house from which she had gone walking in the mountains.

'I think it is time for us to hold a *slekt samling,*' she said, holding up the newspaper to show a photograph of a large family gathering. 'There were over a hundred people at this one. They came from as far afield as Australia and South America to gather at the original family home on a farm near Trondheim. Those of the younger generations had never been there before, but were so enthusiastic about seeing where their forebears had lived. People born abroad always like to know their roots.' Then she added, 'It would be just the sort of family occasion that Ingrid would have loved.'

'I can't argue with you on that point,' Anna agreed thoughtfully, her mind busy as she rose to her feet from her gardening. It would be a project that would require her whole attention and would alleviate the tension between Alex and her. 'But it would take a great deal of organizing – hotel rooms to be booked, catering for a welcoming banquet and then an evening supper and entertainment too. Just think how many cakes we would need for the coffee and cakes sessions!'

'We could manage all that!' Julie insisted eagerly. 'We would give everybody coloured name tags – blue, green, red or whatever – to show which of Ingrid's children they are descended from! Then, the morning after the first grand day, we could have morning coffee and cakes at Ingrid's house, where everybody could look around. I'm sure that would be a highlight of the whole occasion. Afterwards we could give them a farewell buffet lunch here.'

Julie's enthusiasm was infectious and Anna gave a willing nod, already drawn to a decision. 'The whole occasion would be a tribute to Ingrid and much deserved.'

Before Julie returned to Oslo, she and Anna sat down together to discuss all that would have to be done. Alex had willingly approved the idea. A date for the following summer was settled for the family celebration and a list made of those to be invited. Twice in the past year Anna and Alex had been visited by two different couples that were Ingrid's descendants looking for their roots. Anna knew that by sending open invitations to them, they would gather in all other descendants known to them, for the old family unity that had been instilled into their forebears by Ingrid had come through to successive generations.

To Anna's relief, the situation settled down between Alex and her, but although their love life had resumed, the barrier between them had not gone away. She knew from what he said to their children and others that he still planned the move to Spain. She supposed that he thought she would eventually give in, but her mind was set.

Over the next few months acceptances arrived for the *slekt samling* and increased in number as those abroad located cousins and other more distant relatives. The final total was two hundred and ninety-seven. Everything was falling into place. Anna had begun calling the occasion 'Ingrid's Day' and everybody else followed suit. David flew home on a break from the oil rig to play his part in the final preparations.

'What do you want me to do?' he asked Anna when he arrived. He was as tall as his father with tousled fair hair and a well-boned face, his nose straight and his jaw strong. Girls were always phoning to see if he was at home.

'You can do the name tags,' she said. 'There is a different colour for each one of Ingrid's children, so that their descendants will know to which group they belong.'

He sat down willingly to do his allotted chore, but he had a better time later when he and his father discussed the wines to be served at the great occasion and did some tasting. Julie arrived home the next day and together she and her brother finished the last of the stack of name tags.

Then suddenly it was the eve of Ingrid's Day. All the guests had arrived at the various hotels, and American voices were heard everywhere in the town, and also two New Zealand tones. On Saturday evening there was to be a welcome party at Molde's largest hotel, hosted by Anna and Alex. She bought a new dress in blue silk to wear, and when she came downstairs to leave for the hotel, Alex was waiting for her in the hall.

'Perfect!' he said admiringly. 'You look beautiful.'

She avoided his eyes. Nothing could be perfect or beautiful with a separation hanging over them every passing day. But somehow she smiled and they set off in the car to arrive in good time to greet their guests. Julie and David were already there, seated at a table with the name tags, a list of all the guests together with birth dates, home addresses and as much as the family tree as was known. Soon the guests came flooding in. There was tremendous excitement in the air, everybody already enjoying themselves.

Next morning, on a beautiful blue-sky day, coaches called at each hotel to collect the guests and take them to a privately owned and very large house in the mountains, which could be hired for weddings and other important occasions. There the banquet was set on long tables with flower arrangements stretching down the length of each one and the delicious food accompanied by the best of wines. Alex gave a

346

speech of welcome and later Anna rose to her feet to give a summary of Ingrid's life. She was like many of the other women in wearing her national costume which glowed with Rosa Harvick's beautiful jewellery and accessories. Toasts were drunk and there followed speeches in English and Norwegian from a number of the guests. Afterwards, people mingled eagerly both in the house and garden, firstly getting to know others wearing the same colour name tag and then moving on to another branch of the family. Many had brought old photographs with them and copies were being requested and promised. There were children among the gathering and Julie had arranged for them to have organized games and races and various competitions to keep them amused outside. Judging by the cheerful noise coming from their direction, they were all enjoying themselves.

Anna, moving from guest to guest, could tell already that the occasion was a great success. The descendants who lived elsewhere in Norway had all wanted to help and Anna had told the women to make their most favourite confection for the coffee and cakes session. Without exception, these were brought in beautifully decorated circular wooden cake boxes which were heirlooms that had been handed down. One of these had the name *Ingrid Harvik* in its design and another bore Emma's name.

At the close of the evening, after a buffet supper and dancing to a lively band, during which many of the old traditional dances were included, the coaches took everyone back to their hotels.

The next day dawned as warm and sunny as the previous day, and the guests, after swarming on to the ferry under David's direction, crossed the fjord in still glorious weather to where Alex waited with coaches that were there to take them to the foot of the slope up to Ingrid's house. Anna was already there with Julie, setting out cups and saucers and more cakes on the long table, with the lighted candles of hospitality, where so many family meals had been eaten in Ingrid's day. In the warm breeze, Norway's flag fluttered on the flagpole that had only recently replaced the one that Magnus had installed long ago. All but a few elderly people, who were driven up by car, walked up to the house and gave various exclamations of pleasure as it came into sight. Cameras snapped on all sides. Then the guests were all over the house and jostling good-humouredly to look at the wedding photograph of Ingrid and Magnus, which Anna had always kept in its original place on the bedroom wall. One American was desperate to see the family Bible in which Ingrid would have entered her children's names and those of her forebears. Julie took it from a drawer to hand it to him and he settled down to study it, making notes and with his cup of coffee forgotten.

Then it was time to go to the churchyard. There everyone clustered around the two graves that lay side by side. A senior American, a descendent of Kurt of the salmon factory, spoke of the importance of family ties and then laid a wreath of flowers on Magnus's grave. He was followed by Sonja's great-granddaughter, who stood by Ingrid's grave and told how she had grown up longing to see the old house that was always part of her bedtime stories as a child, handed down through her mother and grandmother. Then she laid a wreath of roses on Ingrid's grave. Spontaneously, everybody applauded.

After a buffet lunch in Anna and Alex's garden, where each white-clothed table had been decorated with sprigs of orange rowan berries, everyone departed, all with talk of keeping in touch and hoping to meet again one day. When the last guest had gone, waving out of sight, David turned to his mother with a wide grin and gave her a hug.

'Congratulations, Mama! Everything was perfect! Even the weather!'

Alex put his arm around Anna's waist as he walked her into the house. There she sat down thankfully into a cushioned chair and kicked off her new shoes, which had proved to be more elegant than comfortable. Outside, the caterers had removed the last of their equipment and folded away the chairs and tables into a van, which had now driven away. Nothing remained to show that nearly three hundred people had been milling about there, except for the trodden-down grass of the lawn.

Alex pulled up a chair opposite her and took her hands into his, looking at her with love. 'I learned something important this weekend.'

'What was that?' she asked.

'Every one of those guests said how their forebears had at heart never lost their home-sickness, no matter that they had been loyal to their new land. I believe I would be the same if I moved to Spain and then for some reason was unable to return home again.'

She looked at him, full of understanding. It was the deep-rooted love of country and mountains that seemed to run through the veins of every Norseman she had ever met or read about. 'I would have gone with you in the end,' she admitted.

He nodded. 'I could never have left you anyway.'

Slowly they grinned at each other. Then he drew her to her feet and they kissed each other as if they were young lovers again.

After such a gathering of Ingrid's kin, Anna decided that the time had come at last to hide away Ingrid's original journal as had been requested in one of the early pages, but first of all she herself wrote out a full account of the family reunion and then folded it and tucked it into the journal.

Alex went with her to the old house the following evening to assist her in the task of concealing it. In the house, Anna sat to read aloud the last page once more.

'"My days are running out. Last week I am

sure that I saw Magnus waiting for me by the silver birch tree. I have also heard his footstep on the stairs, and now and again there is a whiff of turpentine, such as always hung about him when he had been painting. When the time is right, he will take my hand and we shall be together for evermore.'"

Anna put the journal into a flat silver box that she had bought specially for it. Then she added the letter that Johan's mother had written long ago. It had been several years before she had felt the time had come to read the words of a much-loved woman, whose son she had married in those wartime days. It had been such a wonderful letter, full of encouragement while expressing love for Johan and wishing him a good homecoming from the war. Anna thought the letter should be preserved and included in the silver box, and she placed it in a protective envelope and sealed it.

Alex was standing by the rosemaling cupboard that two or three centuries ago had been built into the wall. There was a tiny aperture at its side and Anna stooped to insert the box, which slid through easily. There was a little thud as it came to rest. Then Alex inserted a piece of matching wood that closed the aperture securely with no danger of it shifting. It was also impossible to discern.

He returned his carpentry tools to where he kept them, while Anna waited by the door in the evening sunshine. As he reached her, he put an arm about her waist and kissed her.

They set off down the slope. It was probably only a songbird in the trees, but Anna thought she heard a whisper of farewell.